T0129405

Sherry Sonnett

RESTRAINT

A Novel

SIMON & SCHUSTER
New York London Toronto Sydney Tokyo Singapore

SIMON & SCHUSTER
ROCKEFELLER CENTER
1230 AVENUE OF THE AMERICAS
NEW YORK, NEW YORK 10020

DESIGNED BY PEI LOI KOAY
MANUFACTURED IN THE UNITED STATES OF AMERICA

1 3 5 7 9 10 8 6 4 2

LIBRARY OF CONGRESS CATALOGING-IN-PUBLICATION DATA
SONNETT, SHERRY.
RESTRAINT : A NOVEL / SHERRY SONNETT.
P. CM.
1. MAN-WOMAN RELATIONSHIPS—CALIFORNIA—LOS ANGELES—FICTION. 2. WOMEN—CALIFORNIA—LOS ANGELES—SEXUAL BEHAVIOR—FICTION. 3. LOS ANGELES (CALIF.)—FICTION. 4. REVENGE—FICTION. I. TITLE.
PS3569.065398R47 1995
813'.54—DC20 94-29211 CIP
ISBN: 978-1-4767-3847-5

To

M.H.P.

Pass It On

The air was washed-out yellow dust and the valley had no end. Mile after mile, the road lay across the land, a coiled snake someone had tossed away. From the road, dusty fields rolled out and fell away as far as the eye could see, then vanished in the haze that hid the mountains rising up from the Valley floor. Overhead, the sun shone so hot and bright it looked like a blur, a rip in the sky.

I had the windows rolled down and shivered in the wind, a hot, dry, unnatural wind that didn't caress but angled off. San Joaquin . . . here on the back roads, the true Valley revealed itself, ramshackle, rusted wire nailed to slanted poles, curled brown leaves in places man-delivered water couldn't reach. Crows pecked at barren fields, but I couldn't hear their cries. I felt my thirst. What was I doing here? Easy. I was following a man, who, the moment I saw him, I knew: he had what I wanted. The way the fabric of his shirt pulled across his chest, the angle of his hand as he held a cigarette, the tone in his voice when he said the word no. If you had told me three months ago that I'd do what I'd done and then risked coming after him, I'd have said impossible. No way . . .

Or would I? I was at a point in my life where too much was under control. I could feel the longing underneath, tasted it when I went to bed each night. I was certain there had to be one more big thing and I was waiting for it, longing for it to explode through the center of my life. I was ready, more than ready.

Then he came along. And I see now that's the way it happens. The line comes up—and you jump.

Part ONE

Chapter One

It began at a party I never would have known about if I hadn't been working late at my office and still there when Don called. Don is my ex-husband, and his calling a few days after a birthday I'd been trying to ignore, and ignoring it himself, was only par for the course. He had a convenient kind of oversight that allowed him to edit out any occasion that required a special effort to give, emotionally or financially. I sound bitter, but I'm not, because whatever it is in him that keeps him disconnected I also feel in me. Does that sound strange? Well, Los Angeles is full of people like Don and me: social, polite, but somehow disconnected, isolated at the core. Anyway, Don and I are two of a kind and maybe that's why it never went deep enough between us to end in the kind of anger that builds steel walls. I could already see that in a few more years we'd value each other as we never had in love, simply because we had a history, went way back, knew each other when.

We'd say, my God, it can't be twenty years, or, remember that time in Mexico . . .? What we'd want from each other wasn't the truth but continuity, and maybe we'd no longer be able to tell what was real and what was the deluded imaginings of two lonely people.

We had come out together to Los Angeles, six months married right after college on the prairie. It hadn't taken much effort to leave. We needed to get away from that landlocked flatness and we wanted what California promised—the sunshine and glossy cars, the hillside houses behind white stucco walls. We wanted the heat and the surf rolling in, palm trees and eucalyptus, a freeway cloverleaf. We didn't disguise it: we were after the glamour, to be part of a world that ran on money and fashion and a certain sexy ease. The movie business and rock and roll—the obvious lures—drew us only indirectly; it was the Pacific we came for, that crystal blue behind and below a dozen TV detectives, the breaking waves at Malibu as a newly sober celebrity alcoholic walked beside them in *People* magazine, the twists and turns on Mulholland made familiar in a hundred movie chases. We knew that light, hard and vivid, etching distances and boundaries, the jumble of L.A. And when we came we did the usual things: got jobs, bought a condo, made friends, drove up the coast. After a while, we made more money and more but different friends and drifted apart, like two leaves on a rapidly melting stream. That's the advantage of the absence of passion: there's no reason not to stay in touch.

I was getting ready to leave my office when he called. It's a small place on Beverly a few blocks from Fairfax, three rooms on the far side of a courtyard hidden from the street. I had rented the space because it was May and a jacaranda was shedding its blooms in a soft purple rain. The rooms were large, white, a knockoff attempt at what they used to call moderne, with more than enough space for me and a secretary, who just now was a young woman named Holly who wore six earrings in each ear. Vega Johnson: Investments and Financial Planning. Humble but mine own. I have a knack for money, for finding it and making it grow, which was unexpected, considering I come from a family that was always behind, or two steps ahead of, the bill collectors, yoked to a man, my bemused father, who wore a brown fedora and couldn't keep a dime. My own talent only revealed itself when I fell into a job in a stockbrokerage, found I liked it, and turned out to be good at it. I moved up from secretary to assistant and got my license. Surprisingly soon the big commissions started rolling in. But after a while I saw I wouldn't go any higher because women didn't, so I took a calculated risk, stole some of my clients, bought a modem, and set up for myself. I trade now for a small but fairly flush group, some with names you might recognize; I take care of all the loose financial ends, and the word of mouth on me is good. I have more than I can handle. There's something sexy about a woman who's smart with money and also looks good in a tight white suit and three-inch heels. A compelling combination, someone once said. Sure, I use it. It buys me what I want—freedom.

Don said there was a party at a new restaurant on Wilshire in Beverly Hills. Going to restaurant openings was part of his job; he was a V.P. for a public relations company that specialized in business and corporate accounts. He often asked me to go with him. I think he liked the reaction when he introduced me as his ex-wife. But I was tired tonight and he heard me hesitate. His own voice was suddenly exhausted.

"Please come," he said. "I really need to see a friendly face."

"What's the matter?"

"Nothing. Out of the ordinary. I'm just in one of those valleys they talk about." That wasn't like him. I used to call him Mr. Evenkeel.

"You want to tell me?"

"Maybe after. We can drive out to the beach, breathe some air. What do you say?"

I could have said no. Gone home, taken a bath, got into bed early with a good book. I could have done anything but what in fact I did. Even now I can't quite believe that so much hinged for a moment on such an innocuous choice. Maybe it didn't. Maybe fate comes and gets you no matter where you are; you never know what's coming down the pike. Am I sorry, now that I know what I'm capable of? That's the funny thing: no. Not at all. No. It's not that the truth is pretty. But it has definitely set me free.

The restaurant was carved out of space previously occupied by a failed S & L. The architect must have been young, eager to make a name, because the place was busy, insistent, with huge, indecipherable objects hanging off crowded trusses and partitions. The initial impression was of a propped-up airplane hangar, and after a while, I realized that's what they must have been after. It was called "Aeropostale." I gave it three months.

The first person I ran into was Marty Toward. Toe-ward as in foe-ward, he liked to say. We had met Marty our first year out. He's a line producer now, the nuts-and-bolts man who keeps track of the actual money for movie producers too "creative" or spacey to be bothered. But back then he was trying to make it as a production manager, taking any show he could get, working the town, making more connections than anyone I knew. He said he could find us jobs, but only Don was interested. Nothing ever actually materialized, which is the way things go in Hollywood, but ever since then Don had wondered if movies were where he really belonged. Which didn't mean anything except that he wasn't happy.

Marty came in with his wife, Olga, whom I'd met before. Don introduced us, but I was surprised because I usually see Marty with other women. He's a terrific philanderer, very public and up front about it. In fact Don says that if people didn't know about Marty's other women he probably wouldn't bother having them. It doesn't take much to see why he likes people to know. He's fat and nothing to look at: a bullet fish face sort of like my Uncle Jerry, balding and awful taste in clothes, no style, not even funky. But Marty has what they used to call personality and it booms out in a constant stream of stories, gossip, facts and opinions, funny and interesting, startling and provocative, sometimes even tenderhearted. He's always in motion, not at all like a fat man, squirming in his seat when he has something to say, gesturing so wildly you watch out for the water glasses. His whole body is somewhere between a wiggle and a dance, hands in and out of pockets, fixing his tie, rubbing his balding head, slapping somebody's back and his favorite word is a hearty "Sure!" So he doesn't have any trouble getting women, young, pretty, up and coming women, and everyone knows and knows that his wife knows and stays with him anyway, although Don tells me she doesn't like it and once in a while, for a few months or so, her face gets pinched and tense, hectic.

"Hiya, gorgeous," Marty boomed over the crowd, and I could see relief in Olga's eyes that it was only me. I suddenly felt bad that I knew so much about the things she tried to hide. I always feel bad knowing things about people I haven't learned from them or seen for myself. It makes me feel guilty and sometimes resentful, robbed of the possibility of discovering or deducing or filling in for myself. I suppose that's arrogant. Sure, I love to gossip, and some of the most interesting things I know about people I know because somebody else told me, and of course I believe the more facts you have the better. That's my business, gathering facts before I make the deal. But I've learned there isn't any Truth where people are concerned, you don't put all the pieces together and get a whole. So why shouldn't I be allowed the conclusions of my own experience, make up the world as I go along, and who cares that sometimes I'm wrong? I'm willing to pay the price. *La vida* really *es sueño.* Arrogant or not, the head I know best is my own.

"Have you seen Don?" I asked, and Marty gestured toward the far end of the room.

"He looks like hell," Marty said, and suddenly laughed. "Probably because he owes me money."

That was a surprise. I knew Don hated to borrow and also that Marty hated to lend. I wanted to ask him something more, but someone pulled him away and I was left exchanging small talk with Olga—jovial, smiling, completely fraudulent talk—and I managed to spill some wine on the sleeve of her dress. This was especially embarrassing because I see Marty with other women and Olga knows I do. Later, I saw her leave the party alone, while Marty stayed behind chatting up a young woman who looked as if she'd stepped off the set of a nighttime soap but probably sold time on a local TV station. How does Olga manage this with just a pinched face?

I finally spotted Don in the crush at the bar. Somehow, Marty had found him first and I headed toward them. Don was shouting something in Marty's ear but waved when he saw me coming. His face was flushed but drawn and I realized that he no longer looked young but had turned into someone parking attendants probably called "sir." When had that happened? And what about me?

"Hi, babe," he said, "great place, huh? I give it three months."

Marty was already moving away.

"Don't go," Don said, reaching out to him.

Marty didn't look back. "Look, I said I'd call him, I'll call him." His anger stayed behind.

"What's that about?" I asked.

Don shook his head. "Nothing. You know Marty."

"He says you owe him money."

He looked at me. I could see something in his eyes that was new, a low-grade fear, as if he were trapped, a wasp in a coffee can buzzing to get out.

"What's wrong?" I asked. "Has something happened?"

"No, no, I'm just a little stretched. The company is cutting back. I think they'll keep me, but I can't stand the idea of looking for another job. And that woman I was seeing, the redhead, remember? She dumped me, just like that, over and out. And last week I read—I mean I read the whole thing—an article on men who get face lifts. But seriously, folks, I'm doing fine."

"I can lend you money."

He smiled but shook his head. "I need another kind of favor. There's someone I want you to meet. He's around here somewhere."

Don took my arm and we set off through the crowd. "Who? Why?"

"He's got money. Rolling in it."

"Uh-uh. The last one you sent me turned out to be a paranoid—he thought I was funneling his money to the CIA. I almost had to call the cops to get rid of him. Remember?"

"There he is. There."

I turned and followed his gesture. The man was standing facing me, a drink in his hand, talking to a woman with incredibly silky blond hair. I couldn't see her face but I assumed she was flirting because he was smiling in that way that's all about the spark. He looked up, saw Don, and noticed me. The smile broadened instead of becoming hidden. Something in me immediately felt the electricity of attraction. I was startled; I could feel myself automatically tense with the special preparation that comes when something is suddenly at stake.

"Who is he?" But it was too late—Don was already introducing us.

His name was Paul. Paul Lattimer. He had the kind of looks you might not notice if you scanned a room, but once you focused you couldn't look away. There was nothing boyish or pretty about him; the word I thought was "handsome." Tall, which I like, with thick dark hair parted on the side and falling across his forehead in a single sleek line. Later, I would have all the time in the world to study the details: the gradual rise of his cheekbones, the tiny patch of hairless skin near his chin, the gold flecks in his brown eyes. Now he was wearing brown, an easy linen jacket, an expensive silk shirt pulling across his chest. For some reason, I noticed his shoes. They were brown, too, soft leather moccasins and the term "slip-ons" came suddenly to my mind. Unexpectedly, I felt myself stirring. It had been a very long time since anyone made me feel that way.

I smiled and nodded, the ritual gestures you automatically make, but all the time I watched him, already zeroed in, and it seemed to me he knew what I was thinking and was thinking it too, both of us already there, waiting. I turned, but Don was disappearing.

"I've got to make nice to the celebrity chef," he was saying. "Won't be long."

And the woman with the silky hair was gone as if she'd never been. Suddenly, I tensed—what if all that electricity was only in me? The one thing I hate is looking like a fool.

"Are you in public relations, too?" I heard myself asking, hating the sound of my voice, so stupidly superficial.

He shook his head. "No. I definitely have no interest in relating to the public."

I was relieved. It had crossed my mind he might be an actor and I had long ago ruled them out as possibilities. To be alone with an actor is to be alone, or pressed into constant contemplation of the other. Besides, I can't stand people who are so dependent on outside opinion.

"Well, what do you do?"

"I put things together. People, deals . . ."

"Ah. An entrepreneur?"

"No. More—subtle than that."

I smiled. "Something like—what?—a facilitator?"

"Yes, you can say that." There was the briefest of pauses and his voice lowered but became more intense. "In fact, I wish you would. I like the sound of your voice."

Surprised, I looked up at him. There's something very sexy about the direct approach, but it's been my experience that the men who most frequently take it are not the ones who interest me. What, in my fantasies, is all fluid and masterful turns out in real life to strike me as blatant and obnoxious. But this man, with his knowing smile, only drew me in.

"Do you always flirt like this?" I asked, unable to mask the light in my eyes. I knew that anyone looking at us, at me, would know exactly what I had in mind.

"Yes," Paul said, "I can't be trusted at all."

His smile was so steady, so open and confident, I immediately felt the very opposite was true. But his confidence intimidated me and I had to look away.

I felt one of his fingers on my wrist.

"Why don't we get dinner someplace—just you and me?"

I tried to read his eyes. I knew what I was thinking, but I was still unsure about him.

"Don and I talked about driving out to the beach."

"Oh. You and Don are—together?"

I smiled. "He's my ex-husband."

I saw him considering.

"Well, is that what you want to do, drive to the beach with your ex-husband?"

"Not now."

"Good."

He took my arm and I didn't pull away. I think I knew in that moment he was dangerous, that I had met someone who could turn me inside out. But it must have been what I wanted, because I didn't pull away.

When I found Don to tell him I was leaving, he was huddled with two bright young things and didn't seem to mind. I said I'd call him in the morning and we could talk then. He didn't ask why I was leaving, or with whom, and I didn't tell him. Whatever was bothering him would have to wait.

We went to an Indian place on Pico west of Century City. If I learned anything more about him then, I don't remember. I only see his eyes, direct, frank, inviting me in, the smile that offers layers of hidden meanings, and feel my own breathing, shallow, excited, gasping for air.

He followed me home, headlights in my rearview mirror as we climbed the hills. Cool air whistled past me and night moisture fogged the gray-dark glass. I could feel his presence so strongly that I half expected him to slip into the seat beside me, all distances obliterated. But at a red light, my own breathing was the only sound. Then red turned to green, and we drove on.

• • •

He came up behind me as I was putting my key in the lock and stood still, so still it silenced me and I could hear metal engaging metal, tumbling together. The door swung open, but I didn't move. Desire made me vigilant. I could smell the smoke from the restaurant on his jacket and sensed the rise and fall of his chest with each steady breath. I was ready for anything, and I think he knew it, but all he did was reach past me and push the door open further. Together, we walked inside.

I closed the door and snapped the lock, then watched him move through the room. Some people are oblivious to physical space, but he wasn't one of them; I could see him taking in the room, its proportions, the furniture, the light from the lamps I turned on. He wandered over to some desert landscapes I had grouped on a stuccoed wall. I wanted him to like them, to see in them what I saw, the promise of unlimited space and immutability, a peace without the franticness of leaves.

"It's the silence," I said, coming up behind him. "Every time you walk outside. You stop and wait and after a minute it's like looking up and catching the drift of the clouds. Getting in tune with the silence."

Unaccountably, I was blushing when he turned to me, made vulnerable by my fear of how he would judge what I was revealing. But Paul was smiling, with that invitation to enter in, assuming we were already in, a small circle of two.

"You're irresistible," I blurted out.

He laughed. "Wait till you get to know me."

"Will I? Get to know you?"

"Oh yes, I think so. Don't you?"

I nodded, wanting that promise of something more to

come. It was too soon to know if he would be anything more than someone passing through, but in that moment I wanted to believe in the intensity, the romance, the new man in my house.

"Do you want a drink?"

He nodded. "Scotch. Anything."

When I came out of the kitchen, I found him standing at the glass doors leading out to the garden. He was staring at the pool, which glowed turquoise in the moonlight.

"Do you want to swim?"

I opened the door and we carried our drinks outside. It didn't even occur to me to think about a bathing suit. The hum of distant traffic came from somewhere down below but louder still were the night sounds, the crickets, a barking dog, a nearby twig snapping in the warm night wind. I undressed quickly, shy and awkward, and slipped into the water. I wasn't hidden—the lights of the pool spotlighted me from below, clarified me in the midst of black night. I looked up. He was already naked, coming down to the concrete edge of the pool. I saw him silhouetted against the night and, with the moonlight at his back, I could see his cock erect and hard. He entered the water and then he was enclosing me from behind, the water lapping between us, and his arms cradling my breasts. I leaned back and felt the muscles of his legs tense as he found his footing to support us. His breath was on my neck. He turned me to him and I felt his lips and all at once I needed desperately to taste his tongue, to have him in my mouth. He let me kiss him and when I pulled away I threw my head back and breathed deeply and then again. The smell of night-blooming jasmine was in the air, heavy and yet elusive. He ran his tongue along my throat and then I felt his hands cupping my ass, pulling me to him and I pulled, too, wrapped my legs around him and climbed slowly onto his cock, my arms around his neck, held, cradled, safe at last and home. He was deep inside me, moving deliberately, the water all around us. I felt him sigh. What pleasure was he feeling, in that exquisite slow friction? Suddenly, I wanted to know, not only to be giving him pleasure but to be inside that pleasure, inside him as he was inside me, to be so deep inside him I was the blood pumping through him, pressing against his fiery skin, lengthening him, reddening, expanding, finally bursting all bounds and showering out.

Later, in bed, he asked me what I liked.

"Anything. Everything."

He laughed. "That's no answer."

I hesitated. "Well, I like to be teased."

He looked at me and grinned. "Head games . . ."

I was suddenly embarrassed, as if my skirt had been hiked up on a city street. He saw it and stroked my cheek.

"No, that's the best. Two people who are willing to play, who understand each other and are willing to play."

"Do we understand each other?"

Somehow I knew that wasn't what I was asking. Did he want me; that was what I wanted to know. Again, or tomorrow . . . was he around for a while?

"I understand you," he said and pulled me to him.

I see now that I was afraid, and full of contradiction, because surprisingly I stiffened. To be understood is to be known and to be known is to be owned. I saw the look in his eye, that cocksure certainty, a masculine confidence that always set me on edge. He thought he had me. I felt myself withdrawing in the usual way, but then something pulled me back. So what if he thought he had me? Didn't I have him? Why not just go with it, play along, let it all spin out? He's an aberration, I thought, a drunken spree in the middle of a long dry spell. I rolled toward him and felt his hand sweep across my body, then watched as his tapering fingers teased at my nipples. Games, head trips . . . why not play along? What have I got to lose?

I awoke somewhere near dawn. He wasn't in bed and I was afraid that he'd gone. But I found him in the living room, talking on the phone. He smiled when he saw me and quickly hung up. "New York," he said. "They're already at work there."

I didn't move. He was sitting in a chair facing the windows. It was dark, but the sky had grayed enough to see the outlines of trees and the first birds were already singing to each other. He was naked. He held out a hand and invited me to him. He opened his legs as I sat down on the floor in front of him so that I could rest my head on his thigh. I felt his hand brush back my hair, his fingers caress my neck. My cheek rested on his soft skin and I couldn't keep my hands from running over the line of his calves. His fingers on my neck seemed to be quieting me and we stayed that way a long time, watching the dawn reveal all that had been hidden.

• • •

Later, we made love again and afterward I lay in bed and listened to the rushing water as he took a shower. It had been months since I'd heard the sounds of another person in my bathroom and I wanted it to go on forever. When he kissed me goodbye his wet hair brushed across my cheek and cooled me as the moisture evaporated in the dry air.

"What are you doing tonight?" he asked.

"Whatever you want."

I was already hooked.

Chapter Two

I was ten minutes late to a breakfast meeting with Bobby Melner, the only one of my clients who'd tried to make something more of the relationship, and who'd had the good grace to continue the business even after I turned him down. He wasn't a bad sort but there was something of the oaf about him, a particular moistness to the nasal way he spoke, a waistline just an inch or two too high. Still, he had the right clothes (custom tailored or The Gap), car (four-door Range Rover), and house (understated Arts and Crafts) and women flocked around. Of course they did; money is a powerful drug. Hollywood was full of people like Bobby, the trust-fund kids I thought of as merchant princes. My client Bobby Melner, the son of Melner Toys. Sukie Billings of Billings Food. Jordan Meyerowitz of M&W Homes. There were WASPs with names their ancestors had paid to keep out of the papers and money descended, and well-tended, through five generations.

There were Kennedys and Fields and Tisches and a host of lesser lights, all drawn by the desire to play that particular game: the media thing, the glitz, the fame and the Ferraris. Making it in that game you were more than successful, you were *blessed,* singled out, anointed by celebrity. It was as good as being Pope—in fact better, because then you had real power. And better, too, because, heading out to spend a Sunday afternoon around the pool at Kevin's or Warren's or Lew's, you knew the boring, unimaginative family back home would be racked with envy. Siblings would spit. Maybe that's why the Bobby Melners were so voracious for every inch of ground, every nuance of the power game; they were enacting psychodramas scripted in childhood and forever unrevised, despite the armies of shrinks and channelers and hours of shiatsu massage.

Bobby wanted to see me because all was not well in his portfolio. I'd been telling him for months, mostly to no avail, that he was dipping too deeply into his available cash. Given the amount he had, this was no easy feat, but he was growing more desperate to stay in the game. If he wanted to continue getting the best tables in town, he needed to stay in "development," which means optioning scripts and paying writers in the hope he could set one of his projects up with a studio and recoup his advances. This had happened only twice in the past six years and both scripts had eventually been put into turnaround, which is a polite way of saying they'd been rejected. Still, no one in Hollywood would cross Bobby off their list just because of that, as long as he continued to keep his pipeline filled. So he spread it around. And why not? Other rich men's sons spend it all on old masters or cocaine or loose and reckless women, so who could hold it against Bobby that he was giving his to living and generally starving artists, if that's what you can call the pens and traffic cops for hire in Tinsel Town? Of course, you could wish he had better taste and ideas, especially if you were trying to improve his bottom line, but I get paid to do my best, not to work miracles.

He was at a table, talking on his phone as I came into the restaurant. It was a deli on Ventura out in the Valley. The food was nondescript, but it was close to the studios, which accounted for its popularity and the fact that at least six other people were on their phones at other tables, too, giving the impression they were going on to heavy confabs right after their bagels and lox. And the bagels and lox themselves lent a certain legitimacy; show business was a story of deals made in delis or at least by people at home in delis no matter how much they earned, so Bobby's breakfast gave him historical connection. A fine point he would never notice.

He waved and hung up just as I was sitting down, then turned to me and smiled.

"Are you sure? Are you absolutely sure?"

This was his standard opening with me, designed to show he was confident enough to bring up my unaccountable rejection of him and that he had no hard feelings. His manner always suggested that my refusal was the only one he'd ever had. For all I know, this was true. As I said, money is a powerful drug.

I smiled brightly and shook my head in wonder, as if Bobby had just said the cleverest thing. You old devil, my eyes managed to say, maybe I made a mistake after all. . . . Women pay this kind of price to do business all the time. For me it doesn't produce anger so much as a deep and abiding contempt for those ridiculous tiny egos that need so much pumping up. Men are right to fear women; there is often fury behind our smiling eyes.

By the second coffee refill, I was still trying to get Bobby to see why he had to go easy on the cash, at least for the next three months. He didn't want to hear.

"I gotta have the money."

"Is it a script?"

He shook his head. I could see he didn't want to tell me; he had that bad-boy look that always made me feel like the school principal.

"It's land," he finally said. "Up near the Ventura line. On the ocean side."

"You already have a nice house. And the place in Aspen."

"I know. But Susan and I—"

"Who's Susan?"

"Ratelsky. Susan Ratelsky."

He sat back to give me room to be impressed. Susan Rateisky was the girl of the moment according to the gossip columns. Her father had invented a process that was crucial to space travel, and Susan, with the regularity of any man-made celestial object, shuttled back and forth between Houston and L.A. looking haughty and thin. What was she doing with Bobby?

"We saw the land last week. Three acres. Two point five."

"Without a house?" He nodded. "A steal. Look, you have Susan Ratelsky. Why do you need the land?"

"To keep her."

I've never understood how some women have this

power, to attract rich men and make them spend it. To live off men, but in a way that is demanding, rather than dependent.

"You haven't got the money," I said, with a special pleasure at denying Susan. Although I'd guess she wouldn't bat an eye but simply move on to the next eager spender.

"I know I haven't got the cash right now. But what about the trust?"

Bobby had inherited half a dozen trusts that he'd been slowly working his way through, but the one I knew he was asking about, by far the largest, provided only interest; it had been set up so that he couldn't touch the principal.

"What about it?"

"Can't you figure something out? Couldn't I 'borrow' the two and half million, just for a while?"

There wasn't much energy to his asking because he knew his grandfather had made the trust unbreachable for just this reason. Either the old man knew his family really well, or he was cynical about human nature in general. The breakfast ended with my telling Bobby for the third time that of course there was nothing I could do.

But that wasn't the entire truth. A few months earlier something had happened that made me think the money might in fact be accessible. I had transferred three million of the principal to a new account in a new brokerage house, along with an account made up of cash reserves Bobby was going to need for a new deal he wanted to make. When I wired the house for the cash, the person who replied thought I was asking for money from the principal account and didn't question it; he or she simply wanted confirmation of the amount I ordered. Ordinarily,

I would have raised hell at such an inexcusable error, but instead, I corrected the request to specify the cash account. And made a note of the clerk's name. I remember my heart racing as if I'd done something illegal, and I guess in a sense I had. I didn't know what kept me silent, but I didn't want to look at it too closely. It probably meant nothing. But I definitely wasn't going to share the news with Bobby.

I called Don first thing when I got back to the office. I wanted to know everything he knew about Paul, but Don hadn't come in yet. I left a message for him to call me back, but he was notorious for not returning calls so I knew I'd have to keep trying myself.

The rest of the day passed in a haze of desire, that slow liquid state, heavy, like smooth thighs sheathed in silk crossing and uncrossing. I thought of Paul, the moonlight on his skin, the smell of his hair, his look as he pulled me down. I was restless, longing, and I startled Holly by going out for lunch, something I rarely did. I wandered over to Melrose and the dress shops. I wanted something new, sleek, a four-hundred-dollar understatement, cut to cover skin but reveal everything of shape. Not that I especially liked mine. Like most women, I beat myself up for failing some impossible ideal, although one of my secrets is, or used to be, a certain pleasure in my own breasts. Does that sound strange?

Well, one summer, a few years ago, a friend of mine was loaned a beach house in exchange for taking care of it and feeding two huge Russian wolfhounds. My friend invited me and four other women out for a weekend. It was a beautiful house, dreadfully furnished, isolated high on a bluff overlooking the sea. The second afternoon, after a lazy lunch and white wine on ice, the six of us went down to the beach, trailed by the dogs. There was no one else there, it was completely private, so we put down our towels, took off our bathing suits and stretched out naked in the sun. It felt wonderful, natural and right, warm sand blown by a gentle wind, white sunlight on the water, light and air on all parts of my body. The sun and wine made us drowsy, we didn't talk much, and some of us dozed. I dreamed of the first majestic creatures to stride out of the sea, trailing liquid spangles glinting in the light, brave new creatures destined to endure. I woke up after only a few minutes and, raising myself on one elbow, I looked down the line of resting women's bodies, some on their backs, others on their stomachs. The dogs were walking among them. In my memory of that moment there is no sound, the wind has stopped and the sea become silent, a solid sheet of breathing glass. I see only the white light and the Russian wolfhounds on their long, thin legs, making their way delicately among the soft bodies, their long pointed snouts gently nudging arms and breasts and buttocks and thighs, wanting to be petted. There is no sound, just the dogs, walking among the women, nuzzling soft flesh.

That night my friend Diana said to me, "You have the nicest breasts of all of us. They're beautiful."

"They are?" I asked, startled, flushing with pleasure.

"Yes. Definitely."

Alone later I studied my breasts in a mirror. Men had

always told me they were beautiful, but of course I discounted their opinions; they had a vested interest, so to speak. Diana's remark, made I knew purely as an objective aesthetic judgment, made me reconsider. I thought about the breasts of other women I had seen, looked hard at my own and I realized Diana was right, I did have nice breasts, possibly beautiful, and from that moment on I took a certain pride in them. Of course, that was several years ago and now, even though I'm still relatively young, my breasts have begun to sag, so I only had a few years of thinking they were beautiful. I accept this; it would be crazy not to, especially when it's so interesting to watch your own body age, to see the changes and understand what they mean, and to feel a certain curiosity, a bittersweet wonder and resignation, a nostalgia for your own surfaces.

I found the dress. It was a deep burnished color, almost brown, but different from the brown Paul had worn last night. Later, at home, as I dressed and imagined it torn off, crushed and crumpled on the floor, I understood I was ready for anything.

I still didn't know much about him. He asked me to meet him at an office building on Sunset, but when I asked if it was his office he said no.

"Well, where is your office?"

"Why—want to send me roses?"

"Faxes. Obscene faxes."

"What would they say?"

I was immediately embarrassed.

"You'll tell me," he said, into my silence. "Later."

It wasn't a question.

I pulled up in front of the building and sat in the car waiting for him. Unworried, certain of what was to come, I felt the luxury of patience, a contented anticipation. He could be from anywhere, married, with kids, although I didn't think so—but I was certain of his desire for me and that made me unafraid. Did that mean it was all about sex, or only about sex? Would he disappear tomorrow or would I run out of steam? I didn't care. There was some signal he had given me, or it was something he evoked in me, something that came from us together, and it told me to plunge ahead. Completely unafraid.

He was suddenly there, crossing the lighted lobby, coming toward me through heavy glass doors, striding across the pavement to the car. His face was blurred by the light and then hidden in the dark, but already his body and its movements—his walk, the swing of his shoulders, the outline of his thick dark hair—were familiar to me. I had the sense I had known him a very long time. Maybe it wasn't he who was familiar, but this thing he evoked in me, something that had been waiting a very long time to break out and be born.

He wanted to stop at a bar somewhere east on the other side of Highland. He said I could wait in the car but everything about him was intensely interesting to me, so I followed him inside and stood alone as he went toward the back to speak to a man in a bright blue suit. I couldn't hear them, but I felt the insistence in Paul's whispered words and I clearly saw the fear in the man's eyes. I didn't know what was happening. Who was Paul to inspire that look on a man's sweaty face? Was I about to go home with a mafioso, or a lone assassin, or even the neighborhood goon? No, of course not. He was too polished, too suave to make his living that way. At least directly. But I was beginning to realize he was into something, that he did his business, whatever it was, in a different way. And here's the truth: I liked it. I liked that he might be shady, illicit, different from anyone I'd ever known. I wanted to think of him playing by other rules, in some other game, unafraid of power, a coiled spring ready to snap. It excited me and, in the glare of that excitement, I found the same place in me. I was a Sleeping Beauty, waking not to the end of a story but to its beginning, to the willingness to go for broke, the rousing desire to go down a dangerous road, to consciously snap reality in two. My eyes were opening and I could plainly see: I'd been waiting a long time for someone like him to show me the way.

By the time I brought drinks into the bedroom, he was already naked. His back was to me—he was going through my closet. Ordinarily, I would have felt invaded and been angry, or ashamed at anyone seeing the mess my smooth white door kept hidden. But as I watched him standing there, relaxed, one hand on his hip as the other moved the hangers along, I felt a thrill at the exposure. I realized I wanted him to see what was mine; I wanted to show him everything. To spread my legs, unfurl myself before him; I felt he wouldn't judge.

I sat on the bed watching. He turned from the closet,

carrying a pair of black high-heeled shoes. I had forgotten they were there. Cheap and tacky, they were a birthday gift from a man I'd seen for several months; I never would have bought them for myself. When I'd unwrapped them, I'd been furious. He said the shoes were for both of us but it didn't seem that way to me. How dare he give me a gift that was all about him and his desire to turn me into an object for his pleasure! Men want whores in black stockings and lace teddies who will enact only one desire, the desire to please—to please stupid men. The shoes weren't for me, not by a long shot. I'd thrown them in the closet, forgotten about them, and soon that man was out of my life.

Paul sat down beside me. "Put these on," he said. When I hesitated, he ran his hand down my calf and pulled off the low-heeled shoes I was wearing. His fingers traced the line of my instep, the cleavage of my toes. He swung my legs across his knee and reached for the high heels. He held one out to me.

"Feel this. The leather."

I touched the shoe and looked into his eyes. I could see that he was already in some other place, as if he'd stridden out on a new playing field and the shoe he was holding was my invitation to play. He was offering a game that had no hidden implications; it was about pleasure, not about judgment. He watched as I moved my hand over the leather, along the high arch of the sole, up and down the heel, and I saw what he meant: if I allowed it, the shoe could be transformed from something cheap, a contemptible masculine fetish, into something for both of us, a neutral object to which we both gave meaning. Here was the great secret: it could have been *his* shoe on *his* foot or anything we held between us, a look, a gesture, the lightest touch of silk. It was nothing more than the whistle that put the ball in play, and nothing less than a new language in which we two could speak.

I leaned back, supporting myself on my elbows so I could watch as he put the shoes on my feet.

"Now get up. I want to see you in them."

I couldn't stop my smile. I stood up and moved a few feet away from him. His eyes were on the shoes and his cock was stirring. I laughed; it was wonderful to be exciting him, and it excited me.

"Walk back and forth. I want to see you move."

I took a few tentative steps, expecting to feel awkward and self-conscious, but after a moment I was walking easily. I began to swing my hips and soon I was swaggering, my chest out showing off my breasts.

"Come here," he said.

I wasn't ready; I wanted to make him wait. I pointed my toes in a seductive pose, flaunting myself in front of him. I felt gorgeous, strong; I was a magnet drawing him in.

"Come here," he said again. "Please."

I walked back to him, strutting, my hands on my hips. I stood next to him and he looked up and smiled, then drew my mouth down to kiss him. I rubbed one shoe against his leg. He moved back and surprised me by pulling one of my legs up so that my foot, in its black shoe, rested on his thigh. His hands couldn't stop moving. As I held on to his shoulders to regain my balance, I watched him rub the shoe over his skin, slowly back and forth, move it slowly alongside his cock. I stopped worrying about whether I would fall. I hungrily watched his fingers trace the black leather, felt his palm caress my sole, saw his cock beside the shoe. Then, he looked up at me and, his eyes on mine, he lifted my foot and put the tip of the shoe into his mouth. Everything in me dissolved in desire. I saw his tongue as he sucked on the tip, moved it in and out of his mouth, licked the leather, ran his lips over the arch of my foot, his tongue down the length of the long, narrow heel. His other hand was under my skirt, running over my thighs, my ass, between my legs. I was moaning. He could feel how wet I was. I couldn't breathe. I felt light, glorious, that if he plunged his fingers into me, he could twirl me easily, like a plate on a stick. I leaned over and pulled his mouth to me, feasted on that wetness, ran my shoe over his still-hardening cock. Soon, he would pull me down to straddle him and cup my ass to pull me close, as he moved deep inside me and I moved close upon him. And when it was over, and I could still smell the heat of our desire and feel his tongue on my nipples, I was left not knowing: Who did what to whom?

Chapter Three

Wednesday was my day to go see Nathan Broadman. Once a month I drove out to his ranch in the hills beyond Westlake. He had a house in town, but he knew I liked the drive, and so long ago we'd fallen into this routine.

I stopped first at the office. Holly had left a message on the machine saying she'd be late; I could hear tears being choked back, which told me she'd probably been up all night fighting with her boyfriend. Nothing looked pressing so I locked up and hit the road.

There was very little traffic heading up the 101 away from L.A. I called Don from the car. This time he was in but kept me on hold for so long I was beginning to think he was purposely avoiding me.

"Never, baby. You're my one open line."

"Then heaven help you . . . what's been going on? What's wrong?"

"Nothing. Nothing serious. I got into a bind, something

stupid, and Marty bailed me out. You know how he is—he wants his money."

"What's the bind?"

"You don't want to know."

"You mean you don't want to tell me."

"Something like that. But stop worrying. I'm sorting it out."

There was something familiar in his voice, an evasion, an automatic deflecting like an animal shivering against the cold, and I understood in that moment why I could never love him. He was always pushing something away.

"So who's Paul?"

"Ah. It took. Professionally—or pleasurably?"

"I don't know a thing about him."

"Well, he's from New York. He controls a very great deal of money—"

"Whose money?"

"He controls it. If it isn't his, it might as well be."

"So you don't know."

"Not exactly. But I don't think his investors are small time."

"Are they legit?"

"I suppose so. No point in delving too deeply."

"But you'd tell me if you knew they weren't?"

"I take it from all these questions you have more than a passing interest—so would you really want to know?"

I laughed, and it was okay that Don knew he had me. Of course I didn't want to know. In those first few weeks, there were many lines I crossed, but this was one I recognized. A friend might have told me that I was simply ignoring the danger signs, but that friend would have been wrong. I wasn't in denial, I was in desire. It wasn't that a grand obsession revealed itself, or a compulsive headlong recklessness. Instead, I felt something quieter and less threatening, a compelling but detached curiosity, as if I were putting myself under my own microscope, clear-eyed and dispassionate, ready to dissect myself in clinical experimentation. Even then, in some certain way, I sensed it wasn't about Paul, it was all about me. So I didn't need details. I just wanted more.

I turned off the freeway and drove through Westlake toward the hills that ran down to the ocean miles away on the other side. The morning haze had burned off and now the sky was blue, made more blue in contrast to the hills, a vivid green from new grasses sprouted in the rains. The rains were over, though, and soon the green would turn brown, and then become so dry brown would turn to gold, so absolutely dry it would shimmer in the white light, burnished by the sun.

Nathan Broadman was the man who encouraged me to go out on my own; in fact, he made it possible by becoming my first, and now my oldest, client. He said I deserved the chance. I was still a secretary at the brokerage house when we met and he was known to the public as Nifty Natey, the owner of a string of appliance stores throughout the West. When he decided to take his company public, Nathan got me promoted onto the team arranging the financing and the initial public offering. I would have worked twenty hours a day to prove his trust in me wasn't misplaced but, even more, I really liked the work, the number crunching and straightforward clarity of formulas and spreadsheets, the yes-no, one-two simplicity of it all. And I loved the momentum, the adrenaline rush fueling the race toward deadlines, the way my life was honed, narrowed down to the dictates of a single goal. For the first time, I felt carried along by a sweeping tide; I didn't have to row.

But Nathan did more than give me a chance at work. Back then he was married and he and his wife, Margaret, supported a ballet company, gave to the museum building fund, and lived in a house in Hancock Park that had one of the best collections of English eighteenth-century furniture west of the Mississippi. They sometimes invited me for dinner and, although I tried to hide it, I always studied them, as if I were an alien to the planet determined to learn its ways, as if learning its ways could guarantee me what Nathan and Margaret had, that elegant, polished world. Margaret was very like Nathan, understated and warm, and I can still see Nathan reaching over to brush back a wisp of thick, dark hair from her face. The last time I saw her most of it had fallen out as a result of chemotherapy and she had the gray skin and inward distraction of a dying cancer patient. After she died, Nathan went into a kind of retreat, all but running his business over the phone, and when he reemerged you could see he was a different man. There was a silence at his center as if at the end of every conversation there was something more that needed to be said but simply couldn't be. He stood permanently in the midst of what was no longer complete.

As the gravel road wound around a hill, Nathan's ranch opened out across the floor of a small valley. It had been one of the first things he and Margaret had bought when Nifty Natey's began to make real money, five hundred acres and an old stucco ranch house built around an arbored veranda set on a gentle rise with a view of the hills. It was one of those hills that Nathan climbed to scatter Margaret's ashes. I only know this because on the forms we had to file in relation to the estate after her death, there was a question about "the disposition of the body." As Nathan read those words, I saw the breath go out of him and when he answered his voice was stony cold.

Nathan was on the veranda, asleep on a chaise in the sun. He was in his early sixties and only now beginning to show signs of age; even Margaret's death had left his face unlined. But time was doing its work and in the strong light I could see it. He was not a big man, and it had never been his physical presence that commanded. His power came from another source. He was the kind who sat back and watched, his mind hidden but restlessly assessing, and then, like a lizard in a nature film unleashing its tongue, struck. With Nathan, that unfolding tongue was slowed down and deliberate, precise, and it didn't devour but amassed. That's what I admired—the patience, the covert calculating, and then the decisive act.

He stirred. I stepped between him and the sun and my shadow woke him up. He saw who it was and began getting up.

"An old man asleep in the sun. Who would have thought it?" he said.

"Not old. Old-er. But not old."

"Tell my back. I was out clearing brush yesterday. I'm going to pay for a week."

I followed him into the house. It was cool and dark, comfortable and muted, completely unpretentious; I'd been coming to it for a long time before I'd realized how much thought had gone into its furnishings. Mercedes, half of the Mexican couple who looked after the place, had put out coffee; later, there would be lunch on the veranda.

We got right down to work. After all this time, we had a routine. First, I reported on the stocks and bonds portfolio, both his and the trusts for his son, Peter, everything they had apart from the businesses. Then we moved into the properties they personally owned: an apartment house in Los Feliz somehow left over from earlier days, which had been in Margaret's name, the various houses, a co-op and a second long-term leased apartment in New York, a condominium on Maui that was sometimes rented out. For a while, Nathan had also given me the management of two strip malls he had developed with Peter, but I hated the constant headache, dealing with dreams-of-glory shopkeepers and fast-food franchises, and when Nathan decided to sell them—before the bottom fell out of the market—I felt nothing but relief. Next, I covered all the housekeeping bills, which were considerable, then the many monthly accounts, store and restaurant charges, his credit cards. I had all of it on the laptop with me, but Nathan rarely looked at the screen. He said he never would have given me all this to oversee if he didn't think I could do a good job; he trusted me.

It was all routine, but it took a long time and when we broke we were both hungry. Outside, Mercedes and I said hello as she put out Nathan's favorite quesadillas along with rice and beans. There was a Mexican beer I'd never heard of that tasted like thin, rushing gold and, as always, a flan that always left me wondering if I could ask for thirds.

We sat back with our coffee. Beyond the shade of the veranda the sun was hot; it slowed things down. Somewhere behind us, crows called to each other. I thought of Paul. I saw his eyes, the way they held me when he put out his hand, the way they watched as I arched my back so that he would touch my breast. Pure desire swept through me and almost forced me out of my chair. I took a deep breath and the flush passed, but I was certain Nathan must have noticed; how could another person fail to sense the volcano that erupted inside me? But when I looked over, I was surprised to see that he'd gotten up and was going inside to answer a phone I hadn't even heard ring.

I looked out. At the edge of the veranda hibiscus and bougainvillea were blooming, and the flowers attracted a small company of bees. I listened to their steady hum until Nathan's voice drowned them out. I could hear he was angry, questioning, but I couldn't catch the words. When he came back and sat down, he didn't say anything; in fact, he looked as if his mind were a million miles away.

I wanted to ask what was wrong but hesitated. There was genuine affection between us, even what I'd have called love, but it hadn't been built on intimate exchanges. I would gladly have told him about Paul—at that moment, the only thing I really wanted to talk about was Paul—but my friendship with Nathan was based on something other than our personal histories, and I liked that. I hate the people who rush at you, always wanting to tell you things, positively eager to give themselves away. They have no restraint. Nathan and I weren't like that and, somehow, that made things feel more solid, not less.

But he looked troubled.

"Is something wrong?" I finally asked. "Anything I can help with?"

He shook his head. "That was Peter—I don't know why it is but I can't get straight answers out of him—he never does his homework." He smiled, but his eyes remained grim. "I've had him trying to track things down, but . . ."

His voice trailed off. Nathan wasn't a man given to meditative silences, but I didn't feel I could ask anything more.

"Have you heard any rumors?" he finally asked.

"About what?"

"The company. Anything at all?"

I shook my head. Despite the recession, Nifty Natey Enterprises had consistent net profits and paid dividends; all its ratios were good. It wasn't going through the roof the way everything had a few years earlier but it was a solid company. It was true that when Nathan had first installed Peter as president they had teetered on the edge of overexpansion. But Nathan had stepped in and pulled things back, brought down the debt and gotten rid of most of the junk, so that now NNE was one of the most stable companies on the AMEX.

"I hear only good things—the stock's attractive. I've got most of my clients in it."

Nathan shrugged. "Maybe it's nothing. I need to trust Peter more. Maybe I've got too much time to myself to worry."

He leaned back again and looked off to the hills. I

thought the only problem he had was the loss of Margaret, and as I turned to look back at the view toward the hills, I heard what Nathan must have always heard, the loneliness in the calling of the crows.

On the way home, I dialed the one phone number I had for Paul. It was his home; he was still vague about an office. There was no answer. I let it ring, though, and drove for a couple of miles feeling close to him in the effort to connect. It fascinated me that there wasn't an answering machine on the line; every fact was significant because some larger picture, the framework, a context, hadn't yet come into focus. Paul loomed so large but was still a mystery. Who was he, and who would he be to me?

On that day coming back into town was coming back to him. I was hungry for him, kept seeing the look in his eyes as he watched me open up, the way that look gave me the power to open. I felt his fingers trace the line of my throat, my tongue on his belly, his hands on my ass. I heard our breathing in the dark. Energy was moving through me, restless, longing energy, but it didn't fuel me. Instead, it left me craving.

Chapter Four

Time passed. Although I got up each morning, dressed for success, and went to work, I was interested only in Paul. I slowly learned some things about him. He'd come out from New York six months earlier to take advantage of the declining real estate market and what he referred to generally as "other opportunities." He was never specific; there were vague mentions of Arab, German, and Japanese investors; of the mushrooming importance of the Pacific Rim; and once of a possible takeover of a portland cement company. I never pressed for details even though, given my work, it would have been natural for us to talk business.

He had leased a furnished condo in one of the towers on Wilshire in Westwood. It had no more resonance than a suite at a good hotel, although the kitchen was well stocked; it turned out Paul liked to cook. I shouldn't have been surprised. I've noticed that men on their own often take much better care of themselves than women without men. Maybe we think that only the presence of a man justifies the expenditures for good dishes, a deep-cushioned sofa, the permanence of built-in shelves; that if we become too complete, too self-sufficient, no man will ever want us and we ourselves will have no need of them. As if, without need, there would be no desire. I hate that most men don't appear to struggle with these complications. Their thinking isn't usually based on making room for another; they don't live so much in what-ifs. They know how to take care of themselves.

Somewhere in those first weeks, he made white bean chili, spicy and thick with chicken. I watched him move around the compact kitchen, his attention only partially on me as he checked the recipe, measured amounts, and adjusted the flame. I was setting the table and we were talking in the way that people do: *So you're an only child,* and *Well, I was only seventeen, I thought I knew everything*. Suddenly, and from out of nowhere, anger flared in me, resistance; I turned and walked into the living room. I'd seen us as if we were a color spread in a glossy magazine: a modern couple share an intimate moment. But that wasn't what I wanted, not that sort of intimate moment, ordinary and conventional. He was the mysterious stranger and that's what I wanted from him: the chance to break free, to take a risk on everything unknown. I thought, we drift along on superhighways and need pills to take us to the streets below. He's my drug, my passport, my connection. I thought, each world is a map of references, each reference a dream of the voyager. I thought, stop thinking and feel. Feel this desert wind.

Why was it different with him? Why did the look in his eye make me unafraid of the look in mine? Before Paul, I had thought I was sexually adventurous, open to experiments and scenarios, without judgment about what anybody wanted and needed. The men I went to bed with always wanted to do it again and whether I came or didn't—and sometimes I didn't and never faked it—they always knew I liked it, the touching and sucking, the teasing fingers and lapping tongue, that quickening point of desire in my eager cunt. I liked to throw my legs open, unafraid to be seen.

But really I'd been held back, some part of me always watching, ascertaining: Did they want me enough, was I putting on a good enough show? Sex had had an ulterior purpose, had been a means to an end, currency in the transaction between me and men. *Will he still love me tomorrow?* But I didn't need Paul to make pledges of undying love—in fact, I didn't want him to. I didn't want to be that couple in the magazine. And with that agenda gone, I stumbled into an unexpected clarity, free of the anxieties that come from manipulation. For the first time I could strut in high heels, dress like an avid, love-hungry tart in silks and lace that could only be about sex. I went down on my knees without any fear or resentment, unthreatened by the guise of submission, by anything we could enact. I stopped worrying about his using me because, in my own way, I stopped using him. In a curious way, that left me free to take whatever I wanted as long as I wanted. I could lie back and let him lap at my center—I could allow it—and had I wanted him to do it for hours I could easily make that known. And I felt the unexpected power of the one who gives pleasure, as well, felt it every time I opened my throat and took him in and made him moan. The focus shifted to me. To what I could do, give and bestow. I felt my power. My tongue determined his destiny.

I suppose you could say it wasn't about power, it was about trust. You could say I was able to do these things with Paul because there was love between us and that gut-level certainty made it all right to enact dominance and submission, for each of us to take a part, either part, and play it with conviction. And maybe in the beginning I did think I was in love with him. After all, what other categories or words did I have for what I felt?

But I see even then I understood that I wanted something else from him. I just needed time to strip away my fear, to open me up to other possibilities, to make me honest in a particular way.

Paul said he wanted me to meet some friends of his.

"Who are they?" I asked.

"I've known them for years. We've done a lot of business together."

We drove out Sunset through Beverly Hills, then turned onto one of the narrow streets that wind through Holmby Hills and stopped at an iron gate. Paul buzzed, the intercom squawked, and we passed through.

Gaby was standing in the open doorway of a large modern house, silhouetted in the light radiating behind her. She came forward as we got out of the car; she held out her hands and Paul grasped them.

"We meet at last," she said, turning to me. "Paul has told us so much about you."

I felt at a loss; he had never until tonight mentioned her to me. She had a slight accent which I couldn't place; seeing her dark hair, I thought it could have been Middle Eastern. She wasn't tall or particularly slim; there was a womanly heft to the way she filled out the dark wine-colored silk suit she was wearing with a diamond pin I took to be real on the lapel. Her feet were small, encased now in high silk sandals. She had that look some foreign women have of being flawlessly put together; they are the women who know how to tie a scarf and drape a shawl, who leave a trail of subtle and lingering perfume with a name you've never heard of. They may be impoverished but somehow they find the money for facials and massages and scented papers to line the drawers that hold their fine silk underwear. They have the patience and discipline real luxury requires. They know something I don't.

Inside, Gaby led us across the marble floor of the entrance hall and down two steps into an enormous white-walled living room. There were other people there. Charles, Gaby's husband, brought me a drink; he was tall and, although still young, had thick gray hair and was handsome in that way models and successful salesmen are, so handsome that I began to think the money must be Gaby's. She was introducing me to another couple whose names I couldn't catch; Paul evidently knew them, though, and like Gaby, they seemed to be foreign.

Hors d'oeuvres were set out. I realized there were unseen servants in this house and that made me aware of all I couldn't know about it, the rooms beyond this living room and what went on in them, the grounds beyond the blackened windows. For no reason I could name, I felt that things were hidden, unmentioned. I felt myself thrown off. I looked to Paul, but he was deep in animated conversation with the others. I heard him laugh, I watched the muscles of his back shift beneath his jacket as he settled in, and a chilling fear came over me. Suddenly, I hated him for bringing me here, for forcing these people on me. I hated that he had a life apart from me and I hated that he dazzled me; it put him beyond me, as if he were a gorgeous ghost teasing me, eluding my grasp.

We went to a restaurant, a new and overpriced place in Beverly Hills. The others were all distorted as if viewed from the wrong end of a hard metallic telescope. I knew they couldn't see how disguised I was, how distant and separate. I watched Gaby. She was the sort of woman men find attractive. The jacket of her suit was cut low and I could see the rise of her breasts as she leaned in to talk. They looked soft, even powdered, and I thought I caught their scent. Maybe there was something between Paul and her. Maybe they'd been lovers. Well, so what? It meant nothing to me.

Then, just before dessert, I noticed a look pass between Charles and Sando, the man of the other couple. It was more than a look; for a moment, they were staring at each other as Charles ran the middle finger of his right hand slowly around his lips. His mouth was half-open and there was a lazy, challenging look in his eyes. Sando shifted and leaned back in his seat. It may have been a trick of the light but it seemed to me that I could see his breathing deepen.

A few minutes later, Sando said he had to make a phone call and left the table. A minute or two later

Charles got up, to go to the men's room, he said. I waited a bit, then excused myself. I needed to see—whatever there was to be seen.

They were out in the alley, in the shadow of a closed white van. Sando was leaning back against it, his arms stretched out above him, looking at Charles who was slowly, softly unbuttoning the front of his white linen shirt. With each button, Charles eased back the fabric, revealing more and more of Sando's chest. I saw him lightly cup Sando's breasts as if they were a woman's, run his palm over the nipples, pinch them erect. He stepped back a bit and put his hand fully on Sando's cock. I saw in the light how hard it was as it pressed against the fabric of his slacks. Charles's hand found a rhythm and he watched as Sando's whole body began to move to it, galvanized by the energy arcing out of that hand. The fingers of his other hand played over Sando's chest, eased up his throat, caressed his cheek. I heard Charles murmuring, encouraging, exciting; the sounds were a link between them, a rope to which they both were tethered. Then he leaned in and they kissed. Sando's arms were still above him as if chained; his whole body was pressing in, wanting more of Charles. They were moving now together. I heard a belt buckle being undone and a zipper opening up. Suddenly, another sound intruded: a car horn down the alley on the street. It blared again. I was suddenly afraid they'd hear it and turn to see me watching. Silently I ducked back inside.

I couldn't breathe. I thought I was frightened; my heart was pounding. But as I stumbled back toward the dining room and then caught a glimpse of Paul, I realized I wasn't scared, I was aroused. I sat down beside him. I kept seeing

Charles's hand; I wanted to feel it, to be the hand that slipped inside the folds of soft fabric. I touched Paul's arm, my thighs opening unseen beside him. He could have slipped his fingers under my skirt and played with me easily as he continued to talk. I wanted him to. I wanted to feel my palm pressing against his hardening cock. I looked at Gaby, the anger and indifference I'd felt now gone. I saw how attractive she was, the warmth and ease her body suggested, a lushness that promised even more. If Paul had had an affair with her, well, who could blame him?

Charles came back to the table, followed a bit later by Sando. There was no hint of the passion I'd seen. I wanted to say something to them, to tell them that far from being shocked or condemning them, I'd wished that I could join them. Their desire drew me in. I looked around the table at the others. How much did Gaby know? It came to me how little *I* knew: there could be arrangements that were hidden from view, whole ranges of experience I couldn't even guess at. Now it didn't frighten me. I only wanted to know more. But Gaby soon signaled the end of the evening by saying she had to get up early. As I got into Paul's car back at her house, she held the door and said we ought to get together. I made a point of giving her my card.

I was voluptuous in bed that night. I thought of Charles and Sando, saw Sando's straining hands above him, his fingers grasping air, the tanned skin of his smooth chest as Charles's fingers eased the fabric back. I pushed myself deeper onto Paul's cock. I was lava flowing around and through him. I made his body arch.

Later, I wondered again what Gaby knew. And I thought about why I didn't tell Paul what I'd seen. I wanted to protect Charles and Sando, to keep their passion hidden, but it wasn't because I cared about them. In a way still unclear to me, I sensed that in keeping silent I was preserving some possibility for myself. A part of me that had never been awake was rising now, enlarging, and I wanted the way open to follow where it led. I needed to be true to that. I didn't know it yet, but my allegiance wasn't to Paul. It was to desire.

Chapter Five

There were two messages from Nathan waiting at the office.

"I've called a meeting for noon. Can you be here?"

"Of course," I said. "What's it about? What should I bring?"

"Nothing. See you at noon."

It wasn't like him to be abrupt and mysterious. But it also wasn't like him to sound false alarms. Something was going on.

There were other messages: one from Bobby Melner who, I knew from the papers, was still seeing Susan Ratelsky and was probably even more desperate for cash. Another one of my clients was thinking for the thousandth time about bailing out of the movie business; she wanted to know whether, if she lived to be ninety and never earned another penny, she would have enough money to pay the rent. I told her she'd be lucky to get through the next six months and then had to spend a half hour calming her down. It's one of the curious things about Hollywood people: they earn huge sums whenever they work and feel themselves rich, but they don't seem to be aware of all the money that leaks out in the downtime on expensive restaurants, Armanis or Gaultiers, and an ostrich Filofax. They have no idea how many of those houses and cars are supported month to month on kited checks. I must say that from time to time I enjoy having to tell them.

There was also a message from Don asking if I wanted to meet for a drink. He was out when I called back, but I left word that any day would be fine; I'd make the time. The fact was I realized I wanted to see him. He was the one person in my life who knew Paul. I wanted that connection.

I took Beverly all the way downtown and cut over to drive through the Second Street tunnel. I came out onto Bunker Hill, a turn-of-the-century neighborhood that had been completely leveled to build a new downtown. You could still see it, though, in old movies; only a few weeks earlier, I'd watched a young Burt Lancaster ride the streetcar up the long-gone Angel's Flight. Now the hill was a maze of new high-rise apartments and office complexes, all of which turned their impregnable backs on the seedy streets below the hill on Spring and Main.

NNE's offices were in one of the new towers. On smogless days there was a sweeping view across downtown west and south to the ocean, all that brightness in contrast to the offices, which were wood paneled, dark, and baronial, a mix of Persian carpets, American primitive paintings, and vaguely uncomfortable eighteenth-century seating. Nathan's office had a half-dozen deeply upholstered chairs straight out of an English men's club, a ten-panel coromandel screen, and a desk on which he kept a photo of Margaret and nothing else, not even a telephone. I could see it was beautiful but I never liked it; it always made me feel on the verge of making a terrible mistake.

The meeting was already in progress when I got there. Nathan waved aside my apologies. In fact, I wasn't late; they had simply started talking. We were a small group: Hal Marlin, NNE's CFO, with whom I'd had some routine dealings, two young MBAs, the kind of nerdy number crunchers Nathan viewed with resignation as inevitable necessities; and Peter, Nathan's son, who frowned when he saw me.

"What's she doing here?" he asked, without even bothering to appear polite. I wasn't surprised; I knew he'd never liked me.

Nathan didn't look up. "I trust her. And I pay her—I want to take advantage of her brains."

I took a seat across from him, next to Peter, which meant we didn't have to spend a lot of time avoiding eye contact.

"Hal," Nathan said. "Bring her up to speed."

Hal had worked for Nathan for years but he still had the conservative look of an East Coast corporate officer. He didn't have a tan. The upper echelons of the Los Angeles business world, with its rich fabrics and stylish tailoring, its showy hundred-dollar haircuts, had never attracted him; his suits were probably just as expensive and his hair, what was left of it, just as carefully cut, but it all served to blend him in, not to make him stand out.

Hal cleared his throat. "Nathan feels that there's too much stock activity, that maybe someone or some group is making a move on the company. He feels that—"

Nathan laughed. "You sound like my interpreter."

"Well," Hal said, "at this point, all we have to go on is your feeling. I'm not at all sure I agree with you."

"Me neither," Peter said. "I'll go further—I think you're worried about nothing. We should be happy the price is going up."

Nathan sat looking from one to the other. The MBAs—the Suits—were silent but attentive; they vibrated energy, like harnessed stamping horses waiting to be driven.

Nathan turned to me. "Maybe they're right and it is nothing. But my instincts have been pretty good in the past and I don't like this sudden push."

"It's not exactly sudden," I said. "The stock's been steadily increasing—that's part of what makes it so attractive."

"You see?" Peter said. "Anyway, hasn't it occurred to anybody that the stock's rising because of the job we all are doing? Really, Pop, maybe you should give us some credit, instead of looking for mystery men."

His voice was unexpectedly angry and we all shifted in our seats. I didn't see Nathan's face, but I sensed his stiffening. Peter recovered, though, and went on. "Besides, if you need things to worry about, we can come up with plenty."

He laughed but it was artificial. I looked at Nathan. His mouth was tight; he knew when he was being patronized. But he was going to move right on. He turned to Hal, who shrugged.

"Okay, we'll keep an eye on it," Hal said. "But even if someone files with five per cent, you and Peter own more than—I think it was fifty-five point eight at close yesterday. I can't see a long-term threat."

"Well, I don't want any surprises—no strangers in bed with me." Nathan got up and went to his desk. The meeting was over. The Suits were up and out, twin flashes of dedicated ambition. Peter disappeared quickly, too.

"Hal, close the door on your way out," Nathan said. "Vega, you stay a minute."

He sat down behind his desk as Hal left and swiveled around to look out at the view. "They want me to be wrong because they don't want me in the way. Especially Peter . . ." He paused. "Well, it's understandable. A young man wants to make his mark. I just wish he had more . . ."

His voice trailed off. There was nothing I could say. "But you know what?" he said turning back to the room and me. "I hope there *is* someone out there—I've been too bored. Cat and mouse—I need the game."

"Providing, of course, you win."

He smiled. "It goes without saying. But Hal's right—we can't lose. Someone could make some trouble maybe but not really much more. Still, it's my company and I want to know. I want you to get on it."

"Me?" I was surprised.

"The people here will do enough to keep me happy but not much more. Ask around, run the numbers through that computer of yours. See what you can find."

"But I'm no industrial detective. Hire Kroll—that's their business."

"No, I want to keep it in the family. So to speak."

I liked his talking like that; it made me feel connected. I

said I'd see what I could do and left him turning to a stack of memos neatly divided into plastic files sorted by topic. He had two secretaries to keep it all humming along.

On the way out I ran into Peter at the elevators. I had the feeling he'd been waiting for me.

"You don't need to get mixed up in this," he said. "I can handle it."

"Your father seems to feel you need help." I was instantly sorry I'd said it. Peter resented me with something like sibling rivalry and I didn't need to make things worse; that was unfair to Nathan. Besides, I knew Nathan loved him and would have done anything for him, even though they were very different. Where Nathan had the great gift of spontaneity and no stake in being right if it kept him from the best solution, Peter dug in beforehand, then tried to bend reality to make himself look good. Everything became a question of ego. It had gotten him into trouble more than once but Nathan was always there to bail him out.

I also knew he ran with a fast crowd fueled by money and cocaine. I'd once been at a party with him. He was high as a kite, got into a fight with the woman he was with and humiliated her in front of everyone. I remember I wasn't surprised. Although I hardly knew him then, I could see he had the capacity to be cruel.

Now, he stepped back, stifling the anger I knew he felt. He suddenly smiled. "Maybe I do need taking care of. You think you're up to it?"

It was a dirty smile and it only broadened as he ran his eyes up and down my body. I've known other men like him who, if they can't get at you one way, will come at you from another. It was funny, really, that he thought he could assert some masculine superiority or rattle me, as if I was supposed to care about his assessment. I was going to stare intently at his crotch to see if he'd squirm, but the elevator doors opened.

"Well, it's kind of a moot point, don't you think?" I said, getting on. "Because I know you're not."

The doors closed on an unmistakable smirk curling his lips. That, after Margaret, he was the person Nathan loved best in the world was one of those inexplicable quirks of biology, a fact you file away and then step carefully around.

Don and I finally met for a drink in the bar at the Four Seasons. I watched him coming toward me and the old guilt just didn't come. I couldn't help it that we'd once been married and planned a future together; we'd been separated a long time now and we were leading separate lives. He was no reflection on me. He couldn't taint me. So I was genuinely smiling as he corralled the waiter and ordered a double as he was sitting down. And that absence of guilt had a curious effect: for the first time, I felt real compassion for Don. You could almost say I loved him.

"You look great as always, babe. A million bucks."

Today, I didn't mind the P.R. smile and easy flattery. He launched into his news—his troubles at work, where it now looked as if they would keep him on; a woman he'd met with three kids and a heavy mortgage; the news from home, where they always asked about me. He was well into his second double before I got a chance to mention Paul.

"I've told you all I know."

"But why did you introduce us? Where did you meet him?"

"I don't know—around. Some party somewhere. Someone introduced us. I meet a million people. I knew he had money. I thought he'd like you. That you'd like him. In a business sense, I mean."

"Oh sure, strictly business," I said, laughing. "You knew what you were doing."

"Did I? Do I ever?"

Maybe it was the booze but his question tripped him into a place that was deep and closed off. He had the look of someone at the very end of the line.

"Don, something is wrong—what is it?"

He looked up and the professional P.R. man was back in place. "I just need a vacation. Someplace without a phone or a fax. Remote and expensive. Know what I mean?" He downed the rest of his drink, then smiled at me. "So you and Paul are—what? Hot and heavy?"

"Well . . . he's got me going." I couldn't find the words. "He's something . . . new. Very different."

Maybe my talking that way hurt Don or made him jealous, but I didn't want to stop. "He doesn't tell me much about himself, so I'm dying of curiosity. You must know more about him."

He shook his head.

"I met some friends of his," I said. "A woman named Gaby and her husband, Charles. Do you know them, know who they are?"

He said he didn't. I thought about asking him to try and find out, but it felt wrong. Don was part of my past, not this new thing that was unfolding. I let the conversation go on to other things.

"Seen your friend Broadman lately?" he asked after a brief lull.

"Why do you ask?"

"No reason. Just making conversation."

"Why do you ask?" I suddenly felt I was in a sparring match. "What have you heard?" I asked.

"What's to hear?"

I saw I had a lot to learn as a spy; I'd already given too much away.

"I didn't mean that there was anything to hear. Like you said, I was just making conversation."

I'd lost him again. He was looking right at me but I had the feeling he was a million miles away. Maybe the sparring was in my imagination; maybe something else entirely was pressing in on him. Or maybe he just wanted to string things out so he could have another drink.

"Well, have you seen him?"

"Sure. You know I go up there once a month."

I didn't say anything about NNE and the stock; it was my turn to change the subject.

"How's Marty—is he off your case?"

"Yeah, I came up with the money, so we're pals again. With friends like that . . . right?"

After a while, I said I had to go. I left him as he headed for the phones to make some calls. He had that worried look again, like a man who's lost a scrap of paper with some vital information on which his life depends. Despite all the people in his life, he was alone, but I knew I couldn't help him. I didn't have the energy to push any harder than I already had. It's strange, but I see now that you don't know who people are going to be to you until it's all played out. You'd think that Don's real importance in my life was that he'd been my husband. But I think it's turned out to be something else: he was the one who introduced me to Paul.

I wasn't surprised when Gaby called.

"I've been thinking of you," she said, her soft accent drawing out the words. "Come have lunch. We simply must be friends."

We met at the Bistro Gardens. I'd been there before, but it wasn't a place where I could feel comfortable. It had the air of private club with a very select membership—ladies who lunched, businessmen on diets for whom the chef cooked special low-sodium, low-fat but miraculously tasty meals at ridiculously exorbitant prices. These were the people who could step graciously and gracefully around all the little unpleasantnesses nipping at their heels, so insulated from the world that the voices on their answering machines weren't even theirs but the voices of their servants.

I saw at once it was very much Gaby's territory; she was already there when I arrived and seemed to know everyone, half the other customers and the entire staff. She was wearing bright red, a straight-skirted suit with gold buttons stamped with an abstract art nouveau design; it occurred to me they might be real gold, antiques that she'd had especially sewn on. If that were so, it showed an attention to detail—and the money and time it buys to give orders to other people to see to those details—that I could only envy. As we sat down, I took in her smile, the cheerful wave of her manicured fingers to someone across the room, the discreet nod to the maître d', signaling that we were ready to order. I saw that even though she was one of those people from someplace else who are lightly attached, and settle in L.A., where things are always shifting, one's fortunes and status, even the ground itself—the illusions of Hollywood are nothing against the shifting instabilities of the land—she also radiated a kind of permanence, the solidity and continuity real money buys. She could go anywhere and be at home. If trouble came, she would be helicoptered out.

"Oh, I'm a little bit of everything," she said when I asked her where she was from. "French, Greek, Lebanese—even a touch of Ethiopian, although my mother may have claimed that just to be exotic. She was a very theatrical woman—feather boas and beaded shawls, very black eyelids, fainting spells—it was terrifying to be her little girl."

She laughed and I could hear that any terror had long ago vanished. I wouldn't be surprised if right now there was a little old lady wrapped in beads and feathers in one of the rooms of Gaby's house whom she dutifully visited every day.

"And I grew up everywhere. My father and his family had interests all over the world."

I resisted asking just what those interests were but contented myself with speculation: olive oil, diamonds, Persian carpets, the armaments of war. An image came: dark men in suits around a copper table, eating handfuls of honeyed almonds and negotiating price. Where was Gaby? Home with her theatrical mother, studying geography?

She wanted to know about me. I didn't lie, but there wasn't much to tell. In any case, for me, our real subject was Paul.

"How long have you known him?" I asked.

"Years and years. Some mutual friend put us in touch when Paul was looking for investors—I think our first venture was Sea Horse Ranch. Do you know it? In Carmel?"

I did. It was an exclusive enclave of individual houses, each built on three to five acres overlooking a strip of the Big Sur coast, a hidden settlement of reclusive movie stars and buttoned-down moguls. I dimly remembered some scandal briefly connected to it—one of the contractors cutting corners, kickbacks, even Mafia money—I wasn't sure.

"Then an office building—"

"In Phoenix."

"Oh, that came later. After the one in Houston. Charles says we must always say yes to Paul because we always do so well."

So she and Charles had been together awhile and he was more than mere decoration. He knew about her business.

"I was very lucky to find Charles," Gaby said, as if I'd spoken aloud. "He's always given me very good advice. And he's very attractive, isn't he?"

"Yes," I said. "Very."

"Like Paul."

She was smiling at me and the look in her eyes was so steady and sure it engulfed me. I lost all footing. What did she mean, what did she know? Some kind of suggestiveness was suddenly thick in the air, oceans of something unsaid that left me breathless. Any power I might have felt knowing about Charles vanished; the look in her eyes, the easy way she leaned in to the table and let her fingers play over the moist stem of the wineglass, the rustle of her stockings as she crossed her legs, made me think it was she who knew something I didn't. I was afraid. But I didn't know of what. It wasn't about the past, learning that she and Paul had been lovers. It was the future now rushing toward me, as if my feelings for Paul and the ones I was learning through him, and what I saw in the alley, and now Gaby's glittering eyes were deepening mysteries drawing me on. They were all emblems of another world I wanted to explore. And that curiosity, my awakened adventurousness, was its own call to abandonment and release. It was propelling me forward with the steady force of a hot solar wind, blinding me with some new and vivid light, searing away all that had hidden my true needs. That was it: I was longing to rise to a dangerous challenge, to press my body fully at the boundaries and with my flesh make them give way. Only fear was holding me back.

Then, in the moment it took to move my eyes from those graceful fingers on the stem of the glass up toward the line of her neck as it rose from the red glowing silk of her wide, soft collar, I stepped across the line. Without moving, I planted myself in another place. Fear fell away, was brought down to size, as if it were a small neat ball I could shape with my hands and tuck in my pocket. I could feel myself striding forward, all energy concentrated; I was ready to play.

"You and Paul have been lovers, I suppose?" I wasn't afraid of her answer. In fact, I wanted to know, wanted the details. I wanted her to tell me where and when; I wanted him to tell me what she tasted like.

She laughed, an elegant rich sound. "Good heavens, no. Although I've thought about it, I admit. Who would not—I think all women respond to him, *n'est-ce pas?* Some men just have that quality—they intrigue and captivate, present an irresistible challenge. Devastating."

"Like Charles?"

"Ah, Charles . . . he's a special case." She smiled and went on eating her salad niçoise, and once more I was left with the sense that it was I who was in ignorance. After a moment she looked up. "Some women have that quality, too. You, for instance."

I was startled.

"Surely you know it," she said. "It's something to do with how self-contained you are."

She sat back and gazed at me. I had no idea what she was talking about but again I stepped across: I didn't flutter away and protest in self-consciousness. No one, male or female, had ever spoken to me like this and now I knew that I was hungry for it. I felt she wasn't describing me, she was creating me and I gave myself over to her examination. It made me bold.

"I sense you watching," she said. "It makes me long to know exactly what you see."

It was my turn to laugh. "Confusion mostly. Or . . . emptiness—" I stopped, embarrassed at having said it, but then I saw Gaby's encouraging smile.

"Maybe that was true in the past," she said, putting her hand on mine. "But you strike me differently now. I feel you will do something—unique."

"Are you a witch?" I knew my eyes were sparkling as they met hers.

"Oh no, that was my mother," she said with a laugh.

I felt a rush of pleasure, the sharpening and animating energy of flirtation, to be smiling with her over delicious food and heavy silver, surrounded by luxury, to catch us reflected in thin, expensive crystal.

"But what about me?" she asked, withdrawing her hand as the waiter came to clear the plates. "What do you see in me?"

I thought for a moment. "I—I don't know."

She sat back, smiling. "Well, that's an honest answer. And a good one. It means we will have to meet again so that you can decide."

It was almost three when we said goodbye as we waited for our cars. Gaby suggested getting together the following week, again for lunch or with Paul and Charles. There was a vague mention of a party. I nodded yes to everything.

After I left her, I decided not to go back to the office. I was restless and didn't want to focus on numbers and deals and the welfare of my clients. I was excited and, if I had known at that moment where Paul was, I would have gone to him without hesitation and stripped us down, run my hands over his back and across his ass, felt his tongue moist and warm at my breast. But it was all right that I had to wait; I was like a cat stretching out in the sun, luxuriating in the heat of desire.

I didn't know how Gaby fit into it. Of course, I was attracted to her, and some of it was sexual: I was aware of her body, a subtle perfume that was heavy and sensuous, and I felt the suggestion in her eyes. But there seemed to be something else she was promising me, a kind of opulent certainty that was slow and heavy and yet mysterious. Maybe it was only the ledge over the abyss, the place beyond the fear, but she and Paul were somehow pointing the way; they were my ticket to ride. It was all right that I still couldn't see exactly where I was going; I felt myself opening to whatever might come.

Late in the day, I headed east. The lavender twilight lengthening behind me had turned the windows of the buildings I was passing into metallic reflective glass, glimmering with shadows and light, throwing back the world outside, making secret the spaces inside. Street lamps were coming on, single points of pearl against gold and purple and marine. It was the magic hour, that shimmering fragile moment between day and night, light and dark, and it suited me. I felt my breathing slow as the colors deepened. I was poised on the brink, the verge of something rich and unexpected, released from the past into a slowly unfolding present, unafraid of the future. I had been longing to be cut loose, unhinged from confusion and emptiness, and now it didn't matter that I was in someplace new, and without a compass. This mystery cut to the bone and it made me feel certain. A freedom had been set off inside me, a brazen recklessness, and it was as if it was its own ladder, luring me forward, supporting me as I climbed.

Chapter Six

Slowly Paul came into focus. At first, I could only see his fingers reaching out for me, or feel his tongue, or flush with pleasure when I remembered the look in his eyes. His face, though, a clear image of it, eluded me. When we arranged to meet in public places, I half-expected not to recognize him. He was new and strange each time in that initial moment and in some way shocking; it was as if the act of seeing him, his image falling like a shadow across my retina, exploded all my vague senses of him into a thousand shards, sent them flying, only to be reformed an instant later in the concrete fact of his actual presence. In each new meeting there were surprises: he was taller than I thought, or smaller, his eyes were lighter, or darker, he was less handsome, or more. I was lost in a fog of continuous desire for him and yet he was fragmented and floated around me like pieces of a jigsaw puzzle, brief snatches of individual images that needed to be made whole.

But slowly he did become whole for me. I learned to focus; he became specific, developed borders and boundaries, achieved an outline, became himself, Paul. It didn't lessen my desire for him; in fact, that became stronger as I began to understand how deep I was able to go with him. But he became familiar, consistent, and that first moment of seeing him didn't explode the world, it centered it, became the source from which everything else flowed. Being with him became the realest part of all my realities, the electric present tense.

And he didn't entrance me; he made me alert. My senses sharpened, took in all the evidence, and my mind became a calculator, computing and storing. I wasn't deluded. I could see clearly who he was, that his surface polish and self-containment came from something at his center that was hard and icy, detached. It scared me; I felt how easily the crust of that ice could be broken and something violent come surging up.

I saw it one night when we were waiting for a table in a restaurant. Paul had been there before and was well-known; the young maître d', with slicked-back *GQ* hair and a well-cut suit, undoubtedly aspiring to some media biz career, was reassuring him that the table would only be a moment. Another man kept interrupting demanding to be seated. He was one of those boisterous good-time guys you imagine in shirtsleeves at a poker table betting thousands at a time. The man pushed at Paul and the maître d', completely oblivious. Paul stepped back and let the maître d' handle him, but as he did I saw the look in his eye. It was more than disgust or ordinary anger; I suddenly felt how easily he could have unleashed a detached, almost surgical violence. I felt his intensity and for a moment he seemed to vibrate with it. Then he took a breath, and it passed; time flowed again; the sounds of the restaurant returned; the man went back to the bar; we were simply people waiting to be seated. I felt Paul's hand on the small of my back guiding me to our table. Its touch was light and I understood how tightly he held himself in check, what an effort he had made to restrain himself. It frightened me but I admired it, and felt something in me awaken—the fascination with that line, the flash point, and the urge to tightrope-walk down it, to feel its taut vibrations along my tingling skin.

I began to realize my suspicions that there was something shady about his business were right. It wasn't only that he was vague—he was vague about everything. When I asked him where he'd grown up, he said New York, but I never learned if that meant the city or someplace upstate. I could see he had taste and style and knew something about modern painting, but when I asked if and where he had gone to college, he changed the subject. He said his parents were dead. He just didn't want to talk about any of it.

He often made calls around dawn to New York and Europe. At first he closed the door, but after a while he didn't mind my hearing. I couldn't understand much or get the specifics, but there were large sums of money being moved across international wires into various real estate and business projects, currency trading, banking arrangements. He spoke to people named Mustafa and Salvatore and Fumiko; he left messages around the world, which were all returned.

Once, when he came back to bed and I stretched out

along the coolness of his body and warmed him with my own, I joked about money laundering.

"I know you're into something," I said.

"You think I'm mafioso? Or maybe the western branch of the Yakuza?"

"Yes. Or something more—subtle. And maybe on your own."

"A kind of international bandit, strictly independent?"

"Why not? I can see you now—ruthless, cold, manipulating millions."

"Money? Or people?"

"Both."

He didn't say anything.

"I'm right, aren't I?" I asked.

He smiled. "You want to be."

I saw the teasing in his eye, the certainty.

"No. I want to be wrong. I want you to be honest, and true, an open book."

"So we can live happily ever after?"

I laughed but suddenly the mood shifted and I stiffened. He leaned back. I knew he saw my discomfort and was enjoying it.

"You don't want that," he said.

He reached out for me with all the ease of possession and casually ran a finger around my nipple. Despite myself I felt my body react.

"I don't?"

"No. You want me to be hard. Cold. A desperado. You want me to be the opposite of everything you ever thought you wanted."

I didn't answer.

"Don't you?"

He wasn't asking; he was telling. I hated him in that moment, for what he could so easily make me feel and his superior certainty. I wanted to turn away, to slam a door in his face, to cut him completely out of my life. But the tip of his finger held me, its tender circling a whirlpool drawing me down, reeling me in. For a moment, I tried to hide my face but then I turned to him. His eyes were laughing, but something made me wonder: Why did I have to think that it was at me? What would happen if I acknowledged that he was right and cut loose of happily-ever-after? Why not let him point the way? I raised my face to him and I opened my mouth, wanting his tongue.

He held back a moment. I knew what he wanted to hear and I knew it at least as this portion of the truth.

"Yes," I said. "Yes. I do want you to be—bad. Someone who sees what he wants and stops at nothing to get it. Who lives outside the rules."

"You know why, don't you?" he asked, his arms encircling me.

I looked up at him. His smile spread me out, fully extended me into the truth. It was so easy to see once I let go of my need to deny it.

"Yes," I whispered. "Because I want to be that person, too. I'm tired of worrying about what other people think. Or being scared the world won't give me what I want. I want to be brave enough to take what I want. To risk everything, with no fear or doubt. I want to feel that rock-hard certainty."

His hand was running along my thigh. "I knew that

about you," he said. "I was waiting for you to see it, too."

I moved closer to him. This time, I didn't mind his arrogance. I only wanted to see the truth.

"I know it now," I said, my lips teasing at the soft skin on his chest. "I want to be bad, too."

I dreamed I was in a training program of some kind, maybe to be a stockbroker, something that had to do with math and figuring. I could see that success in the program depended on being good with numbers and I suddenly realized that I wasn't. But I didn't see how that could be right and I found myself protesting, "I am, I *am* good with numbers!"

"No," I heard a voice say, "you only think you are."

I awoke with a sense of suspended time, endlessly caught in the sound of that voice, in the moment when I realized that success depended on something I couldn't do. In the morning light, I thought I understood. It was just an anxiety dream; I'd read enough self-help books to know one. It made sense that I should have one; I'd have to be inhuman not to be unsure of what was happening now. But as the day went on I couldn't shake the feeling that the dream was about something else, something that went deeper than Paul, more to the core. For some reason, I kept seeing the bend of the number 9, that sensuous circle and the leg straightening down, pointing down to some mystery I couldn't make out, a world in which all the usual landmarks were gone, obscured, or disguised. A world of circles and lines, mysterious hieroglyphics pointing toward other mysteries I couldn't even see. Maybe that was the world I was entering now, passing through gates I might never find again. And did it make me less fearful, that it was the world to which I wanted to go?

I came home late one night. Paul was already at the house and I found him sitting out on the terrace. He smiled as I sat beside him, but as we talked I could tell something was bothering him.

"A hard day?" I asked.

"Oh, money worries . . . you know how it goes."

"Well, as a matter of fact—in your case, I don't know how it goes."

He didn't laugh.

"Why don't you tell me? Maybe it's something I can help with."

He smiled again. "Only if you can come up with seven hundred and fifty thousand dollars."

"Sure. Let me get my checkbook."

He took my hand and pulled me close. "Even if you had it, a gentleman never takes money from a lady."

"Well, I'm no lady. As you well know."

I ran my tongue around his lips. He leaned back and let me kiss his mouth and cheek and neck. His hand moved to my breast. I rested my head on his chest and we sat that way for a while, watching the night and the city below us.

"This money," I finally said. "You're not in any trouble, are you?"

"No, no, of course not," he said. There was a brief pause. "Well, actually—let's put it this way—the pressure is . . . unusually intense. The irony is I only need it for a few days."

I could hear a dove murmuring somewhere close by. When Paul didn't say anything more I knew what he must be up against; he'd never mention needing money unless things had gotten serious. All the vague guesses I'd made about him in the past few weeks fell into place and, without needing specifics, I simply knew for certain that I'd been right. He shifted beneath me.

"Can you tell me?" I asked.

"You don't want to know the details. I'm overextended. It's happened before, but the people I represent sometimes get very nervous about their investments."

I understood. He'd been threatened and was looking for a way out. But he was trying to reassure me.

"Don't worry," he said. "This has happened before . . . although usually I see it coming. Somehow it always works out."

He kissed me then, at first to change the subject, and then to make it the subject itself. I knew enough not to press, and in a few minutes we got up and went inside.

I'd brought home a surprise, as much for me as for him. On impulse, I'd stopped in a store on La Cienega that sold trashy lingerie and bought a pushup bra two sizes too big along with two sets of falsies. The bra pushed up my own breasts but I used the falsies under and on the sides to make them even higher and pushed to the center. I'd also gotten a deep red silk camisole big enough to slip over my now huge breasts and low cut enough to show the deep cleavage the bra and falsies made.

When I came out of the bathroom and Paul saw me, he burst out in startled but delighted laughter. I laughed, too, amazed at my own audacity, swaggering as I showed off my now enormous chest. He was already in bed, and I straddled him, teased his chest hairs with the silk, let him see my inviting cleavage. He laughed again, reached up and squeezed the sides of my breasts. The foam was soft and gave under his grasping fingers.

"Presented for your pleasure and your use," I said, with anything but a submissive smile.

"Are you sure they're for me? I can see it's doing something for you."

He was right. Even sitting astride him, my whole body was a swagger, challenging, promising, seducing. I loved it.

"I feel powerful," I said, running my hands over the enormous mountain on my chest. "Like a fertility goddess. A huge and bountiful mother. The irresistible seducer of every man's soul."

I pulled back and moved his cock so that I could slide him into me. I pushed his hands away; I wanted to touch myself. I ran my hands over my huge breasts, across the silk and followed its thin tautness at the sides. I pulled a nipple up and out of the lace of the bra and pinched it, teased at it, and ran my palm around it until it was hard. Then I moistened my finger and plunged it into my cleavage and watched his face as his eyes followed my every move. His hips were moving and I could feel him deep inside me. He reached for my chest but I wanted more myself; I arched my back and, as I moved steadily on his cock, I held and played with my wonderful breasts. I could see myself in the mirror that hung across the room, riding him below me, my back straight, my chest powerful and strong. My hands couldn't keep still. Finally, I let him touch me and I put my hands on his as he squeezed and cupped and patted my juicy breasts and felt the softness of the taut silk. Then I pulled him to me and buried his head in my cleavage. I pressed my arms against the sides of the bra so that he was surrounded, cradled in my breasts. I felt him pulling closer, eager, avid, wanting more of that incredible softness. We were pumping together and I felt him find a nipple and begin to suck. The power of generosity flowed out of me and I held him then, encircled him with my arms, engulfed him in my breasts, and we rocked together until we came.

A while later, as I listened to the water hissing in his shower, it came to me there was a way I could help him out of his financial bind. I could move the money out of Bobby Melner's account. If it were true that Paul only needed the cash for a few days, I could have it back in the account before anyone knew about it. Besides, who was to know? No one but Bobby—and I could always find some way to explain it. He'd accept anything I said, as long as he thought I was trying to get him access to his so-near-and-yet-so-far trust.

I rethought the sequence and my breathing deepened as if I were being aroused. I gave myself up to it, and for a moment it seemed that nothing else existed but this strangely stirring possibility. I thought the words, "It would be so easy," and they were like a velvet case I was languidly slipping into, a dark and silky pocket, a narrowing chute encasing and elongating me. I imagined the telephone and the wire transfer form; I heard my voice electric but steady. It would be so easy . . . easy . . . very, very easy.

Then the shower stopped and I came to: Could I actually be considering embezzlement from one of my own clients? I heard Paul moving in the bathroom and the clatter of plastic as he dropped something on the counter. No, of course not; I wasn't serious. Yes, it would be easy, but it would be wrong. Anyway, it was no more than a fantasy, a surprisingly exciting fantasy but no different than the hundred sexual fantasies Paul had set off in me, most of which would probably never be enacted.

He came out of the bathroom, smelling of soap, and I watched him at the mirror toweling his hair and combing it. I raised myself on one elbow.

"Why do you say you just need the money for a few days?"

"Because I know what's coming in. And when. But, listen, babe, it's my problem. Don't you think about it."

He got in bed beside me. We rolled over into each other's arms, ready for sleep. I didn't say anything about knowing a way to get him the cash. There was no point; it would all be gone in the morning, no more than a late-night reverie.

Chapter Seven

By the time I got to the office I was certain I could do it. The very ease with which I thought it could be done seemed like a green light. I'd be a fool not to go ahead. I felt I'd already begun; my heart was beating as quickly as if I'd already taken the first step, and that quickening pace prodded me on. For the first time I understood the lure of gambling, of putting it all on the line, stacking the chips and going for broke. A door had opened and it revealed what I wanted: to take the risk.

I tried to be businesslike and drew up a mental ledger, itemizing the pros and cons. As far as I could see, there would be some danger, but it would be minimal. If my request for the funds were refused, I could always say I'd simply made a mistake and tried to withdraw from the wrong account. If the withdrawal was discovered before I could return the money, I could say it was an honest mistake—and pull out my notes of the bank's earlier error.

No one would push it; the bank people would not want their own slipup known. In fact, I could make an issue of the bank committing that kind of mistake in the first place; a little righteous outrage would go a long way. And I could worry about replacing the money later. Bobby would be very patient if I strung him along with dreams of what miracles that missing money might be working.

I sat alone in my office. I could hear Holly at her keyboard, clicking away, and I could feel the vibrations of traffic out on the street. It was all business-as-usual, an ordinary day. Except that I was thinking of committing a crime, the kind of crime that got people put away. For a very long time.

Had I ever done anything I could call a criminal act? The closest I could come was something that now seemed laughable compared to what I was considering, an incident from the last few years of my marriage to Don. We were doing a lot of speed and cocaine at the time, mostly because it was the new thing to do among the people we knew, although I always enjoyed the rush, the definite acceleration of reality.

One night at a party I was in the bathroom and without really thinking about it I went through the medicine cabinet. I found a bottle of speed, little white pills legally dispensed by a doctor who probably used more himself than he wrote and a pharmacy getting rich on California appetites. On impulse I pocketed the bottle. It was the first thing I could remember stealing; even as a kid, I never stole comic books or candy or shoplifted clothes. I felt tremendously guilty and never told Don. But I used the pills, every one of them, day after day reminding myself of the theft, always with a flush of guilt.

Soon the bottle was empty and for some reason I was terrified to throw it away in my own garbage. I was afraid Don would find it, even if I stuffed it at the bottom of the garbage cans out back. I knew I was crazy, but for days I carried the empty brown plastic around with me, the opposite of a good-luck charm: each time I saw it, or felt it in the bottom of my purse, I felt a stab of fear. Then, one afternoon I spotted a Dumpster behind the Thrifty's on Sunset and I tossed the bottle in. Hurrying back to my car, afraid of being seen, I was finally horrified, not only at the theft but at the lengths I had gone to keep it hidden. It was a true criminal act. I knew it and I felt ashamed.

Still, stealing a bottle of speed from a stranger's medicine chest and hiding the evidence doesn't automatically lead to a life of crime. I could have done a lot worse and not be sitting in my office now contemplating a major felony. And for all I know a lot of major felonies are committed by people who never so much as had a nasty thought—Milquetoast accountants afraid of their wives, little old ladies from Pasadena. What I mean is, you never can tell; nothing is ordained—the good or the bad. Nothing automatically leads to something.

When should I do it? It was a Tuesday, the most nondescript day of the week, when things were likely to be quiet after the Monday rush. Should I wait and bury the transfer in late-week, last-minute traffic? Was morning better than afternoon? How could I be sure the same clerk who'd made the earlier mistake would be there? Wasn't it better that it be someone new, since that first clerk would be especially alert to another error? What if—? I suddenly sat down. It was just a fantasy; there was no way I was going to do it. No way at all.

Still . . . something in me kept coming back.

It didn't escape my notice that it looked like I wanted to do this not for myself but for Paul. Was I only one more desperate woman risking everything, giving it all away just for the love of a man, a man who was shadowy, mysterious, with nothing about him that promised the solid ground of a mutual commitment or anything conventional? After all, I hardly knew him and had no reason to trust him; there was no way I could be sure he'd really be able to return the money in a few days. "A few days"? How in the world could I be thinking about embezzlement with no more to go on than "a few days"?

Obviously, I wasn't thinking. Or maybe I was just thinking in a whole new way. I understand it now, now that so much else has happened. Paul's need for cash opened the possibility, but he wasn't my dope and I wasn't an addict; I wasn't thinking about doing it for him. It was like strutting around in my black high heels or buying the bra and falsies. I had done it initially out of delight that I wasn't threatened by the bimbo image, that I could play with it. But I hadn't just played, I had crashed through that image, broken free to something entirely new on the other side, a sense of a more fundamental female power, my own power, to which everything else, even a cock, was subservient. Maybe this was something similar; maybe there was something new, undreamed of, waiting on the other side. That's what was drawing me on, the irresistible urge to pursue an irresistible desire, to take the risk and be completely willing to see where it led. Paul was the occasion, not the reason. In the truest sense, I was doing it for me.

I stood up; I needed to move around. It was as if I'd been living on a very low flame and had just felt for the first time a sudden burst of higher intensity. A craving developed, not so much for danger as for what danger brought, this burning flame: intensity.

I reached for a legal pad and wrote out the details of the transaction. All I had to do was get up and drop the sheet on Holly's desk. She would do the rest. If it was going to work, it would work; today was as good a day as any, right now as good a time.

I got up and went into the next room. Holly hardly looked up.

"Here," I said, slipping the sheet on her desk. "Whenever you get time."

I went back to my office and sat down behind my desk. Our computers were networked and I set my screen so that I could follow as Holly typed out the order. My heart was racing, but I forced myself to breathe deeply, rhythmically, and soon the slow momentum calmed me. I closed my eyes and felt my breasts rise and fall. I moved and let my hips settle into the cushioned seat. There was an unmistakable sensual stirring, as if unseen hands were caressing me, stroking me, stretching me out in a smooth solid line. I felt myself expanding out past the barriers of stultifying restrictions and inhibiting rules. My fear was gone and in its place was the absolute clarity of complete control.

It was then I remembered Mr. Smith.

I must have been twelve or thirteen. It was one of those frequent times my father was out of work and my mother was tense with the effort to hold down her fear. Our house was always silent and I learned how to hide myself in plain sight, to be hidden away even as I sat down to dinner and handed around the peas. No one noticed me—except for Mr. Smith.

I realize I have no idea how old he was. He could have been young, younger than I am now, but I wouldn't have seen it; whatever his age, he was on the other side of the line that set off all adults. How long had he been watching me before I noticed him? I don't know. He lived in the house next door, and one night as I was getting undressed I saw him in the dim light of his room across the way. He was standing only partially hidden in the folds of a lacy curtain, smoking a cigarette, staring at me. His eyes were dark; in an instant I felt their electric charge spiraling toward me, exposing me, a deer caught in the headlights of an onrushing car. I pulled back and froze. In the silence, I heard sounds from the rest of the house, my mother drying the last of the dishes, my father already stretched out on the sofa with a bottle of booze. But his look riveted me, and all else fell away until there was only the man and his eyes upon me.

I moved forward again, suddenly uncertain—maybe I'd imagined him. But he was there, clear in the dim light. I saw him raise his hand to his mouth and draw on the cigarette. I stared, fascinated, entranced by that enlarging pinpoint of red glowing light. Time slowed and I calmed down. I sensed he wasn't startled or afraid at all, and his lack of fear, of embarrassment at being seen made me catch my breath. It was as if he was extending an invitation to join him far away in a place I hadn't even dreamed existed. His slow drawing in of the cigarette smoke, the way his other hand played on the fold of the curtain fabric, his fingers long and spread—he was saying, "I'm here, I see you. Stay in this place with me." And somewhere deep inside me, without even knowing it, I made the decision to join him, to step fully into his acknowledging gaze. Everything in me flowed toward that light.

I moved further into the window. I'd been clutching my blouse in front of my chest but now I slowly lowered it, tossed it away, and fully faced Mr. Smith. His hand stopped moving on the curtain and he was still, enveloped in smoke which the breeze from the window was curling around him. We were yards and yards apart, but if he whispered my name, I knew I would hear it clearly. My newly developing breasts were still covered by a thin undershirt, and without hesitation, I slowly lifted it over my head. I felt the fabric sliding across my skin, over my nipples and up the soft inner skin on my arms. I was moving as if under water, in slow motion, caught in an endless loop of smooth fabric sliding across soft skin. When the shirt was off, I moved still closer to the sill. My eyes were steady on Mr. Smith's face as he stared at me. I felt no self-consciousness, no sense of being spied upon or used. Instead, deep in my groin as keen as a knife thrust, I felt my power to attract and I understood that it was I who was holding him transfixed.

For the first time in my life, I knew I was whole and powerful enough to have effect.

That was the first of many nights, encounters always ended by some noise from the house, my mother's call, or an extra-loud car on the street. We never touched; he never made any attempt to move beyond our window meetings. During the day, if we saw each other on the street, we pretended not to know one another. How did I know to do that? Was I following his lead, or some instinct deep inside me?

Then one day we were thrown together. It must have been a neighborhood party or something at the church, a backyard barbecue. We caught sight of each other and as usual in daylight looked away . . . now I remember: it was a birthday party. Someone—a child? an adult?—was unwrapping a stack of presents. I watched the mounds of colored paper and ribbons pile up and I was suddenly in a rage. I wanted to tear them all to shreds. My parents were fighting, I hated my house, and I hated that someone else was getting all these presents and attention. I wanted to bolt, run away, disappear from my life forever.

Instead, I stole. Without planning it or even knowing I was about to do it, my hand reached out into the pile of presents and my fingers closed over a tiny box with a gilt foil top. I knew what was inside—a small heart on a chain, all gold and glittering, the kind of thing worn by all the girls who were prettier and more popular than I'd ever be. In an instant, the box was in my pocket. I moved away and heard a burst of laughter but it had nothing to do with me. All was as it was before; no one had seen me.

Except Mr. Smith. Of course he'd been watching me. I

caught sight of him through the crowd and I saw his eyes shifting to my pocket with its slight bulge. Guilt began to creep across my face but, in a flash, I saw his confusion, the hesitancy he felt, and I understood that he could never tell what he'd seen me do. Without fear, I turned to face him squarely. This time it was I who was inviting him to step into this place with me, I who was offering complicity. I felt my power and he felt it, too. I smiled and turned away.

Sometime after this, for some reason that's lost to me, our nightly meetings stopped. But I wonder now about that locket. . . . For all I know, I kept it hidden for years in the bottom of a drawer, or started wearing it when we moved on to the next town. Or maybe I put it back that very day, somehow understanding that it had already served its purpose: to show me the uncertainty in Mr. Smith's eyes and the power that I had.

The sound of Holly shifting in her chair brought me back. I turned to the computer screen and saw she was phoning the bank. I listened to the tones and connecting sounds, and for a moment, but only a moment, I couldn't remember why I was watching the screen. I was suspended somewhere between blind panic and rock-solid calm, and then I was riveted, more focused, clearer than I'd ever been. The bank logged on and Holly typed in the request. I followed the flash of the cursor as it was propelled across the screen, then watched it pulsating as she waited for confirmation. Even then I could have stopped it, called it all back and gone on with my day, which would have been just another day, no different from the rest. I could have stayed safe. But the truth is I had no intention of stopping. It never even entered my mind.

The bank okayed the request. In a matter of minutes, the money would be in Bobby Melner's cash account, the account I could sign checks on. I took a deep breath and suddenly I was panting, gasping for air as if coming up from the deepest deep-sea dive. My hands were trembling. I saw Holly sign off and then could hear her making hard-copy notations about the transaction. The forms would turn up in my in box, I would initial them, and then they would be filed with all the other documentation on Bobby's account.

It was done. I had done it.

I decided to wait twenty-four hours before drawing against the account. By that time, if the bank was going to notice the error, I'd know about it. On a new kind of energetic elation, I went through the rest of the day without doing anything out of the ordinary. I had lunch with a stockbroker who wanted my clients to invest in an IPO for a solar technology company. I told him I'd think about it and called him at five to say yes. I signed checks and returned all my phone calls. And every moment seemed meaningful, heightened, enriched by my secret, by what I had done.

Paul called in the middle of the afternoon and I realized how little I'd thought of him directly. Now that it was done, I was in no hurry to tell him; I wanted to wait until tomorrow when I could go into the account and have the money in hand. And I wanted to see his face. When he said he'd be tied up until very late, I heard myself saying I wouldn't mind a night on my own. It was true. I wanted a few more hours of being the only one who knew what I'd done.

I got home early and cooked for myself, something I rarely did, pasta in pesto sauce and a huge chopped salad. I put on some CDs, lit the candles on the dining-room table, and ate my dinner there, watching the shadows cast by the flames. After, I cleaned up and put everything away, washed the pots and folded the place mat, and all my movements, every breath and gesture, felt effortless, electrically charged. Then I undressed, poured a glass of white wine and went out to the pool. The night air was cool as I let my robe fall from my shoulders and slipped naked into the warm, lapping water.

A half-moon was rising and jasmine was in the air. I lay back and listened to the sound of a small animal creeping through the dense ivy on the hillside. I was surrounded by sounds—the traffic below, insects, an airplane overhead—and yet it seemed very quiet, enveloping, peaceful. I thought of Paul, of what his face would look like when I told him what I'd done and handed him the check. I thought of his tongue and his cock, the arch of his back as he pushed his way deep inside me. My hand slipped between my legs and I slowly slid my fingers over the moist lips. I didn't want to come. I wanted the pressure, to play with arousal, with my own luxurious responsiveness. My body floated and I gave myself up to its lightness. I felt as if I'd been cut free from metal ropes that had bound me to the ground, lashings that had sentenced me to all that was ordinary, shrunken and pale. I was alive now, awakened and voluptuous.

I heard myself sigh. I thought about the future, and just

as I hadn't known I'd had this possibility, I guessed there were a great many more that I had now enabled to come my way. I wasn't afraid; I wanted the thrill of risk. My hand pressed more firmly as I gave myself a sharpening of desire and I floated toward the center of the pool, my other hand gently playing over my breasts, teasing at my nipples. I had acted and I was set free. Now I could really begin to know myself.

Part TWO

Chapter Eight

I didn't say anything when I gave the money to Paul. I simply handed him the check drawn on Bobby Melner's account. It took a moment for him to realize what it was and then, when he did, he simply looked at me.

"It's all right," I said.

He shook his head. "No."

I thought he meant he wouldn't take it.

"It *is* all right," I said, reaching for his hand. "If you get it back to me in a few days, no one will know."

But that wasn't what he meant.

"You don't want to move it in a single check. Void this one. I'll show you how to do it."

With those few words, he confirmed everything I'd suspected about him. I tore up the check and wrote down the instructions he gave me. I didn't ask any questions. There was no reason to; everything I wanted to know was already revealing itself.

I watched his face as he told me what to do. It came to me that things could have gone in other ways. He could have been floored by my gesture and demanded that I put the money back, staggered that I would do such a thing and think that he would take it. Or he could have pulled me to him in amazement and gratitude, and showered me with kisses, admiring my nerve. Instead, he was matter-of-fact, a businessman explaining the mechanics of a deal, and asked nothing about how I'd gotten the money, although of course he knew. I liked that. I liked that he wasn't making a fuss. What I had done had the feel of something inevitable, and what is inevitable never needs a showy display. And in some curious way, the reserve with which we both were acting made me feel safe. If things are quiet, orderly, unemotional, and restrained, then they're manageable, controllable. They can't get out of hand, and lead to disaster. Or so I thought then.

Things were normal at the office. Holly was unusually helpful, which I correctly guessed meant that she and Tom had hit some pocket of mutual understanding. It had been more than twenty-four hours, but some part of me was still waiting for the bank to call to notify me of an error, so I kept myself busy seeing what I could dig up for Nathan. I wanted to help him and I was grateful for the distraction.

I started by checking the on-line quotes; the stock was up a few cents, but so was the rest of the market. I ran a thirty-day history, then three and six months. There was a slight upward trend but no single days that looked unusual and no number-of-shares-traded that appeared especially large or in any way suspicious. If Nathan's instinct was right, it wasn't apparent in the most obvious place.

Next, I called some brokers around town. Everyone knew that Nathan was my client, so it wasn't giving anything away for me to ask about NNE, but no one told me anything I didn't know already. Research on the company was good, the stock was strong. I began to realize I'd have to find some other way to investigate.

Nathan had essentially asked me to become a detective, but that had no appeal for me. I wasn't sparked by an image of myself as a forties private eye, a Bogey with breasts. But I did see another possibility, something more subtle—to be a spy, a hidden covert intelligence operating just beyond and below whatever could be seen. I felt myself becoming liquid, thick like mercury, fanning out into hidden worlds, searching out dark mysterious crevices for silent trackless exploration. Like an invisible spider, I wanted to pull invisible but responsive strings. It suited my new mode.

Of course I wanted to do it for Nathan—because I owed him so much and I really did care about him. But there was this, too: that I wanted to push at, and expand, the limits of my own power.

I stayed busy until suddenly it was late afternoon. The bank wasn't going to call. I sat back and smiled. And as I turned back to the computer screen, I smiled even more; I realized then I wasn't going to give it another thought.

"I'll have the money back to you tomorrow," Paul said, when we met that night.

"So soon?"

"I just needed a twenty-four-hour cushion—you gave it to me."

"Does this happen often?" I asked.

"From time to time."

I looked at him and smiled, then shook my head.

"I don't think I could risk it again with the bank."

"There are other ways. What about your other clients?"

It was, of course, the obvious question, the inevitable next step. For a moment, I wondered if I'd seen this far ahead all along. It was another line and I didn't know if I could make the leap. He saw me hesitate. He pulled me to him and I could feel his breath, his lips on my cheek and the back of my neck.

"It doesn't matter," he said. "Don't think about it. You've done enough already."

I let him hold me and didn't say anything. But I knew that he was wrong: I hadn't done enough. I didn't yet know what I was capable of but I wanted to do more. I turned to him and put my hand on his cock, my palm flat and insistent against the fabric of his slacks.

"We'll be late for dinner," he said, but I could already feel his hips begin to move.

"Don't tell me that you'll mind."

I reached for his mouth, my tongue at once hungry and bountiful. Oh yes, I wanted to do more.

He took me that night to the home of a man who lived at the beach, somewhere on the cliffs just south of Paradise Cove. In the dark, I could hear the surf approaching high tide; all evening, with the doors thrown open, I was aware of its erratic rhythm pounding on the beach below. I was wearing a new dress made of the thinnest tissue linen and I felt the moist breeze lift and fill the folds of my skirt around my legs. Wisps of hair curled around my neck.

The house had been designed to look like a Mediterranean villa perched above the Riviera, with ornate stone balustrades and even gargoyles, derailed somehow in southern California. I could see the outlines of a grove of palm trees around a tiled pool near the edge of the cliff. I knew that any one of those trees, planted recently and undoubtedly brought in full size, had cost more than a good used car. I tried to imagine signing the check that paid for them, and I knew instinctively that whoever had wouldn't even remember how much they cost. What was it like to have that kind of nonchalant ease?

The host's name was Gunther; he said he was from Switzerland. He was about fifty and probably had a wife and children somewhere, but he struck me as a type I'd seen before, the sort of friendless man most at ease commanding, who views the need for female companionship as a strictly practical affair. And Camilla, the Swede who seemed to be his girlfriend, was ordered up from central casting, a blond model out of the pages of *Vogue* with the good sense to dress in the starkest black. That little nothing probably cost three times as much as my sage green linen, but then I had to work for a living.

We crossed a marble hallway into a room with a coffered ceiling and what I took to be fragments of Greek and Roman sculptures on the wall. They could only be genuine. The furniture and drapes were thick and heavy with silk, brocade and velvet; they wouldn't last long in the ocean air. This was a version of Malibu I'd never seen before, one that wasn't about the southern California "lifestyle." To look down from this particular promontory was to survey a wider stage, a larger, more international view. It was the land of luxe and wherewithal, in which antiquities traveled globally, satellite communications hummed inaudibly behind antique hand-carved double doors, and costly fabrics didn't need to be conserved. I was impressed.

Paul had told me that he and Gunther were in business together, but the other guests were new to Paul as well as to me. Almost everyone had an accent of some sort and was clearly very rich. Two of the women had short hair cut so full you knew Monsieur Someone had to trim it every week to prevent it from collapsing. When the men moved, I saw the flash of solid gold. In this crowd Rolexes would be slightly déclassé.

At dinner, I was seated next to an Englishman named Jasper. He was small and stocky, around sixty, and when someone mentioned the electronic highway he asked where it was.

"I'm so out of touch with things," he smiled when it was explained to him. "All my time goes into the collection."

It turned out he collected ancient pottery, which was his connection to Gunther; they'd been friendly competitors for several important pieces. The talk moved to a particular object both of them had bid for and lost.

"It was extraordinary," Jasper explained, "an absolutely beautiful bowl, but very mysterious. No one is certain what it was used for. A ritual object of some kind, an ordinary household item—"

"Or a potter's reject," Gunther interjected. "Which is why I dropped out of the bidding. I like to know what I'm getting."

Jasper laughed. "You dropped out because you'd already bought enough to stock a small museum. I, on the other hand, very much wanted it. I find the ambiguity irresistible—I like that I can imbue it with whatever meaning I choose."

Gunther grunted. "Must you, Jasper? You know I loathe metaphysical discussions."

Jasper winked at me. "My friend here can't abide uncertainty. It distresses him that things may be only, just *only* what they seem. And that how they seem can change at any time."

"Things don't only 'seem,' " Gunther said. "A brick wall doesn't 'seem,' my friend. And it doesn't change."

Jasper sat back. I could see he was delighted he'd drawn Gunther in. "I don't deny the brick exists—of course, the stuff of the world is out there, circumscribing what we do, throwing up brick walls in our path. But isn't it we who call it 'brick'—and how do we know there isn't a way to pass through?"

"Try it," Gunther said. "You'll see."

"Ah, such certainty," Jasper sighed, "the death of so many interesting conversations."

Gunther smiled; they'd probably hit this particular brick wall many times. Jasper's eyes were shining in the candlelight.

"All I mean to say is, I don't think we ever understand in any ultimate sense, although all around us people shout what they think is Truth. Well, I'm convinced there is no Truth, only perspective. And every time we think we've found the 'Real' or the 'Best,' the 'True,' everything shifts and all we can do is scramble to the nearest ledge."

I wasn't sure I understood. "But then how do we know what to believe in? What to live by?"

"Precisely, my dear—the question of the age. How on earth do we know?"

Paul and I stayed behind when the others left.

"Gunther and I have something to talk about—we won't be long," Paul said. "You don't mind?"

I shook my head.

"We'll be in the library," Gunther said.

Of course this house would have a library. Probably with leather-bound books in matching sets and an antique globe from the eighteenth century.

"I'll be fine," I said. I didn't ask about Camilla the Swede, who had disappeared. I wasn't sure if that was a terrible breach of manners or simply the most sophisticated thing to do.

But it didn't matter. I wandered out to the terrace and stood looking out at the dark night sky. Far down the coast to the south, I could see the lights of planes taking off from LAX, their low arcs over the water like the trails of rockets launched in slow motion, making a stately progression. The tide was ebbing below me, but each peak of surf still broke with a clap, highlighted in the light from a half-moon rising steadily among the stars. I could sense the house behind me. It wasn't at all my style and the people in it weren't people I necessarily wanted to know. But still I wanted what they had, the confident stance, the solid ground, antiquities, and talk of finance over the Baccarat.

And I thought about what Jasper had said. Only a few weeks ago, his fascination with what he called ambiguity would have puzzled me, the woman who loved numbers and their concrete clarity. Now I saw what attracted him, the way in which what is mysterious carries us, compels us on, leaves us unrestrained. What is unresolved is free of borders, unbound and unbounded, like the night before me, its horizon visible only as the difference in two inky black tones merging with each other. I raised my face to the moon, now traveling quickly toward its apex. The wind was rustling palm fronds; I could feel it unloosening my hair. I breathed deeply.

"Vega."

I turned. Paul was standing in the door way, silhouetted by the light behind him. He was holding out his hand; it was time to go. If I ever loved him at all, it was in the moment, with the night wind eddying around me and the tide echoing below, as I walked toward that hand, with its certain touch and leading direction, offered in the glow of a rich crystal light.

"What did you and Gunther talk about?" I asked on the way home.

"There's a business we're interested in. I'm not sure yet how it will go."

"Are all your investors like Gunther—and Gaby and Charles?"

"What do you mean?"

"So—moneyed."

He smiled.

"By and large. Yes."

"How did you find them?"

He shrugged. "All sorts of ways."

"But how did you start? Who was the first? How did you get on this track—with these particular people—on this level?"

He laughed. "You want the ABCs."

"To the XYZs. I want to know exactly."

"Well, I don't exactly remember. One thing leads to another."

I knew I wasn't going to get anything more specific out of him—and that was okay. He was my mysterious lover; I was content to let him lead me on. I looked out at the ocean beyond the car window, the smudge of moonlight floating on the water.

"There's a lot of money to be made, isn't there?" I asked dreamily. My words seemed to stretch me out luxuriously.

"Yes," Paul said. "Of course, you have to start with something."

I heard the opening in his words, the curtain pulled aside, the rock rolling away to reveal the mouth of a brightly lighted cave, shadows dancing up the walls to hidden heights above.

"I'll put together a list of my clients. That's a good place to start, isn't it?"

He smiled and ran his hand over my thigh. "Yes," he said. "It is."

As easy as that, so easy, requiring no more effort than to push myself off from the edge of a deep, cooling pool on whose surface I could lie back and float. In slow increments, I had been getting ready, turning toward the unknown, and now the fear of consequences was no longer running me. I wasn't going to hold myself back beforehand for fear of getting caught, or learning something I wouldn't like, or being taken someplace I didn't want to go. Any place I went would be unknown, and that in itself was the challenge I wanted. I was ready to be in the flow.

Paul's fingers found my flesh beneath the linen. They were cool and I held them there.

He stretched out across the sheets and I lay down beside him. He reached for me but I pushed his arms above his head and held them there, my fingers binding his wrists together.

"What do you want?" he asked.

"Be still. Be perfectly, absolutely still."

He smiled and lay back. I opened his mouth with my tongue and I felt his breathing deepen. I pulled back and slowly ran my hand down the thin fragile skin of his underarms, across the hairs now fully exposed, down the smooth side of his torso. His hips began to move.

"No, I mean it. Be still."

I looked down the length of his body, exposed and vulnerable now because his arms were pinned. My fingers glided over him, just barely touching his warming skin, across his stomach, down his thigh. His eyes were watching me, studying my hand, trying to will its touch. I slowly spread his long legs and I let my fingers hover over his balls and rising cock but I didn't touch him. He raised his pelvis, straining for my hand but I pulled it away. I smiled when I heard him moan, and when I looked in his eyes, he smiled, too, unembarrassed by his need. I leaned in to him, my lips fluttering over his neck and cheeks, my tongue licking at his ear, across his eyes. I ran my breasts over his chest and I didn't mind when he raised his head to watch my nipples graze his skin. He moaned again. I could feel his desire, the straining intensity he was barely able to contain. I knew how much he wanted to move, to throw his arms around me, press me to him, plunge into the relieving friction of my hand and cunt. I was very wet; his need inflamed me and began to carry me along the same rising tide. I let go to it and realized it was what I wanted, to be suspended with him in that space that is pure desire, so keen, so intense, you are forced to surrender to it second by second or be driven mad.

Chapter Nine

At the office, I put in a call to Jennie Berger. We had met when we worked together at the stockbrokerage; she moved over to NNE at the same time I went out on my own. Now she'd worked her way up to corporate secretary and head of shareholder affairs. I knew she was the person to talk to about who owned what of NNE. I could just have asked for the latest rundown—for that matter, I could have asked Nathan's assistants to print one out for me, but something told me to do the schmooze. I invited Jennie to lunch.

We'd been friends of a sort back when we'd worked together. We'd both divorced around the same time and suddenly found ourselves with oceans of free time to fill, so for a while we went out to dinner after work and movies on weekends. Once, we drove up to Santa Barbara overnight and bought each other too many margaritas. Then, something happened—I met a man, or she did, or maybe the new rhythms of the new life just took hold, and with less time to fill we realized there wasn't much to hold us together. We'd been out of touch for a while.

We met at a Japanese restaurant in one of the new towers downtown because Jennie said she didn't want the hassle of moving her car. I'd forgotten this aspect of her, the easy insistence that the mechanics of things be arranged for her convenience. She had a way of demanding things that was always a challenge, and I could never decide if she did it because she got something from the struggle to prevail or because she expected to be denied and wanted that confirmation.

"You're looking well," I said as we sat down. It wasn't true. She had always been thin; she was almost gaunt now. I didn't think she had lost weight, but all the lines had shifted, been planed to a hard edge.

"You, too," she said. "I love that rust color on you."

It struck me how automatic these compliments were, the way in which women always compliment each other on how well we look. "That dress is great." "Don't you look nice! Your hair—did you have it cut?" Even my clients who throw a fit if a man in a business situation so much as mentions their hair or their clothes, who explode if they even get a hint that how they look figures in any way in their careers—do this with other women, fall into this mutual complimenting. Why do we do it? To put the other at ease—or to disarm her?

"It's been a long time," she said.

"Too long." I didn't mean that, either.

"What is it about this town that makes it so hard to stay in touch?" she wondered. "It's not as if I have a million other things to keep me busy. Although maybe you do."

I wondered if I was wrong to hear reproach in her voice.

"Well, business is good. Better than I expected. It does keep me pretty busy."

"You were very smart to go out on your own. Of course, you had Nathan behind you. There wasn't much risk with such a big fish on the line."

This, too, was something I'd forgotten about her—the one-two punch of accolades given and then quickly withdrawn. *Yes, you were very brave to cross the Pacific in a canoe, but then you did have all that wood beneath you.* Well, I was here at this lunch for a hidden reason, so I could rise above the flash of anger I felt. It was an interesting lesson in the power that comes from hidden agendas.

"I was still terrified. Don't you remember? He would have dropped me in a minute if I couldn't do the work."

"Not much chance of that. No, from where I sat, you made it look easy. You decided to do it, you did it, it worked."

I laughed. "If you knew how many nights I didn't sleep. And the months when I worried I wouldn't make the rent."

She was nodding, but I could see she wasn't listening; she'd formed some idea of who I was and how things went for me and now she was locked into it. She wanted to know about my clients, if I had any glamorous ones, and when I told her about some of them, fudging on the names, I could see it was only grist for her mill, the one that was all about everything I had and everything she didn't. She wasn't only locked into an idea of me; she was locked into one of herself: she who would always be denied.

"And other things—how are they?" she asked.

"You mean men?"

We both smiled; what else could she mean?

"Well, lately, it's gotten—interesting."

"Lucky you. Who is he?"

I wasn't going to give her any details. "Just a man—we'll see where it goes."

"I'm jealous. Ugly, but true."

Her saying it didn't make it all right. And she didn't have to tell me she wasn't seeing anyone; I could see the restless loneliness gathered all around her.

"Well, there are other things," I said. "Look how well you've done."

"You mean the job? I could do it in my sleep. I thought it was what I wanted but I see now I only knew what I didn't want. The Midwest, my ex-husband, children—all those 'no's.' "

She suddenly stopped, embarrassed, betrayed by the plaintiveness in her voice. I didn't know what to say and I don't think she wanted me to reassure her. Judging by how she regarded me, she would have found it condescending. She took a deep breath and a sip of wine and recovered quickly.

"Look," she said, once again back in charge, "is Nathan trying to tell me something through you? Has he sent you to check up on me?"

I laughed. "No, not at all."

"Then why do you want this list?"

"I've got so many of my clients in NNE, I just want to

know as much as I can. And it seemed like a good excuse to get together."

She made a choice and decided to believe me. Maybe she no longer cared what Nathan thought; maybe it didn't matter.

We moved on to other things, traded gossip and small talk until, toward the end of the meal, she brought out the shareholder information she had put together for me.

"There are so many names," I said, looking down the list.

"Well, there are the large holders, of course—pension funds, mutual funds and institutions, but NNE is considered very solid. That attracts a lot of small investors. They add up."

"And you keep track of every one?"

"Me and the computers. That's my job."

"Well, is there anything unusual here? That I should know for my clients?"

She appeared surprised at the question, and I worried that simply by asking it I had given too much away. I had yet to learn the extent to which most of us are unaware of the ways in which we can be, and are, manipulated.

"Like what?"

"I don't know. You tell me."

She looked down the list and shook her head. "Nothing."

"I'm just curious—who's new now?"

"Here, I've printed out a cumulative for you."

She unfolded an eleven-by-fourteen sheet broken up into columns.

"It tracks who's new each quarter and who falls off. See? The new ones this quarter have asterisks."

There were about twenty names, including one of my newest clients, for whom I'd just bought a thousand shares.

"Did you set up this sheet?" I asked. "It's really very clever."

She nodded, but I could see it gave her no satisfaction. She'd become pinched somehow and narrow, shut down to feeling, even good feeling, maybe because so much of what she felt caused her pain.

There wasn't much else to say. When we parted, neither of us bothered with the conventional noises: *Let's do this again,* or *I'll call you soon.* I hurried away from her. Some part of me feared contamination, as if her dry bitterness could invade me. When had that happened to her? And had I been like that, heading in that direction, teetering on that edge? Well, it didn't matter. I had met Paul and now my life was opening out; I was moving through a new landscape, discovering the roadway—creating it—as I went along.

I gave Holly the list of shareholders and asked her to find out as much as she could about the names on it, especially the ones who had come on in the last two quarters. I made a copy for myself and was getting ready to go over it when the phone rang. It was Gaby.

"I'm in your neighborhood shopping—is there the remotest possibility you could come and join me? Isn't it ridiculous—I'm completely overwhelmed by all these choices!"

She was at a new shop at Sunset Plaza. I'd passed it a few times and could see it was the kind of place where even the T-shirts were over a hundred dollars and the saleswomen, mostly gorgeous young aspiring actresses, were as well dressed as the wealthy customers.

"I know I'm terrible dragging you away in the middle of the day—but you must rescue me—please!"

It wasn't exactly in my neighborhood, but it was close enough. I said I'd come.

She had just emerged from a dressing room when I arrived. A saleswoman was fastening a complicated closure on the back of a green dress.

Gaby turned fully toward me.

"Now tell me honestly—what do you think?"

She was beautiful. Her dark hair was down, caught at the sides with small gold combs; her mouth was red and glistened in the light.

"Does it make me look too fat?"

I looked at the dress. It seemed designed for nights at the theater or a special dinner, some elegant occasion. Made of a soft, clinging material, with the subtle sheen of silk jersey, it showed off every curve. When she turned sideways I could see the rise of her belly and the sweep of her bottom; folds of fabric fell across her breasts in a subtle soft drape.

"It's lovely," I said.

"The color—it doesn't make me look pale?" She turned again, showing herself to me.

I shook my head. "Not at all."

She smiled and moved closer to me.

"There's another I want to show you—come talk to me while I change."

I went with her to the dressing room, a large carpeted cubicle behind a louvered door. The saleswoman offered to help her, but Gaby said we could manage on our own. She was filled with questions for me—how I'd been, what I'd been doing, how things were with Paul. I answered as I stepped behind her to unfasten the dress's closure. She pulled her hair aside and as she did I caught the expensive scent rising up from the exposed skin of her neck. I stood back as she stepped out of the dress. She was wearing a silk camisole, an off-white color trimmed in ecru lace. There was no bra; I could see her nipples and the outline of fullness beneath the silk. I looked away. I'd felt myself wanting to cup that fullness in the palm of my hand; it frightened me.

The second dress was as beautiful as the first and she looked as wonderful in it. She laughed and said that since she couldn't decide, she'd better have both.

"Thank you so much for coming," she said, her hand on my arm as we walked down the street to a café for cappuccino. "I don't know why, but your opinion is very important to me."

I watched her as we talked and drank our coffee, her eyes subtly outlined to emphasize their width, the glossy hair pulled back from her smooth temples, the heavy gold earrings that rested on her neck when she inclined her head. What did she really want from me? And what did I want from her?

She mentioned Paul. "He says you're thinking of investing with us," she said.

"He did?" I asked, her words an alarm bringing me to. I was immediately terrified that he had told her about Bobby Melner's account and what I'd done. I tried to disguise it, but she saw that something was wrong.

"Shouldn't he have said?"

I tried to appear relaxed. "What else did he say?"

"Nothing. Just that."

I didn't know if she was telling me the truth. I was suddenly adrift, alone, swinging over the abyss, hating her, and him, for talking about me when I wasn't there, for leading me down this strange terrifying path. It was their fault, Paul's fault, that I had crossed a secret line, irrevocable, into some territory from which there might be no escape. Had he exposed my secret to the world—had he betrayed me?

"Vega," she said. "What's wrong?"

She put her hand on mine. I looked up at her. She was smiling. As suddenly as it had come, my fear fell away. What if he had told her; what if she did know? She herself was part of it; she couldn't hurt me. She was in a sense my ally. We were in it together.

"I'm fine," I said, not pulling my hand away. "Low blood sugar, maybe. Let me buy you an eclair."

She shook her head; she was late to meet Charles. I knew it was irrational but I felt a stab of jealousy. I said I would stay and pulled the check to me. She gathered up her packages, leaned down and quickly turned my face toward hers and kissed me on the lips. I automatically opened my lips and for a moment felt her tongue.

"Goodbye, my dear," she whispered. "I'll call you soon."

Feeling shot through me, a shock of fear, or of excitement. She was already walking away. I was relieved. I thought then that I needed time to sort things out, to understand what I wanted. But I think now I already knew. I simply needed a slower pace.

• • •

In one of the towns we lived in when I was a girl, there was an apartment building I passed every day on my way home from school. I knew that rich people lived there. High up, the apartments were set back with terraces; from a distance, I could see potted trees, a vine-covered trellis, a stone urn cemented to a parapet. It must have been spring, some period of warmth, because on one of the terraces the French doors were thrown open and heavy white drapes billowed in the breeze. Each day I saw them, the yards of fabric lifted and let down soundlessly, signals to me of dark inner space. Who lived inside, and what happened there? I felt afraid, as if the knowledge of another world would devastate my own. And yet I couldn't look away, entranced by those billowing folds, twin rippling magic carpets. I wanted to fly toward them on every intake of suspended breath. I couldn't look away.

I printed out the list of my clients for Paul. I was surprised to see there were more than thirty names; I'd stopped counting at the first fifteen, the point at which I'd known I'd be all right. I could remember those first months of fear, a year and a half of pressured uncertainty. The business from Nathan paid for the office rent but the rest had to come from somewhere else. And I'd had to hire a secretary immediately, even if there was little work, because I thought that without one it would be too easy to mistake me for a bookkeeper. I knew I was up against the woman thing.

I remember worrying that I would be relegated to what I thought of as the distaff side when the first client after

Nathan was a woman, someone he in fact referred, a wealthy widow who lived on a couple of acres in Palos Verdes under the tallest eucalyptus trees I'd ever seen. She was always dressed for golf, asked very few questions, and nodded with what I took to be distraction as I patiently explained her finances to her. I made fun of her, what I judged to be her frivolous existence and I suppose, also, that I was jealous; she'd been left a very rich woman with a financial portfolio and tax structure that had been carefully thought out.

But she surprised me. She found an error that I'd made. It wasn't significant, nothing was lost, but it was stupid of me, clumsy, the kind of thing that could easily make a client walk. To myself, I tried to excuse it with all the pressure I was under, but I knew that the one thing I couldn't allow the pressure to do was let me make mistakes. It was a warning and I heard it; I forced myself to concentrate no matter how worried I was.

There was another lesson from her. When she pointed out my error, and as we discussed it, I realized she hadn't been distracted during my explanations; she'd been bored. In fact, she'd already known every item on every line I showed her and every facet of the larger picture as well. Then I realized I had made the sort of assumption about her I'd worried that people would make about me. I think she knew it, knew I'd condescended to her because—what?—she was a woman, an older woman, an older woman dressed for golf? She never mentioned it; she was too polite. And I was never so foolish again, which is why I've done well with the movie crowd and even some rock and rollers. The ones that look like they're off the street, in torn jeans and matted hair, with tattoos over three quarters of their bodies, both male and female, who often turn out to be making millions—at least this year.

That woman was no longer a client; she had died a few years earlier. She'd ultimately referred two others to me and their names were in front of me now on the list. They'd all come in a variety of ways; some had been with me since that first dicey year. Now I was preparing to use them. Not "use" them. I forced myself to see it for what it was: I was preparing to steal from them. I waited, but those words had no weight; I couldn't connect with the guilt they should have evoked. Despite myself, my mind skittered away: I was only borrowing the money, which would only seed my own investments. I would make it up to them; I would in fact take them with me into this new possibility of high returns. Hadn't I already tested the waters with Bobby Melner, and hadn't that worked out? No one would lose anything; no one would be hurt.

But even those words had no meaning; they paled before a brighter flame. I could imagine my fingers on my computer keyboard, a pen in my hand altering codes and numbers, my lips uttering words to make real all that I could manipulate. I felt the thrill of that danger, the vivid brightness of the crucial moment, the rush of pushing toward that danger, the tempering that comes from not turning back. I wanted to abandon myself to that secret source. I wanted that power.

I glanced down the list again as I prepared to pack it up. I saw Nathan's name and stopped. I didn't need to think about it; I knew I couldn't include him. I couldn't give him up. I thought it was because of what I owed him and the shame I'd feel if he knew. But I see now it was more selfish than that. I needed him as a kind of mooring, so that I could point to one good thing I was doing, one gesture that was clean. He was the ballast that would keep me afloat. I would protect him. Even more, I'd help him all I could.

I gave the list to Paul.

"Is this everyone?" he asked when he'd looked down it.

For a moment, I couldn't remember if I'd ever mentioned Nathan to him. I decided I'd remember if I had.

"Yes," I said, "everyone."

He turned back and scanned it again.

"What?" I asked at his silence.

He shook his head.

"Nothing. It's good—a lot of names."

He patted the bed beside him. "Let's go over it. Tell me what they have and we'll see what we can do."

I sat down.

"I need to ask you something first," I said. "I saw Gaby today—did you tell her what I did?"

He didn't say anything.

"It's all right if you did," I said.

"I didn't. No. I just mentioned that you might have some money free."

I nodded. "Do you speak to her—I mean, often?"

He looked at me. "What are you asking? Are you jealous?"

"No. I'm not."

I was surprised to see that was the truth. I didn't want them not to be in touch; I wanted to be part of it. I couldn't stand to be left out.

I relaxed beside him.

"Actually," I said, "there's something—I don't know—intriguing, about you and her—and me."

He laughed. "Oh, I see. It's all right if you're there, too."

I was smiling. "Of course. It's my fantasy—you don't think I'd let the two of you have fun without me."

"Does that really interest you?" he asked. "You and me and another woman—is it exciting?"

"I'm afraid to say yes."

"Why?"

"Because then it may happen."

I was challenging him, and he knew it; he also knew I really was afraid—not of him, but of the part of me that wanted to push through all my boundaries. I recognized the look in his eye; he thought he had my number. He ran a finger around my lips. I opened my mouth and took his finger in, sucked on it, ran my tongue along its length, licked at the webbing along its base. I felt him moving and looked up at him. I had his number too.

It was surprisingly easy to lift large amounts of cash from many of the accounts I oversaw. For instance, one of my clients was a painter who'd had a spiritual awakening and gone off to live on an island in the Pacific he described as "suburban Bali," not to paint like Gauguin, but to meditate and fish and do little else but wear seashells in his hair. He hadn't done anything new in years, but the highly stylized, almost abstract, portraits of street people and the generally down-and-out he had done before he left had lately become trendy and, since he'd been a speed freak back then, his current dealer had hundreds of paintings and drawings which were now bringing in high prices. The cash was flowing, and all of it through me.

Another client was a burnout victim. When she came to me she had just started a jewelry business that was so shaky I offered to take my first fee in trade. Then a friend of a friend of hers gave one of her pins to a friend of a friend of someone in the movie business and the next thing she knew her jewelry was hot. Everyone had to have a piece of it. She got reams of publicity from all the magazines that are always desperate for fodder and to announce the next big thing, and overnight she turned into an industry. It nearly killed her. By the time she decided to quit, she said she hadn't slept in months. But she'd made a small fortune and, when she went off to a cottage in northern California and a man who'd been a lumberjack and was now writing an organic gardening column for the local newspaper, she turned it over to me. In addition to managing what she already had, I handled the royalties that still came in on a few designs she'd sold to a national maker and, as long as I increased the monthly checks I sent her, she didn't ask any questions.

Not everyone made it so easy. Like Bobby Melner, most of my clients were very much in town and not all of them had a big cash flow, but enough of them did at any one time to give me what I needed.

We started relatively small, two hundred thousand dollars Paul needed for a week. I took it from one of the widows for whom I'd just done a six-month review, so that even if Paul held it longer no questions would be asked. That transaction set a pattern we basically followed for everything else we did. I set up a new trading account I called OMNI. It was designed to look like a pool account, something I could use to trade through on behalf of all or any number of my clients for anything that required more than any one of them might have available alone. I liked the challenge of setting it up, the beauty of the spreadsheets, and I could see that this legitimately was a good idea. The problem, of course, was that I didn't tell any of my clients that their money was being used—and put at risk—in this way. And I certainly didn't tell them that the "investments" I was making were in transactions that I knew wouldn't stand much scrutiny.

That first money went into a currency buy that began at a bank in the Bahamas.

"Where is it going from there?" I asked.

"The less you know, the better," Paul said.

I hesitated and then kept silent. It was obviously some kind of money laundering and I didn't want to know where the dirty money was coming from. It occurred to me that most of Paul's investors probably had the same kind of willful ignorance, and I had a moment of contempt for us all, for that part of me that wanted to be insulated from the facts. I hated what I saw as my contemptible passivity, the weak need to keep myself in the dark. I wanted to be stronger, strong enough to embrace the truth.

True to his word, Paul returned the two hundred thousand within the week. I cleared the pool account and moved the original sum back to the widow. I was amazed by the profit to me: Paul said not every deal would be as lucrative, but this first one netted me almost fifty thousand dollars. I felt dizzy that it could be so easy, that this kind of money really could be available to me. I didn't know what to do with it. My first impulse was to go for something extravagant—a down payment on a Rolls Corniche convertible, a diamond necklace, an English eighteenth century armoire, more Armani suits than I'd ever be able to wear. I could even reline the pool in original Malibu tile or redo the kitchen. But having the money to get any of that, or a hundred lesser things, made them somehow uninteresting, as if I wanted only what I could not have until the moment I could have it. Besides, I hated compulsive spenders, the ones without a shred of restraint, driven by glossy lying ads.

Instead of spending I saved, and I drew a secret satisfaction from the restraint this showed, to have that money available and not to spend it. I liked holding myself back from running wild; I was gratified to see that I could be cool and responsible. I created a hidden account, for both trading and investing; its password on my computer screen was NIGHT. Buried under layers of electronic camouflage, NIGHT grew quickly as the weeks went on, and as it did, it became an entity, assumed a shape, until I almost thought there was a real person behind it. "What would be best for NIGHT?" I found myself wondering, or, "Would NIGHT approve?" I tried to visualize this secret identity, to give it a human face. Was it male or female? A parent or a child for whom I was creating rock-solid security? A partner or a lover? Was I winning the world with my skill and daring?

After a while I stopped asking those questions. I saw that NIGHT didn't need a human face or body. NIGHT wasn't a person, place or thing, but an enveloping atmosphere, a state of mind I was more and more assuming. I could close my eyes and feel it, the sense of pushing off into dark and heavy water, of lying back on the knife edge of an insistent current, of giving myself over to a whirlpool's eddying embrace. No, NIGHT wasn't a separate entity or even a separate part of me, some hidden aspect of who I had become. NIGHT was my desire, my appetite for more, the thrill of real transgression: my most fully realized self.

He took me from behind. I wanted him to do it, wanted to be split open in that way, accessible. His fingers found my asshole and then moistened it; I felt his cock press into me. It hurt, but when he asked me if I wanted him to stop I said no and raised myself higher. He pushed slowly, slowly, and, as we rocked back and forth, his voice was in my ear, almost cooing to the rhythm of his tender thrusts, as if to a much-loved child who needed gentle care.

"Oh, sweet girl, sweet girl . . ."

His hands cupped my breasts and pinched at my nipples; one moved across my stomach and teased gently at my clitoris. I sighed, shuddering at his touch. I felt his breath, his mouth and tongue on my neck, and turned and strained to feel his lips with my own. I felt that I was floating off the bed, adhering to him, held against him by his mouth and his hands and his cock easing into me. I was opening, becoming larger each time I let go to pain, and as I surrendered to it, again and again, I felt a flowing out, as if gorgeous ribbons were being pulled from my chest and floating up to heaven, as if all of me was streaming out beyond the borders of my skin. I was huge, boundless, vast enough to take him all, to encompass every inch of him. He was inside me now, moving easily, no longer needing to hold back, and I could feel his gratitude with every plunge into my most secret space. He held me fast, one hand on my breast and the other on my cunt and I came that way, to the murmuring of his voice: Oh, sweet girl, sweet girl.

Chapter Ten

Holly did a good job of tracking down and identifying most of the names on the NNE shareholder list. Of course, many of them were familiar to me: the Broadmans, other insiders from NNE, well-known investors and various institutions. Aside from my own clients, there were others I knew: Don was on the list, as was his friend Marty Toward. This wasn't a surprise; Don had started buying NNE when it first went public and I assumed that Marty had followed his lead. I could see that Marty must be doing well in the movies; his stake in NNE was substantial. Don's stake had also gone up in the last quarter, which did surprise me; I couldn't put it together with his need for money. He'd been broke enough to borrow from Marty, something I knew he hated to do, and yet he hadn't sold any stock and in fact had bought additional shares. Of course, in a sense that was smart. The stock was solid and generally trending up; it was better to hold on to what he'd bought low and even to add more at current prices. But I never thought of Don as smart in that way. He was someone who couldn't hold on to things; they slipped through his hands. For a moment it crossed my mind that he was part of the conspiracy which Nathan was wondering into existence. Don and Marty and who knew who else.

But, after all, I knew Don. It wasn't that I thought he wouldn't take part in something covert; I could see him, like me, turning on to the idea of secret manipulation. But this particular conspiracy would destroy Nathan and that was something I didn't think Don wanted. He wouldn't want to protect Nathan; he'd want to protect me. I was a kind of psychic anchor, part of what kept him on track.

Still, I was curious, so I put in a call to him and left a message. Actually, I was relieved he wasn't there; the truth is, asking Don about his finances wasn't something I wanted to do. I could hear him bristling, shrugging it off, pointing out to me that *As we are no longer married, Vega dot dot dot.* Well, he had a point.

There was one name on the list, though, that did surprise me: Judd Mallory, an actor I'd seen for a while after my divorce. As I thought about it, I realized he was the man who took me to the party at which I'd seen Peter Broadman stoned and obnoxious. I didn't remember their being friends but they must have been, which would account for Judd's name being on the list.

But I couldn't just mark him off. Sitting at my desk now, I kept remembering. When I met him—at somebody's house, around an empty pool—he was a year or two past what had been a big break: he'd been cast in a miniseries playing the lead's younger self. He'd had almost an hour's screen time and had made a big splash, but it was still a question which way his career would go. He had the sort of dark good looks often called "smoldering," with wide-set eyes that were at their most glamorous and compelling when they were stony, expressionless. Even when he was at his most engaging, you had the feeling he was watching you; when he smiled, some part of him was always held back. That was his big plus as a movie actor, because the audience could project onto him whatever they needed. Like every other woman, I responded, and it wasn't just on film. He had it in person, too; you could see the challenge, almost an insolence, in the way he held himself. He made you feel the compelling excitement of being both frightened and attracted.

I saw he was still living in the Briarwood, an old Hollywood pile on the northern edge of Hancock Park. I was tempted now to call him. Actually, I couldn't remember much about what had happened between us, why he liked me, what we did, how it ended. Maybe that's what intrigued me, that I couldn't remember. The more I thought about it the more there seemed something I wanted to go back to. Without knowing quite what it was I dialed his number. After all, I had the excuse of investigating NNE.

"Oh, Vega, sure—a blast from the past."

He sounded as if I'd woken him up, or maybe he was stoned. I realized I'd heard that drugs and booze were the reason he'd never quite delivered on the career that he had promised. I knew he still worked, turning up in low-budget horrors or as a guest star on one or two TV episodes a year, but stardom, even a busy career, had passed him by.

"I just saw your name," I said, "and it started me thinking about old times."

I hadn't prepared a better reason, but he didn't seem to question it; maybe he thought that any woman who had known him once would want to come around again.

We played catch-up for a while and as we talked I began to feel an unexpected kind of excitement. I was picturing that challenging, promising look in his eye, but the arousal I was definitely feeling wasn't tied to him exactly. It came from the game I was playing with him, the motor of my secret purpose and manipulation. I was hovering over Judd like a superior intelligence and I felt the thrill of that covert power. The idea of sex with someone who couldn't guess at my hidden agenda—that very detachment was exciting. It made me move in my chair, and each movement, each circular swing of my hips was a lasso, gathering in a hard-edged energy. I wanted to keep it going. I suggested that we get together.

"Sure," he said. "Come on over anytime. Now."

I laughed. Only an actor, a drug-addicted, unemployed actor, would be so scheduleless and completely amenable.

"It's eleven A.M.," I said.

"Is it?" I could hear him stretching. "An excellent time of day."

The Briarwood had been built in the thirties and still had its original art deco entrance and moldings. Legend had it that it had been owned originally by a silent screen star, an actress whose lover had shot her former husband in the lobby. It was at once both seedy and expensive, catering mostly to show-business types who needed furnished places short term—writers and directors in from New York, young Hollywood hopefuls who shared the rent, rock bands off the road to cut an album. There were some long-term residents; the youngish ones all seemed to have dogs named Rodney and Larry and Jane, while the older people looked like maître d's at old-time roast beef restaurants or costumers who had dressed Loretta Young. I went up in the elevator with an old woman whose hair and makeup were exactly like Joan Crawford's in her heyday. I realized this woman had been young in the forties, had copied that style and never altered it. Maybe she had come to Hollywood to be a star; maybe she was just a fan, one of those people in the crowds at movie premieres, waving, hoping for a smile or an airborne kiss. Now you could see the ghost of what she must have looked like, her forties face and style, superimposed on the old woman she had become. I knew which one she saw when she looked in the mirror.

Judd's apartment was at the end of a long, thinly carpeted hall. The building was quiet; people were either at work or not yet out of bed. I hadn't been there for years, but it felt very familiar; something about that hallway had stayed with me. I couldn't shake the feeling that it was important I remember what it was.

He opened the door barefoot, wearing only jeans. I couldn't help but notice first thing that the top button at his waist was open. I saw that his stomach was still flat and hard; the sun that had tanned it had also bleached the hairs that gathered thickness as they disappeared below his zipper. I didn't know if he had done it purposely, but it was sexy if he had; I liked that he might be putting it out as a kind of advertisement. For a moment, I thought about Paul. I didn't yet know what I'd come to Judd's for, but whatever it was, thinking of Paul wasn't going to stop me. I didn't wonder why; it was enough that I knew it.

I followed Judd into the living room.

"Well, Vega," he said, turning to me with his slow Hollywood smile, "funny how things keep coming around."

I saw him whole now. I could tell he still worked out, but his skin had lost a certain smooth elasticity; it was coarsening, becoming thin and dull. The real surprise, though, was his face: he had lost his looks. I couldn't help staring. He was the victim of a too-rapid ripening, one of those men whose handsomeness is held as if by torque, in a tension that time comes along and snaps. But it wasn't only time that had done damage—I saw the bottle of Scotch on the coffee table and the half-empty glass, the powdered mirror and razor blade, the seeds and stems scattered on the stained carpet. All those chemicals had cut deep lines in his face, hardened his features into an angular mask; he didn't look old but was completely without a trace of youth. It was the face of a convict who was doing hard time. I guessed he could only play the heavy now, and not even the central one; he was a featured player sent out to do the dirty work, the enforcer or the psychopath, brought in for a scene or two.

There was a stillness in the room, even though he had music on in the bedroom; the air felt wound down, vacant, an empty atmosphere. He sat in an easy chair, and motioned me to the couch. He was rolling a joint. I said how long it had been and he smiled as he licked the paper; he didn't seem curious about why I'd come. I forced myself to make conversation, although I think he would have been perfectly happy to sit there and smoke in silence. His lack of interest was creepy; he reminded me of a fat spider nodding lazily to whatever stumbled into his web. *Far fucking out . . .*

After a few minutes, I began to wonder if even sex would get him going. There simply were no vibrations. In fact, I had the feeling that if I reached for him and unzipped his fly, if I helped him shimmy out of the easy envelope of those low-slung jeans, if I massaged his cock and sucked on it or put my nipple in his mouth and brought him deep inside me—he would simply nod and smile, his disconcerting vacancy still intact. His eyes were still beautiful but they looked blasted out.

I didn't want to stay. If there was any excitement to toying with someone, it couldn't be someone who was barely there. I turned down the Scotch he was pouring for me and quickly brought the conversation around to NNE and Peter Broadman.

"I see him from time to time," I said. "Are you still friends?"

"Yeah, sure. You know Peter—once he gets his hooks in . . ." He flashed that Hollywood grin.

"What do you mean?"

I waited while he held the smoke in and ignored the cough as he let it out.

"Peter was always out there—you know?"

"Like how?"

"I don't know—mean. Pull the short hairs and not think twice. But you got to balance these things—he takes good care of me."

"You mean the stock?"

"What stock?"

"NNE."

He looked over at me, focusing. "Oh, sure . . . my investment for a rainy day. Peter's pension . . . Peter picked a pack of pickled—people." He laughed as if it were the funniest thing in the world. "Really a pack of very pickled people." He laughed again, then looked at me.

"You know Stella?" he asked.

"Stella who?"

"Jordan . . . Stella Jordan . . . she was always around."

"No. Who is she?"

He was staring down at the table, his eyes unseeing. I'd lost him. His fingers were curled around the arms of the chair; I guessed he was holding on as the chemicals kicked in. After a while, he put the joint down in an overflowing ashtray and looked fully at me.

"Stella!" he suddenly roared. It was Brando in *Streetcar*. "Stella!" he boomed again. Then he laughed and shook his head. "Pretty good, huh? Sure. I coulda been a contendah."

He laughed again, but it was hollow, and I wondered how many actors had made that same cry, full of longing, not for Stella but for Brando, for all they wished to be and feared they never would.

"So Stella—does she know Peter?" I asked.

"You would want to say Peter knows Stella. Now *I* know Peter but I'm just one of many—small potatoes, fucking small potatoes. Stella Jordan, though—there's the deal."

"What deal?"

He was staring again. I had no idea what he was telling me, or even if it was anything at all.

"What's the deal?" I asked again.

His eyes were closing. For a moment, they widened again and he looked at me, puzzled by—what? The conversation? My very presence? I didn't know if he could possibly be as far gone as he looked, but there was no point in staying. He looked up when he heard me stand.

"Well, Vega," he said slowly, "you look great. You haven't changed a bit. Still hot . . . very hot."

Some of the old look was in his eyes but it was a strictly mechanical flirtation. I smiled and mumbled something about next time. He nodded; I could see my staying or leaving was all the same to him.

"Come by anytime," he said as I left. The door closed behind me and I shivered at the emptiness enfolding him again.

I walked slowly to the elevator. The hallway was still quiet. Again, I felt its familiarity, that sense of something waiting to be claimed. It was only when the elevator door swung shut and I was traveling down that I remembered what it was.

We'd been going out for a couple of months. Judd was erratic; he wouldn't call for a week, then phone at midnight and ask if he could come over. I always said yes. It was in that chaotic time after the divorce and I needed the company, needed a man's desire for me, even though I suspected the only time Judd thought about me was in the sixty seconds before he made the phone call. He always brought dope, "the best sinsemilla" and "dynamite cocaine," and as we got stoned I stopped noticing his actor's self-obsession, and that none of our conversation, such as it was, ever reached beyond the walls of whatever room we happened to be in, or even much beyond the bed. He had a druggy sensuality; he'd close his eyes and run his hand slowly over my skin with the intense concentration of a blind man discovering an exquisite new world. It always excited me. He was made for pleasure and he was offering it to me.

One night he called and said he was having people over and why didn't I come by. When I got to his place in the Briarwood, you could smell the grass in the hallway. There were about ten people in various stages of getting high: a thin blond German actor, an older woman whose head was almost shaved, an incredibly tense couple who hardly spoke to each other. The light was dim, and as I smoked and drank, I felt as if I were under water, as if we all were thin sea grasses swaying in the slow, heavy current of the music and drugs.

The tense couple began to kiss. They opened their mouths very wide and licked and sucked each other's tongues. Their lips were far apart; I saw inches of tongue, the underside blue veins straining as they stretched to swallow each other, two snakes dueling to the death. It didn't excite me; it was ugly, pornographic, and its blatancy, the lack of subtlety, was frightening. I tried to make myself look so that the sudden pounding of my heart would stop, but a shudder of revulsion swept through me and I had to look away. No one else seemed to notice them. Judd was stretched out in an easy chair, his eyes closed, a joint dangling from his fingers. I could hear laughter from the kitchen as someone searched for food. I was alone. Suddenly, my ground gave way; it all slipped out of my control as if a hidden hand had sprung a trap-door and I was falling helplessly through space. I took a breath but I couldn't regain my footing. Nothing seemed real; everything was dangerous.

I sat for some time, waiting for it to be all right, but I couldn't get back to level ground. Somehow, I stood up and went into the bathroom. In the mirror, the skin on my face had turned powdery, an unhealthy grayish blue. It looked sprayed over my bones in a hurried makeshift way. I ran my wrists under cold water and splashed some on my face. It's the grass, I told myself, only a drug, everything's fine, you're perfectly safe.

I came out of the bathroom. For a moment, its bright light made me blind in the twilight of the living room but slowly things came into focus. The couple was now on the floor. They were fucking. Their clothes were still on but both had pulled down their pants and I could see their asses as they ground together, in sharp movements, staccato, with a kind of grim determination. I watched the whiteness of their buttocks against their dark slacks as they rose and fell; it became disembodied, the whiteness of a pulsating membrane, edgy for relief. I felt threatened, about to be engulfed, and anger surged up in me; why couldn't they restrain themselves? What right did they have to inflict their desire on the rest of us?

I looked over to Judd and my breath caught in my throat. He was still stretched out in the easy chair, but now a woman was on the floor in front of him kneeling between his legs. One of her arms had disappeared up his pants leg; I could see the rhythm, feel it in me, as she massaged his calf. She bent and delicately lifted his other foot. Her tongue moistened her lips, licked slowly at his ankle; she separated his toes with her slow fingers, lapped at the crevices between them, sucked deeply, ran her tongue along his sole. I looked up. His eyes were closed and his head was thrown back. I saw then a man was standing behind him, leaning down and over him. He was unbuttoning Judd's shirt. He moved in the same slow way the woman did, as if swaying underwater, as if to elongate every stroke and touch. His hands slid slowly inside Judd's shirt. Judd moved beneath the searching fingers and the cloth fell away, revealed the muscular torso, the hairless nipples, the smooth and suntanned chest. Judd sighed, accepting it all, and reached back, his arms over his head, and with his hands pulled the man against him, cupped the man's ass, firmly held him in. The man was stroking him, the fingers of one hand buried in Judd's thick, long hair. He leaned farther down; his lips played along Judd's neck and collar bone as both his hands fanned out toward Judd's waist. His fingers met the woman's other hand and together they pressed in on the fabric covering Judd's enlarging cock. I realized Judd's foot was buried deep between the woman's legs and the man was pressing his own cock at the back of Judd's head, against the chair. All three of them were moving to the same slow rhythm, each lost but locked together in the same slow unhurried heat.

Judd opened his eyes and saw me. He smiled lazily, his dark eyes heavy and inviting. He held out his hand to me. I didn't have to think. I shook my head: no.

"Come on," he sighed, "come on."

The man and the woman both looked over at me. They were smiling. The woman shifted her weight and I could see the outlines of her breasts as she turned toward me. The man opened his lips and I saw his tongue; he straightened and began unbuttoning his shirt. Suddenly, I realized my heart was racing: I was terrified.

"This isn't my scene," I managed to say.

"No?" Judd said, still moving to that rhythm. "That's funny, I thought it was."

He closed his eyes and I knew that I'd ceased to exist for him, for all of them. I looked around. Everyone else had caught the scent of sex, and it wouldn't be long before all of them were doing it, moving together, undulating, flesh against flesh. My panic flared; I turned and before I knew it I was running down that hallway, the look in Judd's eye hounding me. I was so frightened I couldn't wait for the elevator but took the stairway down. The cold night desert air on the street slammed into me, a solid sheet that sideswiped me and sent me reeling. Hours later, I was alone in the dark on my living room sofa with no memory at all of how I'd got there.

For days after, I kept telling myself it was the grass that had made me paranoid and panicky. Only a drug, only a drug . . . But I kept seeing the three of them, the slow, patient rhythm. The woman's hair as she bent over to suck at Judd's foot, the feel of it brushing lightly along his sensitive skin. The man's lips as they moved down the long neck, their whispering heat and promise. I felt sacked as I pictured it, undone with desire. Why then had I been so frightened? What had made me run? After a while, I thought I knew: I hadn't been warned, no one prepared me, and anyway orgies weren't my thing, I liked my sex private.

But now going down in the elevator after all this time, I

suddenly realized what had scared me that night. It was Judd. I could see him—the movement of his legs as they sought out and submitted to the woman's touch; his fingers spread across the man's behind, pulling him close, holding him in place. I saw the knowing look in his eyes as he held his hand out to me, the borderless invitation, his open shirt falling away from the smooth skin of his long, narrow torso, his body completely at ease, relaxed, so totally relaxed. In that dim light, he was stopping time. His whole being was clarified, concentrated on a single purpose, not the finality of orgasm, but on intensity, intensity elongated, made everlasting, intensity as the vehicle into an ever-present now. To join that triangle of pleasure was to give myself over to a place in which there is no discrimination and therefore no defense, a place without controls. That was it, what had terrified me—complete abandonment, that voyage out of self.

But not anymore. I had gone through the looking glass and was entranced now by the very things that had frightened me, the unknown, the risk it took to let myself go. I was a changed woman, no longer afraid to take my hands off the steering wheel and give myself up to the road. And maybe that's why I'd come to see Judd: so that I would know it.

I taught Paul how to tease me. To let his fingers hover just above my skin, pulling back when I raised myself, avid for his touch. To let me feel his tongue just beyond the reach of my mouth and my own pleading tongue, or lightly skim my breasts and tingling nipples. To run his hands over my thighs and belly and make me raise myself up to him, in a frenzy for the pressure he denied me. I taught him how to keep himself close but just beyond my reach and make me crazy for his full embrace. I wanted to ache with the most intense desire, to feel every cell in my body alive with ardent need. I wanted to be undone.

I'm lying across the bed. He stands naked a few feet away, the hairs on his chest thin filaments as he moves in the light of a single lamp. I raise my arms above my head and cross my wrists. He ambles toward me, looks down with detachment and curiosity. I am his interesting specimen, to be probed, subjected to tests so he can measure my reactions. I need to break through that look. Sounds I have never made before escape me, I raise my chest and offer up my breasts, arch my lower back, my legs spread wide so he can see how wet I am, pink and juicy, ready for him. His eyes rest on me and I am consumed, my world come down to a single moment, an urgent necessity—the feel of his hand. His voice is murmuring in my ear, encouraging, promising, his breath a tantalizing taste of his barely withheld touch. I beg him with my eyes, plead for a single tip of his finger. His outstretched hand falls and I am heartbroken, bereft, desperate. I will do anything to earn his touch. I am mad, a wild animal raging with exquisite pain, and I offer myself up to it, allow it to take me again and again to the crest of what feels like certain obliteration, the point at which I'll shatter if I don't feel relief. But that point always contains its own surrender and as I let go to it, moment by moment, again and again, I hang suspended in an ecstatic silence, the eye of the storm, a desperate equilibrium found anew, again and again, until that moment when he gives me what I want and lets me feel the pressure of his hands, his lips and tongue, until he kisses me and sucks and comes deep inside me and we move together as one up the glistening slope.

And no matter how long he holds out, now matter how long he keeps himself from me, he always gives in too soon. Too soon.

Chapter Eleven

Paul said he had to go to New York.

"Why?" I asked.

"Business. I'll be back in a few days."

We were at his apartment and, as he packed a small suitcase, I realized how few personal things he had around him. No photos, a few books on business, nothing that gave a hint of who he really was. This was the man on whom I'd stopped closing the bathroom door; how was it possible to be so intimate physically and still not feel an equal emotional connection? It was very strange: I didn't worry about what he felt for me, whether he was "in love" with me, felt none of those old insecurities, but I didn't feel any certainty about us, either. I had no sense of permanence; I never thought about the future. I knew something was going to happen, but I didn't wonder what.

"What's the business?" I asked, my hand lingering over

the silk lining of a jacket he was taking with him.

"My usual, Vega. You don't have to know the details."

"I don't want to be like the others."

"Who?"

"All your so-called investors. I'm not afraid to know the truth."

He glanced at me and smiled.

"Nobody wants to know the truth. What people want is confirmation of what they think already. Or a way to justify what they want to do. Or something that stamps them special and different."

He tossed a shirt into the suitcase.

"Nobody wants the truth."

"What about you?" I asked.

He shrugged. "I want to make a lot of money. And I don't much care how I do it. I don't need to dress it up and make it look pretty."

"Well, neither do I."

He smiled again as if he knew it all.

"Don't be so condescending," I said. "It makes me hate you—all that self-assurance."

He didn't say anything.

"If I don't know just what the deal is, I'm not really part of it," I said. "It makes me feel like a child who can't play with the grownups."

"What do you want—to be my partner?"

"Why not? Look, I know with all this cash it must be drugs. And all that goes with it."

"What might that be?"

"I don't know."

"There are other things besides drugs."

"Like what?"

He smiled again. It was infuriating.

"I'm not afraid to know."

"But you don't know what you might find out."

"That's the point—I'm willing to take the risk."

He was looking at me. I couldn't read his eyes. They could have been angry, or skeptical, or simply assessing new possibilities.

"I tell you what," he said. "You bring me something worth being partners in. Then we'll talk about it."

There was an edge in his voice, a steeliness. I'd heard it before, sometimes when he was on the phone keeping all the balls in the air, making sure it was all getting done. More than suppressed anger waiting to explode, it was a steel door coming down, invulnerable, implacable, determined to prevail. But that voice didn't make me submissive; it challenged me. I knew the only answer to that steel was a metal of an equal strength, and I couldn't pretend I had it in me—at least not yet. But I was turning out to be a very quick study, and who could say how far I could go?

I dropped him at the airport but didn't go back into town. I needed to think. I drove past Venice and Ocean Park, then turned down to the ocean and kept heading north. The sky was gray, the wind strong and cold, moist, and the waves were thick with sand and foam. There wasn't much traffic and I kept to the right, without a need to hurry. Malibu drifted past, a blur of houses huddled on the ocean side and, on the other, looming hillside veined with impossible, invisible roads. An old blue pickup kept me five miles below the speed limit and I didn't mind.

Driving was the only place I could let my mind be blank.

I stopped somewhere north of Trancas, parked on the ocean side, and wandered down to the sand. The beach was deserted. I walked north beside the pounding surf, following the curve of the coast. Wind-scattered sand eddied around me as I watched a pelican diving for fish just beyond the breakers. I breathed deeply. The taste of salt reminded me of Paul, his taste on my tongue, but I put it aside. I needed to think about him apart from the sex.

When he said that I'd have to bring him something worth our being partners, of course Nathan had crossed my mind. But I knew my need to keep that clean was still stronger than any temptation. I wasn't going to give Nathan over.

There was something else I wanted to think about: the steeliness I saw in Paul, the cold invulnerability that at once attracted and frightened me. I saw his face, calm and determined, without a trace of doubt. He looked cold, but was he? Maybe there was some other way to see it, as a kind of austerity, a necessary distance, in the way a scientist needs distance and detachment in order to make accurate assessments. Maybe there was a kind of detachment that wasn't cold but hot, a disconnection that increased passion, even bred it, actually made available a new kind of energy, focused, burning with a deeper intensity, like a laser's concentration.

Paul's self-containment was compelling. It drew people to him, drew me and kept me fascinated. I thought about his touch; he couldn't be indifferent. There was almost a purity about him, a single-mindedness, clear and unmuddied; free of self-doubt, he didn't think, he acted. And that was the source of his strength, that there was no gap between thought and action, no blurring, undercutting doubt.

But was that the truth? How could it be a good thing to be without doubts and self-questioning? Weren't we taught to think before we acted, to consider others? Was that only a self-sabotaging courtesy masking self-denial, the reason we failed ourselves again and again, and sold ourselves short? I didn't know. How could I know? All this was so new to me; I couldn't find the familiar landmarks, the means of orientation. Jasper had said there is no truth, only perspective. But from what vantage point was I looking, and what exactly was I looking at?

I walked faster, wanting not to think. After a while I found some rocks and sat looking out to sea. Wind shredded the fog and far out I could see a circle of sunlight shining through on to the gray churning water. It disappeared, then emerged again as the fog reformed. Something in that light suddenly claimed me and I stared at it, hungry for its warmth. Then, slowly, it began to move toward shore. I sat still, in the grip of a terrible need to have that light shine on me, as if it were a shaft that could drive through me and rivet me to earth. I looked up, searching for the break in the grayness the light was coming through, but I saw only fog, and then when I turned back to the surface, the circle of light was gone.

The phone rang in the middle of the night.

"Hello," I said, only half awake. There was silence; then suddenly a sob, quickly followed by another. I sat up, completely awake.

"Who is this?" I asked, my heart racing.

I heard another sob, the gasping intake of breath. It was a man. He was crying, more than crying, sobbing like a child, the sobs coming from a place that I knew was very deep, and old.

"What's wrong, what is it?"

I was almost shouting. He couldn't catch his breath. He was saying something but I couldn't make it out—"I can't" or a name—something buried by the terrible sounds in his throat.

"Please," I said. I couldn't hang up. The pain in that voice was a claim on me. It made its own demand.

"It's all right," I heard myself saying, and I could feel the tears starting in me. "It's all right. . . . Who is this? Who?"

The line went dead.

I jumped out of bed and put on the overhead light. For a moment, I thought it must have been a dream, a nightmare, that I might even have been holding the real phone in my hand but dreaming those terrible sobs. But I knew in my bones that someone, real and in pain, had been on the other end of the line. Who was it? Did I know him? Maybe it was a wrong number, or a random dialing by a desperate near-suicide.

I couldn't go back to sleep. I walked through the house turning on the lights and drank some wine to calm me down. Shivering, I stood looking down at the city below me. After a while my breathing, the fear of every shadow set off by those disembodied cries, eased off. But I couldn't shake the sense that I knew that muffled voice. But who was it? Who? And what answer could I ever make to those unbearable cries?

• • •

Nathan wanted to meet in town instead of at the ranch. I went to his office and we moved quickly through the monthly accounts. He was preoccupied and waved away the apologies I made for not turning up anything about a possible predator.

"And you won't," he said. "You're not the only one I've had working on this, and no one has found anything." He paused and looked out at the hazy view. "They're very clever."

I smiled. "Maybe they don't exist."

"When in doubt, assume the worst," he said.

There was a delighted smile on his face; he looked sharp and devilish, like a man who was rolling up his sleeves for a delicious task. I realized how much he was enjoying this and that maybe it was worth it if it was doing so much to energize him.

But I didn't expect what came next. Peter and Hal came in; evidently there was a meeting scheduled I didn't know about. Nathan said I was to be included, then made an announcement.

"I'm thinking about spinning off NNE real estate," he said matter-of-factly. He paused, then went on quietly, "I'd like to know your thoughts."

Over the years, NNE had amassed significant real estate holdings, both developed and undeveloped land set aside for future stores, stores built by others that could be converted to NNE outlets, warehouses, garages, and other properties. This all was carried on the books and made up a good share of the company's worth.

Peter looked stunned. "You can't be serious. It's a terrible idea."

Nathan turned to Hal, who said, "I agree with Peter. I

don't know that it would ever be a good idea, but now—when real estate prices are so low—you'd be weakening NNE to a significant degree and the new company's assets would be virtually stagnant."

Peter interrupted. "Why in the world would you even think about it?"

Nathan ignored him and continued looking at Hal, who went on. "I can tell you that NNE shareholders won't like it, no matter how many rights you give them in the new company. And the Street—well, frankly, Nathan, I think they'd laugh." He hesitated a moment, then went on. "I can't imagine why you're even mentioning it. It doesn't make any sense."

"It does to me," Nathan said.

Both Hal and Peter spoke at once. I watched Nathan listening to them and realized why he was putting this out; he wanted to shake things up, create some tension, to see who was flushed out by the prospect of NNE making such an unexpected, even self-destructive, move.

"I'm just thinking about it," Nathan said. "We'll see where we go from here."

That's what I didn't know: how far he was prepared to take it. Did he only want to float a rumor, or was he actually willing to take it to the brink?

I left with Peter and Hal. I could see Peter's fury. After Hal disappeared, he turned to me, almost pinned me against the wall. "I need you to talk him out of this," he hissed in my ear.

I pulled away from him. "I don't care what you need. As if I could, anyway."

"You'd better," he said, moving closer again.

"Oh, that's good. I'd 'better.' "

"Just do it."

There was contempt in his eyes.

"Or what? Are you threatening me?"

He laughed.

"That's exactly what I'm doing, Vega. And you'd better keep it in mind."

"Fuck you," I said, before I could stop myself.

He laughed again. "Just talk him out of it. It's a stupid idea and I won't let him do it. I don't want to hurt him—but I can't let him do it."

He turned and hurried down the hall. I could have shouted that Nathan probably wasn't serious, that it was a ploy to flush out any predators, but if he couldn't figure that out himself I wasn't going to help him. Besides, I was completely on Nathan's side; if he wanted to have some fun, I didn't want to be the one to ruin it for him.

But Peter's anger stayed with me. Even as I laughed off threats from him, I realized I didn't know exactly what he was capable of. For a moment, I was afraid of him as women are often afraid of men, at least in the abstract, of their superior physical strength, the very real possibility of being overpowered, hit, beaten. I felt the usually buried place in me that always feared a remorseless juggernaut. How many times in the past had I backed off because that fear was running me? What hadn't I said; what flattery had I offered, what impulse in me had I abandoned?

No more. I wasn't going to back off, to retreat out of fear. I closed my eyes and saw the way: to confront and not to run, to feel the fear but move forward nonetheless. I began to breathe deeply, and a euphoria began to build inside me, a momentum, as if the greater my appetite the more there was to eat, as if the more I took on the more I could support. Oh yes, I had it in me. To go up against Peter. And even more—to go up against my fear. That was what I saw in Paul and that was what I wanted—not the money but this, the rush of breaking through my fear.

I went out to dinner alone and then stopped at the Beverly Center to drift through the shops. I thought about NIGHT's money but I wasn't tempted to buy anything; there was nothing I needed. I smiled; it was very clear to me that I wasn't greedy and I liked that, the dignified restraint. I just wanted the special blankness that looking through the racks can bring, a kind of holiday or blackout to kill an hour or two. Besides, NIGHT's money was being held in readiness, even though I didn't know for what.

I wandered into a store that sold clothes for men and women. There were only a few people in it but one of them was a man who immediately caught my eye. He was very dark, his skin a bronzed brown that could have been Latin or Indian, and he had long black hair falling loose halfway down his back. He was tall and thin, with a narrow face, and when he looked up I saw his eyes, very black and thickly lashed. He was beautiful, and that beauty had its own power; I thought he could be an Aztec prince or a Great Plains chief—or a Colombian drug dealer, the elegant white linen suit sort portrayed on TV shows.

His hand was resting on a stack of shirts. His wrist was exposed and on it was a bracelet, a wide cuff of silver and turquoise with an intricate filigree surrounding the stones. Something in me quickened at the sight of it. I looked at him again with new interest, that he had made the effort to put the bracelet on, a masculine adornment. I had never been with a man who was a peacock, the type you saw all over L.A., the ones who strutted in tight pants and open shirts, flashing gold rings and chains, who so plainly wanted you to look at them. That wasn't my type at all. But I could see now I was excited by a more subtle version of it, by the idea of a man decking himself out, draping himself in flowing fabrics, in silks and velvets that invited touch, in clothes that consciously showed off a wide chest or a flat stomach or a long and muscled leg. An earring, a bracelet, something completely unnecessary except as an embellishment of masculine appeal.

He was moving out of the shop and I decided to follow him. He had several shopping bags; he'd already bought a good many things. I wanted to know what. As I drifted along behind him, I speculated; I could see him showing me his purchases, trying things on, asking what I thought. That's what was exciting me, that a man would adorn himself in order to please me, that together we would have a secret understanding, give a secret but definite meaning to certain clothes and objects, not the obvious things like my black high heels or his bikini underwear, but things more subtle and innocent. "Does it excite you, the way this particular shirt pulls across my chest? Do you want me to wear this bracelet? Do you want both of us as we move through the day to be aware of that bracelet and know what it's about, what it offers and promises? Because if you do, I will. I want to please you in that way."

He got on the escalator and took it up to the top floor. He was heading for a cup of coffee. I got on line behind him, our bodies only inches apart. He was wearing a black linen sport jacket; it would have been so easy to pull it aside and slip my arm around his waist. He sat down at a table and I took one not far away and watched him as he took out a magazine, sat back and crossed his legs, turned the glossy pages over slowly one by one. One hand brushed back the long dark hair cascading across his eyes. I saw him raise the coffee to his mouth and drink; I watched his tongue lick lightly at his coffeed lips. It would be so easy to get up and go to him, to take the cup from the long, slim fingers of his elegant hand and press my lips against his palm, to stand leaning down to him, my fingers trailing along his extended throat down toward the smooth skin hidden beneath his collar, to kiss him fully on the mouth. Why not do it, take the steps to bridge the distance between us, not simply the physical distance, but the distance of desire? Why not awaken him to the irresistible reality of what I now felt? It would be so easy, to get up and sit beside him, to tell him he was beautiful to me, to press my cheek against his with the utmost tenderness, a tenderness that may be only possible with a total stranger because it relies on nothing, is attached to nothing but our own yearning need to express it. I could suggest we leave together, or even better, guide him into a hidden corridor and unleash a sudden passion, feel his hands tearing at my clothes, ride him as he leans against the wall. It would be so easy to let desire flower.

He was checking his watch. He got up. My eyes followed him as he went toward the movie theaters; he was going in. For a split second, I thought that I would chase him, really pull him back and offer my embrace, but I looked away. When I turned back, he was gone and I let him go.

I sat for a while, finishing my coffee. I was floating in a subterranean river, which I now understood was always there, a river of possibility always flowing beneath the surface of daily life. Like most of us most of the time, the man I had followed was oblivious to how strongly that river flows beneath us; with a single gesture, a whispered word, I could have shown him how close he stood to its claiming tide. It was the river of desire, which we keep safely below us, controlled in its banks and levees, so controlled that we can put on our silks and bracelets, all our ordinary adornments, and stand removed from the desire they betray. We can refuse to read their codes, stand back and not be swept away. We learn to be restrained, to hold ourselves back from surrender to that surging tide. But it is always there, awaiting us, tempting us, dark waters lapping at our feet, ready to break through and carry us away.

Chapter Twelve

There were three messages from Bobby Melner when I got to the office the next morning.

"He was furious when you weren't here the last time," Holly said. " 'Where the hell is she?' Like I'm your mother."

The phone rang again. Holly answered it.

"Just a minute," she said, and gave me a one raised eyebrow look. Bobby. I went into my office to take the call.

"I've got to see you," he said.

"Sure. What about?"

"I can't say over the phone. We have to meet."

I smiled. If Bobby needed some cloak and dagger, I was willing to play along.

"You want to come here?" I asked.

"No."

"Where?"

"Not my office. Or the house . . . Look, there's a church on the corner of Wilshire and Normandie."

"A church?"

This wasn't exactly where I thought of Bobby.

"There's a parking lot behind it. Can you meet me there?"

"If that's what you want. When?"

"Now. I need to see you now."

There was no mistaking the worry in his voice.

"You want to give me a hint? Should I bring any papers, any files?"

"No. I'll meet you there in twenty minutes."

I hung up. He'd obviously done something bad—promised money he didn't have to a screenwriter and was worried now that he'd look bad all over town, or he'd bought something for Susan Ratelsky that he couldn't afford. I'd find some way to bail him out.

Before I left the office, I asked Holly to track down someone named Stella Jordan.

"I already did," Holly said. "She's on the NNE list."

She handed me a copy. Stella Jordan had ten thousand shares, a substantial amount, and an address in the Valley. I slipped it in my purse.

I drove south to Wilshire and then headed east along what optimistic city fathers had once called the Miracle Mile. This was the part of Wilshire that was really a boulevard, a wide and winding corridor that had once been lined with hotels and apartment houses but was now shadowed by office buildings put up in the glow of the expansive seventies and eighties. Now, in the downturn, these buildings, desperate for tenants, had a derelict air. Some of the old apartment houses were empty and boarded up, awaiting either the wrecker's ball or some influx from the Pacific Rim to spur restoration; others had already been given a paint job and were advertised as vintage L.A. art deco. These, too, were mostly empty. The whole street had a dusty, used feel, not so much the old Los Angeles transient feel of new arrivals alighting a moment before finding a permanent home, but the sense that it was all finally gone and everyone was in a holding pattern to see what would happen next. The spaciousness of the boulevard wasn't expansive now; it was desolate.

Bobby was waiting for me when I found the church and parking lot.

"This isn't exactly your beat," I said to him. "How do you know this place?"

"A woman I used to see—in AA—they have meetings here all the time." He waved that aside. "Let's go somewhere. You drive."

He got into my car. I headed west on Olympic, through Koreatown.

"So what's going on?" I asked.

"I did something stupid," Bobby said. He was drumming his fingers nervously on the dashboard; I could see he had no idea he was doing it.

"I sort of guessed," I said. "Well, tell me what it is and we'll figure something—"

"Pull in over there," he suddenly interrupted.

He was pointing to a strip mall with a 7-Eleven. I turned in, and he jumped out of the car and disappeared inside. A minute later he was back with a six-pack of Diet Coke and a half-dozen packs of sugarless gum. He flipped open the cans and gave one to me, then unwrapped two or three sticks of gum and stuffed them in his mouth. I shook my head when he held a pack of gum out to me. He unwrapped another stick and managed to get that in his mouth as well. His moist mouth was chewing fast, but it didn't seem to calm him down. He ran a hand over his eyes and I realized he was more than worried; he was scared.

"Well?" I asked, as he finished the soda and opened another.

"I'm in trouble," he finally said.

"I can see. Look, it's all right—you've overextended before and we've always found a way to cover it."

"It's different this time."

He was looking out the window. It didn't matter that all the signs were in Korean; he wasn't registering them anyway.

"Remember that land? At the beach?" he asked, turning back to me.

I nodded. "Two point five."

"Right. Well, I really wanted it."

"For Susan."

His fist hit the dashboard. "It isn't fair that the trust is set up the way it is. It's my money—no one should tell me if I can spend it. It isn't fair."

I felt my contempt for him rising. He was such a child, a rich kid thinking he had it all coming.

"So what did you do?"

"A couple of months ago I was introduced to this guy named Richard Arzell. Dick. You ever heard of him?"

I shook my head.

"He made a fortune in shopping malls in the south. Developing, leasing. Well, somebody said he was looking for movie projects—we should get together."

He spit the gum out into the wrappers he'd saved, then chewed on new pieces. I saw the used wrappers in his hand; I couldn't help wondering where he was going to leave them.

"So we met. I told him I had all these projects the studios wanted just ready to go except they needed a little more development money. I took him to some parties, introduced him to some people whose names he knew—he was real impressed."

"I bet."

"Well, then I told him I had a script, a whole package, an action thriller perfect for worldwide, and why involve a studio—we could do it ourselves, make a profit on foreign and video even before we shot a frame. All I needed was some money to get it all going."

"How much money?"

Bobby didn't want to say.

"Not two point five?" I didn't think even he could be that stupid—or that daring.

He shook his head. "Five hundred thousand. Enough to move into preproduction."

"Only you didn't. You took the money—"

He nodded.

"Right. It was stupid. I admit it. Stupid." He leaned toward me. "We've got to come up with it."

I heard that "we" but resisted the urge to point out to him that at the moment it was his problem, only his.

"Does he know what you've done?"

Bobby nodded. "That's the worst part. He knows and he hasn't done anything."

"What do you mean?"

"He offered me a deal. I can either come up with the money—which he knows I don't have—or sort of go to work for him. 'Put yourself at my disposal,' is how he phrased it."

"What does that mean?"

"Otherwise he'll make a big stink, even go to the cops. . . ."

"What does that mean—at his disposal? What does he want you to do?"

"Introduce him around."

"So? What's so bad about that?"

I could see him hesitate. "I don't think he wants to make movies," he finally said.

"What does that mean?" I asked.

"I think the recession's hurt him. Big time. He's been hurting for dough and I think he sees Hollywood as a cash cow. He said some things—what he wants is to meet people with access to cash. Distributors. Record people. I think he wants to siphon it off."

He stuffed all the gum wrappers into his pocket, then looked up at me, his eyes pleading. "Don't you see? I can't do it—he'd own me. And how can I betray the people I know—the relationships I've built up over the years. My good name!"

He slumped lower down in the seat. I wanted to say, what a time to call upon integrity. As if he had had any to begin with.

"He also wants me to introduce him to Jonathan Carland."

"Who's that?"

Bobby looked at me as if he couldn't believe it. Hollywood people are always like this, amazed when you don't know every aspect of their world.

"He's one of my oldest friends. He ran Tiger Head Films when they made that string of hits—remember?"

I shook my head. This time Bobby didn't notice.

"But he got out of production into financing. He says that's where the real power is. He runs his own department at a bank downtown and puts deals together for them, big deals, like when Hikado made the run on Megalomedia." He popped open another can of soda. "I can't introduce Arzell to him. I'd be finished in this town. Please, Vega, you've got to find the money."

"You think Arzell will let you go even if you pay him back?"

I could see that hadn't even occurred to him. I was almost sorry I had said it. But not quite.

"He's got to. That's all. He's got to. I made a mistake. It was stupid. But I can't be expected to pay for it the rest of my life. No one could ask that—it wouldn't be fair. I mean, even the Mafia lets you pay them back—they have a code of honor."

I sat looking at him, a man completely without a compass or a patch of solid ground. He didn't want to protect his old friend Jonathan Carland because it would be wrong to give him up to Arzell; he was afraid to do it because if the word got out he would be finished in Hollywood. He was a pleader, a deserver, someone who should have it easy but now he had caught a glimmer of just what the real world could send at him and he was collapsing under it. So it was up to the rest of us to serve and save him; it would never occur to him to do it himself. And he didn't care what the solution was as long as it got rid of the problem.

"Can you get the money? Can you find it?" He was really desperate.

I could have said no and let him go under. Richard Arzell would use him and then get rid of him, or toss him to the police, and Bobby, a rich little boy whose main accomplishment was that he could get a table at Spago, would simply be gone. And no one in Hollywood would think about him or remember, because he wasn't a player anymore and Hollywood lived in the highly impermanent Now.

"I'll try," I said. "I'll see what I can do."

"Oh, that's great, great."

His relief was visible, his mouth moister than ever. Already he was beginning to feel the problem was gone, that by giving it to me he was coming out from under.

"I'll find a way to thank you. I promise you I will."

What a fool, I thought, he doesn't even see it: there is no out from under. His real trouble was undoubtedly just beginning, but I didn't have the heart to tell him.

I called in to the office after I dropped Bobby off at his car. There was a message from Paul; he would be back by evening. I was glad. I needed to talk to him about this thing with Bobby. On impulse, I took out Stella Jordan's address. I knew there wasn't much point in my pretending to be Nathan's detective, his spy, but I liked the idea of the continuing pursuit, of operating beneath the skin. And Judd Mallory had linked Stella to Peter Broadman; I wouldn't mind turning up something to use against Peter.

The address wasn't far out in the Valley; I could be there in twenty minutes, just enough time to think about Bobby.

Of course, there was no way I could legally come up with the five hundred thousand dollars. Bobby must have known that, although I could see he was in the kind of denial that made it possible to know without knowing. His weakness, his moral rationalizations and unwillingness to take responsibility, filled me with contempt; it made him an uninteresting, unworthy object. But I could see there was a lot to be said for holding someone's fate in the balance. Bobby was dangling from my fingers like a puppet on a string; his movements, his fate, depended now on me. He thought he was making himself safe from Arzell; he didn't see just how completely he had turned himself over the moment he rushed to find someone else to do it for him. But that was all right; I didn't need his recognition of the power I now held in order to feel my own delight. I alone held the higher perspective and that was fine with me.

Bobby probably thought I'd figure out how to tap his trust and I liked the irony of my already having been to that well. It was too risky to try it again, but I could bail him out on my own—NIGHT had more than enough money, which, in a further irony, had been seeded from Bobby's account. I sat for a while with the realization that I had the resources to move on that scale, the power to decide.

I turned off the freeway and drove about a mile north of Ventura Boulevard, through a middle-class neighborhood. The neat rows of houses had been built in the explosion after World War II and an occasional lone orange tree in a manicured front yard was the only ghost left of the miles of desert and orange trees that had been replaced. I found Stella Jordan's house; it was as neat and nondescript as its neighbors. This was the San Fernando Valley I had always secretly been drawn to, the miles of conformity, anonymous and ordinary as the streets and towns I'd grown up in. But here I didn't see emptiness in the anonymity; I saw an absence of pressure, imagined a life somehow free of complication, of the curse of ambition and the need to move up. Of course I knew it must be fantasy, that to knock on any door would be to open up lives as complex and full of drama as any daytime soap. But that reality didn't diminish what attracted me, modest expectations, the absence of ambition.

I parked a few houses down from Stella Jordan's. An unseen dog was barking as I opened the car windows and sat thinking, drawing up a mental balance sheet of pluses and minuses about Bobby. Once I helped him, he would have something on me, even if he didn't know the details of just where the money was from. This didn't seem like much of a drawback, given Bobby's lack of brains and his cowardice. I could see those weaknesses would always make him unreliable, but if I planned for that, never put myself in any position where I needed anything—anything at all—from him, it didn't seem like much of a risk.

A dark American car pulled up in front of Stella Jordan's. Two men got out and rang her doorbell. I watched as they disappeared inside. What Paul would know was how to bail Bobby out in such a way that we—Paul and I—would own him. Because I could see that was the opportunity I was being handed: to use Bobby in the way that Arzell had wanted to and of course to get rid of Arzell.

The front door opened after a few minutes and the men came out, got into their car and drove away. A few minutes later, a man and a woman pulled up; they too disappeared into the house and reemerged a few minutes later. A lone woman rang the bell followed by two teenagers, boys in cutoffs and extra-large T-shirts. It wasn't hard to figure out what was going on: Stella Jordan was obviously a drug dealer camouflaged in middle-class suburbia. So much for my dreams of Valley simplicity.

I started my car, drove past the house, and turned the corner. I knew now that Peter Broadman was mixed up with drugs. It could be that he was simply one of Stella's customers, but somehow I didn't think so. Stella owned shares of NNE, a lot of shares. That suggested complications, hidden knots to be untied. I didn't need to knock on Stella's door today but I knew I would. I almost laughed. All in all, I was having quite a day. Possibilities were all around.

Part
THREE

Chapter Thirteen

"I've come across something interesting."

Paul and I were at dinner at a restaurant in Westwood. It had opened a few years earlier to rave reviews and you couldn't get in, but now the crowd had moved on. The food was still great, an L.A. mix of Tex-Mex, French and Asian, only now they were happy to see you and always had a table.

Paul had taken a cab in from the airport and I'd met him at his apartment. By the time I got there, everything I'd watched him pack had been unpacked and put away; the apartment, like him, offered few clues and showed no traces. But for the first time, his mystery wasn't simply intriguing or exciting. I also felt wary, on the alert. He was a good teacher: I was learning to hold something back.

I'd noticed it when I was getting dressed to meet him. I put on a new dress in a deep wine color made out of a heavy, almost metallic, knit; it flowed and clung at the same time. I stood back and checked myself in the mirror, fastened on a necklace of thin copper disks, brushed out my dark hair, deepened the brown of my eyelids. I was evaluating, calculating: I wanted to attract him not only to arouse him sexually, but also because his wanting me might in some way be . . . useful. I was surprised; I didn't know quite what I intended. I had no plan, no definite idea, but an unsuspected part of me was obviously making provisions for a time I might need to trade on whatever desire I could evoke. The woman in the mirror smiled. It gave me pleasure that I was saving up for a rainy day, and not just in NIGHT's account.

It turned out Paul already knew who Richard Arzell was.

"Sure. A lot of action in the South—real estate, construction. As a matter of fact, I know someone who did business with him a few years ago over a tract near Little Rock. He needed help with the unions. And I've heard rumors that he's trying to get something going out here. In Bakersfield. That could be interesting. I ought to go up there and take a look at it."

"We could go together, make a trip of it," I said. "We haven't been away together at all."

Time away sounded good, but I also liked the idea of staying close to Paul and learning what I could.

"Bakersfield isn't exactly romantic," he said, smiling.

There was no mistaking the look in his eye, or the answering one in mine. Like fish swimming to another part of the tide pool, we moved effortlessly and instantly to the point of sexual connection. It was so easily there we didn't need to force it; in fact, there was a particular pleasure in moving toward it and then choosing to retreat, like children rushing for the wave, then evading it with a thrilling laugh. After a beat, Paul smiled; I sat back and picked up my fork.

"Anyway, Bobby's right to be worried about Arzell," Paul continued. "He has a nasty reputation."

"Should we leave him alone?"

Paul almost laughed. "I thought you liked it dangerous," he said.

"I do. I do."

I could see him speculating. "Actually, men like Arzell are often very easy. Nasty little egos, very big fears. The kind who roll over at the first sign of real trouble."

"What is that—'real trouble'? You'd threaten him, hurt him?"

He looked at me. "Does that bother you?"

I shook my head. "I know it comes with the territory."

He was studying me. "The details wouldn't turn you off?"

I was suddenly angry. He was challenging me, and no matter what I said now I'd feel like a fool—needing either to protect a ladylike innocence or pretend I was indifferent to blood and violence.

"They might turn me off," I finally said evenly. "But that wouldn't stop me."

That was the truth. It had been the truth since the moment I met him.

He nodded. "Tell Bobby you've got the money for Arzell. I'll give it to you."

I nodded. I hadn't told Paul about NIGHT. Instinctively I knew it was better that he not know.

"And then we'll get Bobby to give us his friend Carland," I said.

Paul laughed. "You're way ahead of me."

"It's obvious," I said, but I was pleased.

"You set up some kind of contact," he said. "I'll take it from there."

"No. I want to do it," I said. "I want to bring Carland in."

He looked over at me. I took a sip of wine.

"You said if I brought you something worthwhile. The way I see it Arzell alone qualifies. So Carland is really a prize. And I want to bag him."

"Just how would you do that?"

I shrugged. "I'll figure something out."

I said it with much more nonchalance than I felt, but an expression I liked crossed Paul's face: admiration.

"I bet you will. What about setting up a system at the bank? It's complicated, it has to be done right. And you've never done it."

"You'll show me." My hand was on his thigh, moving up. "You're a very good teacher."

He smiled and nodded and ran his tongue over his lips as he held still and concentrated on the path of my hand. I couldn't stop smiling.

"And when I bring him to you, we split him down the middle." With a final tap, I pulled back my hand. "Fifty-fifty on whatever moves through him."

"Oh, really?"

"Yes."

"You're full of surprises, Vega."

"Only since I met you."

He reached out and let his fingers brush across my chest. He was teasing me and I liked it. I liked looking into his beautiful eyes and openly acknowledging the desire bubbling underneath. I liked playing with it in a public place, tantalizing ourselves with what had to be deferred. And tonight there was a new layer, a sense that I was keeping secrets, that I had something to hold back. It didn't deaden my desire; in fact, it inflamed it. I was alive to the freedom such withholding confers.

"Is it a deal?" I asked, leaning so close to him the hairs on my arm responded to his electricity.

"Partners," he said, and I closed my eyes as he lifted my hair and pressed his lips to my perfumed neck.

He sat on the edge of the bed. I knelt in front of him and pushed his knees apart. He leaned back and supported himself on his elbows. I took him into my mouth and sucked. I cupped his balls in the palm of my hand; the fingers of my other hand moved lightly across his chest, teased at his nipples, plunged into his open mouth. He sucked them as I was sucking him. My tongue was drawing him out, making him larger; I ran my teeth gently up and down the shaft. My hands were restless; they skimmed across the taut flesh of his belly, ran down his thighs and calves, outlined the muscles and tendons, the arch of his foot resting on the floor. My hand moved under his ass and I played at his hole. He moaned and I pushed him down, my hand beneath his ass holding his hips up to me, the other hand playing up and down his chest and stomach, feeling him spread out before me, smoothing him out, sanding him clean. I breathed in, excited by his smell, the secret smell hidden in the crevices of his body, the smell of sex as I spread my own knees and felt how wet I was, how open. I took him deeper into my mouth, more deeply than I'd ever done. I felt that I would choke but instead of pulling back I opened further, and wider, more. He was moving rhythmically, thrusting deeply, purposefully, and I could feel myself going out to meet him, my mouth and throat a widening tunnel, an enlarging passageway, warm and moist and welcoming, an expanding chamber which had no limitation.

It wasn't difficult to put together a file on Jonathan Carland. He'd made a splash in the business press in his mid-twenties when he'd become president of Tiger Head Films, one of the boutique mini-studios that had sprung up as the old studios declined and released a string of hits, low budget, mostly thrillers directed by a man who had been a set designer and suddenly blossomed as an international cult director the French had practically made into a national hero. Carland had benefited, and articles about him in *Fortune, Business Week* and *The Wall Street Journal* all said he was the best of a "new breed," sophisticated taste coupled with a brilliant business head. I couldn't see what was so sophisticated about a string of low-budget thrillers, but other people seemed to think it was all very hip.

It was Carland's background that interested me most. Like Bobby, he'd been raised rich, but Jonathan's family wasn't simply rich; they were patrician, bulwarks of the American aristocracy. His ancestors appeared to have founded the whaling industry in Rhode Island and branched out; every gas lamp in Providence had once been fueled by a Carland company. His great-grandmother's house at Newport, one of the few palatial "cottages" built by a local, was now a museum and open to the public. *Business Week* had a picture of him lolling on the front lawn. I could make out a portion of the house behind him, a French chateau of ornamented rosy granite and beveled glass. There was a strip of manicured and perfect lawn sweeping down to a private piece of ocean where even the waves were probably genteel. Carland was smiling, and that smile contained all the ironies, at once claiming and deprecating his impressive history. *So old-fashioned, so useless,* he seemed to be saying, *but it's still my heritage. And don't you forget it.*

Instinctively I knew that, unlike me, Jonathan Carland had never felt like an outsider. He had never hung back afraid to say or do the wrong thing. He couldn't imagine what it's like to buy something, a suit or a leather case, knowing it's too expensive, but suddenly desperate to have it because having it will elevate you into a higher region where everything is clean and fine and ordered and all about quality and beauty, and then you get it home and the next day are plunged into guilt about what it cost—you really can't afford it—and then even more harshly plunged into doubt about whether it's even the right color or cut, or whether one more time you've made some error of taste and judgment so that, as always, you are fated never to have just the right thing, never to have control.

Carland couldn't know those doubts. Looking into his smiling eyes in the photograph, I knew he would take control for granted. No wonder he had left movie production, which was all about courting "talent" and pleasing the public, for the downtown banker's world in which he held the purse strings. I guessed, rightly as it turned out, that he had moved from Beverly Hills to Pasadena or San Marino, from the glitz of the west side to the staid, old-money northeast of downtown. Some of his movie friends probably saw this as a kind of retreat, an unaccountable quirk, as if anyone who walked away from all that glamour must be flawed in some way. But I didn't think Carland saw it like that; he understood he was moving toward, returning to the center of real power.

The only unexpected item in Carland's biography was that he had been married and divorced twice and was presently single. The picture-perfect staid home life that usually came with his territory had obviously eluded him. That was in my favor. I didn't yet know just how I was going to get to him, but the fact that there was no wife to keep track of what time he came home at night definitely seemed a point in my favor.

Nathan called and invited me to dinner. He'd made a reservation at Chasen's and was already there when I arrived. He didn't see me as the maître d' led me toward him, and so for a moment I saw him unguarded. It was a shock: sunk in the deep leather of the booth, he seemed small and shrunken, tired and, above all, alone, lonely. The energy he'd had in his office the last time I'd seen him was completely absent; his shoulders were slumped and he was staring down at the table, lost in thought. I didn't know if something had happened, or if the frailty I was noticing for the first time was now always lurking underneath. He looked up and his lost look was gone, replaced with a smile as he straightened up. And I forgot it, too; I wanted to forget. I wanted Nathan strong.

"You're looking very well," he said, after we had ordered. "Very—what is it?—vivid."

I smiled. "I like that."

"What have you changed?"

"Nothing."

"Women always say that. At least Margaret did. After she bought a new dress or did something to her hair."

"Well, we like to make it seem effortless. Entirely natural."

"With her it was."

I loved him in that moment, loved his love for her.

"Did you know when I met her she was designing dresses?"

"No. I had no idea."

"For a little company downtown. On Eighth and San Julian. She'd gone there right out of high school."

"Margaret? I thought she'd been born rich."

He shook his head. "A younger brother and sister. Her father long gone. And the mother drank."

"Margaret?" I said again.

"I was just thinking about opening a second store. I remember I had a big Lincoln, black with tan leather upholstery. Her mother looked at me and saw nothing but dollar signs . . . but Margaret—she wouldn't be rushed. She was good at the work, she liked it. Why should she get married?"

"She could do both."

He shook his head. "In those days, if you got married, especially to someone with money . . ." He shrugged. "It was just assumed she wouldn't work."

"So she chose you."

"I don't know . . . she chose to get married to someone with money."

"Nathan. She loved you. Anyone could see that."

"Later. But in the beginning I'm not so sure. She was a good girl—she wanted to take care of her family. The unselfish thing."

Nathan had never before talked to me in such a personal way and I didn't know what to say. It came to me how arrogant we sometimes are: we think that what we see is all there is and that it's always been the way we see it.

"Later, when I knew she loved me, I felt so guilty that my money bought her, robbed her of her chance."

"But she was happy with you. She had a good life."

"But she might have had a better one. Been a great success. An American Chanel. How do I know?"

He suddenly looked up at me, with an expression on his face I'd never seen before.

"I hate money. What it does. I hate it."

His voice was intense, almost violent. He heard it, too, and for a moment, he was staring at me, his eyes puzzled and helpless before the rush of his own feelings. Something was wrong, very wrong. My hand reached out and rested on his sleeve. I didn't know what else to do. He shook his head at his private vision, and we sat like that, as if the rest of the world had disappeared. I wanted to fix it for him, whatever it was, but I didn't think I could, and I hoped it was enough that I sat now beside him, my hand on his sleeve, trying to tell him he wasn't alone.

Finally he picked up his drink, and as he moved I withdrew my hand. We were back to normal. He took a sip.

"You didn't say much about the spin-off idea," he said.

"I don't take it seriously."

He smiled. "Of course not. I don't expect anyone to think I'd actually do it. But I want them to worry about what else a crazy old man might get up to."

"Peter's worried," I said carefully.

At the sound of his son's name, that helpless look crossed his face again.

"My only son," he whispered, and the sound of his voice was shocking because it was so naked: anguished, confused, and vulnerable. I heard contempt and longing and above all pain. Here was the real depth of what he was dealing with, the terrible isolation that came from Margaret's death and Peter's reckless ego.

Somehow the conversation moved on. Nathan took a breath and changed the subject; I gladly followed him away from the abyss. We ate our food and talked about unimportant things. He had only wanted my company. I left him in the parking lot and watched him recede in my rearview mirror as I drove away. But I held on to the expression I'd seen on his face and it made me more determined to track down whatever line about Peter had opened up in front of me. Somehow Peter would have to go because Peter was hurting Nathan. I was determined to do whatever I could to protect Nathan.

I rolled down my window so that I could feel the night air. Life was a seesaw, a roll of cycles in endless motion. When I was younger and inexperienced, Nathan had been there to show me the way; he gladly shared his strength with me. Now the scales were tipping in the other direction and as Nathan aged and weakened, I was ready to be there for him. It seemed inevitable that it would come to this, and Nathan's need quickened me, was an impetus, a source for my momentum. It felt like a perfection that Paul had come along and awakened hidden appetites and hidden strengths in me, and I could use them now to help my friend. Of course, there were things I'd never tell Nathan—about the money, about doing something I shouldn't. But those words—*something I shouldn't*—I didn't know what they meant anymore, since everything I was doing was making me stronger, moving me toward the woman I had the capacity to be. How could I turn away from that widening new prospect? How could I refuse to become the woman I was meant to be?

Paul had asked me to meet him in the bar of a hotel in Westwood. He wasn't alone. A woman was with him.

"This is Jane," he said, as I sat down at their table.

She was young and very pretty, with light brown hair that rippled back from her face in soft waves before falling to her shoulders. The deep green of her silk dress shimmered in the muted light of the almost empty room. She smiled as Paul ordered a drink for me but didn't say anything. I noticed her hands were very small, with finely shaped nails that were painted a dark red; one of her fingers was lightly tracing circles in the moisture that had accumulated at the base of her glass. I looked from her to Paul, waiting for one of them to give me a clue to their relationship, but Jane remained silent as Paul and I made small talk about what we'd done that day.

"How do you know each other?" I finally asked.

Paul laughed and I turned to him.

"We don't exactly," he said and, seeing I was puzzled, went on.

"She's here for us. If we want her."

I started to ask what he meant, but then it came to me.

"I've taken a room upstairs," Paul continued. "If we want to. It's up to you."

I instantly flushed. He had given me no warning, caught me so off guard. Anger flared. I didn't like that he had found this woman and arranged it without consulting me, that he'd been able to prepare but had not allowed that to me. And yet, as I took a breath, I realized that in a way I'd asked him to do this, to do for me what I could not do for myself.

"I need a minute here," I said. My face was hot, flushed; reality had changed, heightened, and I felt myself heavy, thickened with fear, and with excitement. As much as I wanted to lift my glass to drink, to take in that cooling, calming liquid, I sat still, afraid I'd visibly tremble.

"Take your time," Paul said. I knew he saw my nervousness and was enjoying it, but I didn't mind; after a few breaths, I saw I liked the edge, the fact that he was pushing me. I wanted to be pulled in to something new. I knew my eyes were sparkling.

I turned to Jane.

"Are you a prostitute?" I felt ridiculous asking her so plainly but I needed to know and it would have been worse asking Paul, talking over her.

She smiled and nodded without embarrassment. Unlike me, she was certain of why she was there and felt no shame. I risked raising my glass and, as I drank, I stared at her. She wasn't at all self-conscious and when she calmly sat under my gaze it took my breath away; I was suddenly aroused by the realization that the only reason she was there was to please Paul and me. I'd always had contempt for men who went to prostitutes. It's so alien to what most women want from the sexual transaction, so impersonal. Now I saw what was compelling in that very impersonality, the desire that flares when the act is stripped of any pretense of emotional reciprocity, stripped of everything except erotic gesture, the pursuit of pleasure, its demands and dictates, sex itself. That was the prohibition, even for a modern woman, against sex without love.

But here was a woman before me, a real woman in a green silk dress, willing to do whatever we—I—wanted. And if I didn't skitter away in fear, if I allowed it, it was exciting, incredibly exciting, to contemplate being in emotional control, distant, above entanglement, and to surrender at the same time to the whirlwind of desire, become even more able to surrender because it is desire removed from, severed from love and all its complex, inhibiting burdens.

I looked down at the table; Jane's hand was lying flat on its edge, only a few inches from Paul's arm. What would I feel if she reached over now and ran her fingers lightly along the fabric of his linen jacket? Or if he slowly skimmed a finger across the thin, fragile skin of her inner wrist? I took a breath. What if both of them did that because I asked them to? What if they did it for me?

I sat back. I saw the three of us as if from a camera positioned high on the ceiling, so close around the cocktail table that our knees were brushing and we could feel each other's heat. I felt inside me all the barriers of convention that separated us, an iron curtain bisecting an inch or two of air. But those were the barriers I wanted to break through, all the old limitations that kept me bound in doubt and hesitation. I wanted to sail free, to penetrate the borders and let desire flow.

I put down my glass. Paul put his hand over mine, and I realized how stiffly I'd been sitting, almost afraid to move. I forced myself to turn in my chair.

"I'm not sure," I said, looking at him. "But I think I'd like to go upstairs."

He nodded and quickly paid the bill. I suppose I was waiting for him to make one complacent gesture, something that smacked of a man and his harem; if he in any way made me feel this was about him, I knew that I would bolt. I needed to thread my own way, not to think but to feel my way toward an opening, toward the inhibiting boundaries that had always blocked me and then to find a discovered passage through.

We were silent in the elevator. Jane stood apart from us. I watched her as she focused on the illuminated floor lights counting upward. She was well dressed and obviously had money. I recognized her black high-heeled shoes; I'd seen them in Neiman's only a few days before. I wondered what was going through her mind. I realized it didn't matter; she had no need for me to wonder, or to ask. Paul put his arm around me. As I let myself lean against him, it came to me that I had hoped he would do this—but that it would be with Gaby. She was the one I'd seen when I let myself think along these lines. But maybe this was just as well. It was so much simpler. Jane came with no complications, no ongoing ties to my life, or Paul's.

The room Paul had taken was large, with a queen-sized bed set in an alcove and a sofa and easy chairs. Someone had already turned on two or three small lamps and their light threw shadows against the neutral-colored walls. I watched as Paul drew curtains to close out the south-facing view. I understood why we weren't at his place or mine; this room was exactly right, an elegant stage set, an anonymous arena for whatever we would do.

"What happens now?" I asked, sitting down. It was a nervous question, bubbling out of a mix of fear and excitement, both indistinguishable, beating quickly through me, a prelude, a fanfare, percolating.

"Whatever you like," Paul said. "What do you want?"

He came and stood behind my chair. I knew if I turned my head, my cheek would brush up against him. His fingers found me, were on my neck and throat, and I could feel myself inclining to him, stretching like a hungry cat for his touch. I looked at Jane as she looked at us; even this, to sit back with Paul behind me, to close my eyes and feel his familiar touch, to let her see my inclining body, even this was to have begun.

Paul's fingers were more insistent now. "What do you want, baby? Tell me what you want."

I looked up at him. "I want to watch. I want to watch her undress you."

He smiled, a laugh deep in his throat, and leaned down to kiss me, his hands stretching me out, drawing me up to him, his fingers skimming my throat and then my breasts. Something in me gave way and I felt myself straining for him, for his mouth and tongue and the pressure of his hands. He pulled away and looked at me, his eyes huge and liquid brown.

"That's what you want, is it? Is it?" It wasn't a question, it was a grappling hook, a coiled rope pulling me up and on. "Is it, baby, is it?"

"Yes, yes," I whispered, and all restraint was gone.

He took off his jacket as he walked toward Jane, who was sitting on the edge of the bed. He sat beside her and she turned toward him and slowly unbuttoned the top button of his white, heavy rayon shirt. His hand brushed her hair back, and then he looked at me; he watched me watching them, watching him as Jane opened his shirt and slipped her hand inside. I could feel what she felt, the smooth warm skin; I saw him twist to make the most of her touch. My breath caught. A part of me was still in flight, from Paul's naked chest responding to another's touch. Was it jealousy? Or fear—of what would be unleashed inside me if I continued watching her fingers slide back the open wings of his shirt, run across his shoulders and down the muscles of his arms, if I followed her red-nailed fingers as they circled his waist inside his belt, then deftly moved toward the buckle and slowly, carefully began the zipper's separation. Her hands moved as mine would have, in slow arcs, awakening, teasing, pleasuring. I felt myself rising and going toward them. Paul was looking at me, and as I moved closer I saw that he was letting himself go, giving himself up to what Jane's touch was making him feel. I stood behind her and reached out to him, my hand brushing back and forth against his cheek; he kissed my palm and ran his tongue along my fingers. I felt his whole body sigh. What was he thinking? Of all the possible perspectives on what we were enacting, which was the one that right now was setting him in motion, sharpening the knife edge, an exquisite enlivener?

His eyes were closed; for a moment I had a stab of fear that he was sealed off from me, was using me, that I was nothing but an object in his private scenario. But my own desire was insistent and I didn't want to shrink back. I wanted to take what was being offered. Wasn't this what sex was always about beyond the body's connections—private minds charged by private dreams, the sources of obsession? Why should Paul's fantasies be in any way a threat to me? Why not allow him whatever he was thinking, give him permission to use what we were doing in any way he wanted? If I did, I would be free to do it, too. I saw it now: my fear—of being used, controlled, judged—had been controlling me, inhibiting me, keeping me down. But why should I take my cue from, give up my power to what I was afraid someone else might do or think? I could seize my freedom, the freedom not to be threatened, not to care what anybody thought.

I took a step back, wanting to see them both. I felt a wide and slow expansion, as if the river of desire were broadening out into a slow and steady current, in which I could slowly turn and stretch, luxuriate in time itself, now becoming a honeyed flow. My hands began to move and, without any embarrassment at all, I teased at my nipples beneath the fabric of my dress, ran slow circles across my belly, pressed deeply into the recess between my legs. I was steps away from them but all distance was obliterated in an immediate connection. My willingness to step onto the field with them dissolved all separation.

Paul's shirt was off and Jane, kneeling, removed his shoes and socks. He lay back, and I could see his stomach, the V-section of skin revealed by his open waistband. His unclothed chest, the way his belt fell open and the heavy buckle pulled back and revealed only just so much, and his now bare feet—all that inflamed me, as if his slacks had no other function but to hide and therefore highlight his sex. He was tantalizing.

I turned to Jane.

"Undress yourself," I said to her. "Slowly. Very slowly."

Paul leaned further back on the bed. He was rocking in a steady rhythm. His cock was hard and he pressed at it.

"Come here," he said to me.

I went to him, leaned down, pressed my own hand against his, and we kissed. I held my hand against him as I turned to watch Jane take off her dress. She was wearing a black silk teddy trimmed in lace. I motioned her to me; I suddenly needed to touch it, to feel the soft fabric, to run the tip of my finger along the delicate outline of lace. My other hand still held Paul, and I felt him move against me. I knew what I wanted now. To slip off his pants and make him naked. To see his hands reach for Jane's breasts and run my own fingers over his as he cupped them in their full black silk. To make his body arch as my hand moved firmly up and down his cock, and then to turn to Jane, to help her out of the teddy, to brush her nipples erect with the back of my hand. I wanted to offer her and Paul up to each other, to spread them out before each other, open, ripe, impelled by desire, under my gaze. To see them kiss and to put my fingers between their lips, to feel their tongues, and then my own lips and tongue on theirs. I wanted to see Paul enter her, to lie beside them and to watch the shaft of his cock move slowly in and out, to see, to smell their moisture and glistening pink flesh. I wanted to embrace them as they embraced each other, and then I wanted them to embrace me, to feel their hands and lips and tongues glide over my heated skin, to feel her breath on my neck as he entered me. I wanted to be unsure where I began or they, to make with them a new configuration, in which touching and being touched were one and the same, an endless moment of intensity, a flowing circle of undifferentiated drenching desire.

Chapter Fourteen

I called Bobby and said I wanted to see him.

"Sure, sure," he said quickly, and then, lowering his voice, "is everything taken care of?"

"I'll tell you when I see you," I said. "I'll be at your house in an hour."

I didn't give him a chance to ask anything more. And I didn't give him a chance to tell me not to come. He didn't know it, but he'd already begun doing what I wanted.

Bobby lived above Beverly Hills in Franklin Canyon. I turned off Sunset and soon was heading up the narrow road into a rustic area of fairly new and expensive houses. The canyon walls came steeply down into their backyards; I could imagine a time when the road I was driving was only a stream bed, a natural path created by winter runoff and the deer and coyote that came to drink while the water flowed. There were a hundred canyons like this one, slicing through the Hollywood Hills, which traveling west became the Santa Monica Mountains and ended at the sea, all of them subject to landslides and fire but worth it to the people who wanted privacy and the illusion that they lived in the country and not in the middle of the Southland sprawl.

Bobby owned what he too frequently reminded me was the oldest house in the canyon. It had been built before World War I, as a low-profile retreat by a chastened associate of the Dohenys in the wake of the Teapot Dome Scandal. At one time, it must have been the only house on the winding trail that branched off the main canyon road. A beautiful example of a California bungalow, it was all brown shingle, large windows, and deep overhangs to shade against the sun. Sitting back from the road on its own gentle bluff, it looked small from the driveway, but once inside you realized it was grand in a perfectly understated way, its airy dimensions made warm by the teak and oak paneling that lined most of the downstairs rooms. There was an inglenook at the living-room fireplace and two original Tiffany windows of lilies and iris in the dining room; all the light fixtures were copper and iridescent glass, also original, made for the house. At one time, it was the only house in Los Angeles I truly wanted for my own, and as I now rang the doorbell, it occurred to me that the way things stood I could probably have it. But it might be my taste was changing. I was content to wait and see.

Bobby threw open the door and pulled me inside.

"Did you find the money? Arzell called—he's going to nail my hide."

I could see that panic had taken over in him.

"Relax. I found the money. We'll get Arzell off your back."

"When? I have to tell him."

"That's what I want to talk about."

I had followed Bobby out to the rear terrace which extended almost to the canyon wall. It had a low railing built of stone brought over from the Arroyo Seco in Pasadena and it was paved in large brown tiles fired in a pottery in northern California. Bobby had told me all this with enormous pride, and I had to give him credit; he had made the house and its gardens a work of art. Looking at him, and thinking about how I was going to make him twist, I tried to keep in mind that he had this in him, too—the ability to bring this beauty into being.

Bobby may have been scared but he could still manage breakfast; the remains of a bowl of yogurt and granola and a basket of fruit were on a round metal table, as well as the morning papers: the *Times,* both L.A. and New York, and the trades, *Variety* and the *Hollywood Reporter.* There was a stack of magazines on the ground near his chair and a small TV was on a side table, its remote ready to zap between all the morning shows. I knew this was what he did—collected news that was really all high-class gossip, even the business news about which studio heads were out and which were in and what media conglomerate was buying or selling or joining forces with what technology conglomerate to form yet another multimedia multinational. Everyone felt they were at the dawning of a new era, a beginning-of-the-next-century paroxysm that would throw up titans and visionaries, and for people like Bobby it was all a race to keep up, to get in on the ground floor.

I watched him as he poured a cup of coffee for me. I was relaxed, willing to take my time. There was a particular delight in bringing him around slowly. He thought I was going to save him; I wanted to see his face when he awakened to the truth of his condition. No wonder I wasn't nervous; I was completely in charge.

"Like I said," I began, "I have the money—"

"You're fabulous, Vega, fabulous."

"But you know Arzell isn't going to fade away. What you did was illegal—he's going to have that over you."

Bobby's fingers started drumming.

"Shit," he mumbled. "Shit."

He was looking off at the hillside. I paused, but he didn't say anything else. It came to me that there were many people like Bobby, the ones who freeze like deer in car headlights, unable to act when fear looms up and claims them.

"But there's something I can do about that," I finally said.

The drumming stopped. "What?"

"I have a friend who could take care of Arzell."

"What do you mean?" he quickly asked. "What friend? How?" For the first time, I could see Bobby focus; his eyes narrowed and he looked directly at me. "Why would he want to take care of Arzell—for me, I mean?"

"Not so much for you. He owes me a favor."

Bobby's eyes narrowed further. "Come on, I'm not stupid."

Oh yes you are, I thought. "No, really," I said, "it would basically be as a favor to me." I paused. "Although I suppose there might be something my friend might want you to do. Sometime. At some point in the future."

Bobby sighed. "I see."

He was beginning to, beginning to understand that there might be ongoing consequences to what he had done. He was a child who kept wanting to dance away but the mean old adults kept holding him back. He was drumming again and his foot had started tapping. I sipped calmly at my coffee. There was a morning breeze blowing down the canyon and I turned my face toward it.

"I don't know who your friend is," he finally said.

"No reason you should, do you think?"

He was staring at me. "Where'd you get this friend, huh?" I could hear a new tone in his voice, a new assessment.

I smiled. "Just lucky, I guess."

He suddenly sat forward. "Jesus. How the hell can I say yes. I don't know who this guy is, what he'll want from me—"

"Not to mention what he might do to Arzell."

It was stupid of me to say that, but I couldn't resist. It was the part of me that wanted not just to roll over Bobby but also to show him in stark clarity all his moral failings. That was childish on my part and I made a note to try and jettison any need to be self-righteous. Like Nathan, I had to concentrate on being victorious, not on being right.

"Look," I said, "my friend isn't a goon."

"But what about me—what he'd want from me? He could think I owe him for the rest of my life."

That's right, he could, I thought. "All I can tell you is, I don't think he'd want anything that would jeopardize your standing. In the community. I think my friend would want to keep you—viable." I paused again. "Besides, what choice do you have?"

For a moment, his eyes flared and I saw hatred for me, a messenger from the unjust world which had put him in this predicament. Then he slumped. He didn't have the imagination to see any alternatives and so he quickly resigned himself.

"All right," he said. "Tell your friend all right."

He got up and went to the railing of the terrace. He was looking at the steep hills up the canyon, covered now with dried and brittle grass.

"There's just one other thing," I said, and stopped. I wanted his full attention and waited until he turned toward me.

"I want you to introduce me to Carland."

At first he didn't get it. "He's not for you, Vega, not your type."

It occurred to me to ask why; the answer could be useful information. But I let it go.

"That's not why I want to meet him. I just want you to introduce us."

"Why? What's your interest in Carland?"

"Maybe he needs a financial adviser."

Bobby laughed. "You're out of your league."

I sat quietly. "How do you know what my league is?"

He stopped and looked at me. Slow as he was on the uptake, the wheels were now beginning to turn.

"You want what Arzell wanted," he said slowly.

"Yes."

His eyes were moving like a trapped animal looking for the way out. He came back and stood at the table.

"If I wouldn't do it for Arzell, why should I do it for you?"

I saw that I would have to spell it out for him. "Because

if you don't, Arzell will destroy you in this town. Whereas if you do, Arzell disappears as a problem and life goes on pretty much as before."

"Except for Carland."

"That's right. Except for Carland."

Bobby turned away again. "I can't do it."

I thought about telling him to get real, that he had to, that in fact we both knew he would. I could stand up, toss my head and tell him it was a done deal. But I wanted to play out the scene, to watch him maneuver as he tried to escape the fate that he himself had set in motion. I wanted to enjoy the new clarity I had, the calm certainty that I could and would get what I wanted.

My silence made him edgy. He sat down and leaned toward me. "Jonathan and I go way back." His tone was confidential, as if once I heard what he was revealing, I would understand. And let him off the hook. "And it isn't just that he's a friend. It's more than that—he's—I just can't do it. I can't."

"Well," I said quietly, "that's your choice. Save him rather than yourself. Although I can't believe that's what you really want to do."

He looked at me and there was real anguish in his eyes. I had a sudden flash that there was something more to Bobby's resistance, something more than ordinary ethics.

"Is that what you want to do?" My voice was calm, gentle, almost motherly. "Come on, Bobby, you can tell me."

"No. I can't."

"Yes, you can. You can."

His shoulders caved in and he began to cry. I sat back, gazing at him. I really did feel compassion for him, for his panic in the sprung trap pressing in on him. Poor boy, poor pitiful boy. He looked up at me and wiped his eyes. Then he began to talk.

"I know him from prep school. Since we were fifteen. Not that we were friends—he was always the golden boy, way above me. A real aristocrat—the ones who send their tweeds to be patched in England for the same money most of us spend for something new. You know what I mean?"

I didn't, but I wanted to learn.

"Of course he went to Harvard. Where else? I'd hear about him once in a while—from someone who spotted him in Harvard Square, or from a distance in New York. Then, I heard that he was going into movies—which I was trying to work up the courage to tackle—and that clinched it. Like the seal of approval. If it was good enough for Carland, it was good enough for me.

"By the time I got out here, his name was already in the trades. It was like in prep school—he just stepped onto all the right tracks. It came so naturally. You couldn't even be jealous.

"Well, I ran into him a couple of times—at Musso's, once at a screening. I had to remind him who I was, but I didn't mind, that's just the way things were. . . ."

Bobby got up again and turned toward the canyon wall. "I don't want to tell you this," he said.

I didn't say anything. What he made of the circumstances he had created was entirely up to him. But I wasn't surprised when he came back, sat down and started talking again.

"It was at a party somewhere high in the hills above Malibu. It was raining, had been for days, so everyone was jammed inside. I was there with a woman I hardly knew; I lost track of her in the crush. You could hardly move. There were a lot of drugs and everyone was stoned. Me, too. I almost fucked some woman I'd never seen before right on the stairs; only the flow of the crowd pulled us apart. It was so weird—I was in that twilight-dawn place from all the drugs, where desire comes and goes and both sides of the curve are perfectly all right. You know?"

I nodded. His eyes were directly on mine. I felt how much he needed me at that moment, needed a companion to give him the courage to travel down this particular road.

"Well, things shifted and when I opened my eyes there was Carland, just disappearing behind a slamming door. I was surprised—it didn't seem like his kind of crowd, but even more—his face—it didn't go with any Carland I'd ever seen before. He looked furious, twisted—the face of someone completely out of control.

"It sounds crazy—I must have been very stoned because somehow I didn't react to that face. I just thought, what luck running into Carland like this. . . ."

Bobby was shaking his head, his eyes gazing down through his words to an invisible irony. "So I opened the door. It was Carland all right. And he was slapping a woman he'd thrown up against the wall—more than slapping her—punching her. I mean, I saw his fists sinking into her soft belly. In a second, I was stone cold sober. And I knew it wasn't some drugged-out foreplay: it was a rape. Definitely a rape . . ."

His foot started tapping on the tile of the terrace.

"The girl saw me and screamed for help and at the

same time Carland turned to me. His eyes were huge, on fire—I couldn't move or look away."

His voice had gotten very quiet and when he went on, I heard a genuine puzzlement. "I know it sounds crazy, but standing there, I knew that what I wanted wasn't to help the woman or to stop Carland—I wanted—recognition." He stopped.

"I don't understand," I said, when he didn't go on.

"I wanted Carland to acknowledge me, not just me, Bobby Melner, but someone he needed. Someone who could help him now." He looked at me. "You see? I wanted Carland to need me."

His sudden laugh cut across the morning stillness of the canyon. Maybe he'd gotten past the most difficult part, because now he went on faster. "When Carland turned, the woman broke away. The front of her dress was torn, like a jagged lightning bolt from collar to waist. One breast had come out of her black lace bra. She threw open a French door and ran outside; Carland yelled and went after her. I didn't think—I just followed. Not to help the woman. To help Carland."

He looked up but not at me. I don't think he wanted to see what I was thinking. "She was terrified, yelling, but the rain and the music muffled her screams. She jumped off the terrace into the brush on the hillside. We could see her in the light from the house, scrambling up toward the road. One shoe had come off. I could see a torn stocking and a long scratch down the back of her leg. She was trying to get to her car. We chased her and caught her there. It was easy. The car was a small hatchback—somehow, we stuffed her in the backseat. She'd left the key in the ignition—Carland got behind the wheel and I raced around into the passenger seat just as he skidded out onto the road.

"She was crying in the backseat, pleading for us to stop and let her go. Carland didn't say anything and neither did I. I thought maybe he just wanted to give her time to calm down so she wouldn't make a scene when we took her back . . . I don't know—I couldn't even look at him.

"Then, suddenly, her hands were around Carland's neck. She was screaming, half pulling herself into the front, half pulling him into the back. The car swerved and I was trying to pull her off when suddenly everything slowed down—there was this eerie—smoothness we all felt at the exact same time. That's the last thing I remember—her head snapping back to look out the window as the car flew off the road.

"I came awake to raindrops pelting my eyelids. I'd been thrown from the car. I managed to stand—I heard rain pounding on metal only a few yards below me. I saw Carland—he'd been thrown clear, too—he was already creeping down the hill through the mud to the car.

"The roof had somehow been sheared off in the crash. We could see her body still huddled in the backseat but something looked wrong, very wrong, even beyond the grotesque way she was twisted." Bobby hesitated. "It took us a while to realize. She'd been decapitated."

He was very still.

"We were paralyzed. It didn't seem possible that in the driving rain and dark we could see so clearly, but there right in front of us—it looked like a cross section—the veins and tissue and muscle—all neat, precise, like in a biology textbook. Or when you dissect a frog. The blood, still stunned, hadn't begun to spurt. But as we watched, a dark redness, swelling, like a tide, slowly oozed out. And then it gushed, in pulsating eruptions as if the heart still beat. Even in the dark we could see it, the vivid red . . . I was in a dream, watching as it mingled with the black rain, became diluted as it ran down the naked shoulders and chest, until it formed a river between the naked breasts."

Bobby was pale. I wondered what it took to live every day with that image locked inside him.

"Carland backed away—I saw the terror on his face. I felt it, too. But then, as if we were both operating on the same frequency, we began tramping through the mud—getting rid of our footprints and the impressions our bodies had made when we landed on the ground. I tore off a shirttail and wiped the steering wheel and every other surface of the car clean of fingerprints. The wind in the storm was playing tricks; I kept hearing the engines of other cars coming along the road but no one came. I forced myself to watch as Carland pulled the woman's body from the backseat, then wedged it in again in some semblance of how it might look if she had been driving and the crash had thrown her into the back. Blood was everywhere. But I didn't once question what we were doing. And I felt no fear, no fear at all. . . .

"We walked for hours in the rain. Down to the coast highway. Some cars went past but I knew no one would take any notice of us—there are always men along that stretch of road, homeless hitchhikers coming down from San Francisco, farm workers heading up to Oxnard. No one gave us a second look."

Bobby got up and started pacing.

"It turned out Carland had rented a house on the beach.

That's where he met her—she took him to the party. We stripped off our clothes and as soon as they were dry enough, we burned it all in the fireplace—everything, even our underwear, socks, and shoes. By now it was dawn. He poured out two stiff drinks and we made small talk, about nothing important, not even the movie business, like two strangers passing the time waiting for a plane. It was all so odd, so strange—reality kept cutting out, or changing as if color slides were clicking in one after the other in front of me. As if the ground kept giving way, but everything was fine. Then he drove me home."

He came back and sat down, his fingers fiddling with the stack of magazines. "Two days later, there was a small item in the paper. She was a secretary from Redondo Beach, twenty years old. Beth. Her name was Beth. No one knew Carland had picked her up. And the rain had wiped out all traces of us. Probably the police weren't even looking anyway, because the autopsy showed high levels of drugs and alcohol. They ruled it an accident. Case closed."

He stopped and I thought he was finished. But his shoulders suddenly slumped and he rushed on.

"There's one thing though—when I can't sleep—"

He looked up at me. "Vega, neither of us looked for the head."

His eyes looked desperate for me to understand. "It's crazy—but it's like it haunts me. The newspaper story didn't say if it had been found. I mean, was it in the car, or had it been thrown out like us, into the dark? I stumbled on the way down to where Carland was crawling to the car—maybe I kicked it, or even crushed it with my weight. Jesus . . . Sometimes I dream about it—tumbling down the hillside, her eyes still open and the mouth blood red, like a scream. . . ."

He got up again, mostly to get away from the image in his own head. I heard him take a deep breath and when he began talking again I knew he had closed the door one more time on what he couldn't bear to see.

"I didn't try to force things with Carland. But he began to invite me to things once in a while—screenings or business parties. And a couple of times he sent some promising things my way. He was helping me, you know? His way of saying thanks. And I never brought up that night to him, never referred to it in any way at all. I never asked if what I walked in on that night was the first and only time he got rough, or if that's the way he likes it. Although, a couple of years ago, when I mentioned his name to a woman I was having dinner with, she got this look, like a sudden whiplash—I don't know—it made me think she had seen Carland like I did—out of control. It doesn't matter. I helped him and I've kept his secret. So we have a real thing between us now—a real relationship. A friendship. Since we were fifteen."

His eyes were pleading and for the first time I saw real anguish in them. Poor Bobby; he had so much at stake. It wasn't as simple as not setting up a friend. In some convoluted way, helping Carland, and Carland's gratitude, had become Bobby's moral ballast; it was a source of pride to him. He had come through when the golden boy needed him and it had been recognized. He had been acknowledged. So now he wouldn't simply be betraying Carland; he would be betraying what he thought of as the finest part of himself. I could hear how he must have rationalized over the years: the girl probably had it coming, they never would have had to chase her if she'd just been quiet and not panicked, it was her fault the car had swerved off the road, her fault that she was dead. What purpose would have been served by their telling that they were there? The girl would still be dead. No, he and Carland had only avoided unnecessary trouble in the aftermath of an unfortunate accident. Anyone could see that.

"Now do you see why I can't introduce you?"

I shook my head and sighed. "I'm sorry, Bobby. No."

There was almost a tenderness in my voice. I could afford it; I knew that Bobby would cry some more and say he couldn't do it, but soon enough he'd recognize his new reality. Some people, when they're trapped, feel in the pressure a power surge and rise to the occasion; they fight to find the way out. Bobby lacked the circuitry, the synapses, for the power to surge across; he got waylaid by the pressure, collapsed, and became willing to do whatever it took to get out from under. And there I was, showing him the way.

When I left him, he looked as if he was going to be sick, and maybe he was. But in a little while, a very little while, he would have a whole new set of rationalizations and he would find the way to form anew a different moral world. I didn't think the new world would last long either. Something would happen and the solid ground would one more time give way as he tried to justify. The truth was clear: Bobby had no bottom line.

Back at the office, I looked again at the picture of Carland in *Business Week*. It had been taken after that night; now I knew what was behind that open, untroubled smile. Did he even remember, or find himself sacked by a sudden glimpse, an echo in the rain? Was he, too, haunted by the missing head? I could guess now why his marriages had fallen apart and why he was alone; he couldn't keep entirely hidden what was rotten at the core. I looked again at that beguiling smile. What did he dream in the still dead of night?

I sat thinking. I could probably pick up the phone and in a few hours have him in my pocket. It would be so easy, almost too easy. And I couldn't think of it as blackmail because he was no innocent. Far from it. Carland deserved it, for Beth and however many other women he'd done it to. He deserved whatever box I could find to put him in. It was actually a pretty retribution.

I got up, went to the window, and watched patterns of sunlight through the leaves of the jacaranda. Was I so different from Bobby? Wasn't I rationalizing, casting reality in whatever light I needed to justify what I wanted to do? For a moment, I was adrift: What was reality, where was solid ground? *There is no truth, only perspective.* If that was true, then I had no more to go on than what felt right to me. I had the responsibility; I was the one who had to excavate solid ground. I sat down again and closed the magazine. The answer was inside: even up the score.

But even then I knew that wasn't my only motive, or even the main one. I wanted something more, something simple but absolutely solid and it had nothing to do with Carland or money or even Paul, with any of the particulars life was bringing my way. It had to do with something deep inside me, my growing desire to keep going, to press farther, to see how much farther it was to my farthest shore.

Chapter Fifteen

Paul made some calls and eventually got to Arzell. He said he was interested in the Bakersfield property. I could only hear Paul's side of the conversation but I knew Arzell was telling him it wasn't for sale. When Paul insisted, I gathered Arzell tried to dismiss him.

"I don't think you understand," Paul said. "I'm doing *you* a favor. I think in time you'll see that."

He waited while Arzell argued. I had the sense he wasn't listening; he already knew which way this scenario would go and was simply letting Arzell recite his allotted lines.

"I tell you what," Paul said. "Some friends of mine will be around to see you. Why don't we speak after you've talked to them?"

He hung up, cool and confident, and one more time I saw what he had that I wanted, that particular assurance, the kind that comes from the repeated experience, the unimpeded exercise, of a strong and certain will.

A few days later, Paul told me that Arzell had agreed to meet him in Bakersfield.

"What did you do to him?"

"Not me. My friends."

"What did they do?"

"Nothing. Just told him about me and my plans, that's all."

"Come on. Tell me."

"Well, you know you can't turn an honest man. But the world is full of people who slip over the line. Some more than others."

"And Arzell is one of them?"

Paul nodded. "Bobby was right—he's in trouble. Big trouble. And not just from the recession. It turns out he likes to gamble. Been going to Vegas for years—a very high roller. I guess a man's got to do what he's got to do to cover heavy losses."

"And you just happened to learn about it."

He nodded.

"From some friends? In Vegas?"

He nodded again.

I smiled. "And then sent other friends to share the news with Arzell."

His smile was very broad.

"You certainly have interesting connections," I said.

"Right," he said, and laughed. "What else matters in this world?"

We drove north out of the Southland over the Grapevine to the San Joaquin Valley. As we came out of the mountains and dropped down to the valley floor, Bakersfield appeared far in the distance, dreamlike in the haze, a crumpled sheet opened out on a bed of irrigated and conglomerated farms, agribusiness as far as the eye could see. I met a cowboy once at a party in the hills above Hollywood; he said he'd moseyed down from Bakersfield and he had a demo record, a guitar under his arm and silver tabs on his denim shirt collar. It was that sort of place, home to beer-drinking shitkickers doing the Texas two-step on Saturday nights. But there was also another layer where the stakes were very high, a world of agribusiness, oil and natural gas, cattle and land. The money didn't live in Bakersfield, but it certainly did business there.

Before we knew it we were in the outskirts of town, passing refineries, granaries, stockyards, and neighborhoods of one-story stucco homes with rusting refrigerators in the front yards and pickups up on blocks.

The land Arzell wanted to develop was north of town, east of the Interstate. It had been part of one of the original Spanish land grants, the Rancho Tejilda, which had stretched from just north of Fresno to the southern mountains, down the center of some of the richest farm and grazing land in the world. The holding had been converted by descendants of the original family into the Tejilda Land and Cattle Company, which had boomed after World War II, when all those stucco houses were built for returning GIs. But the company fell on hard times during an extended recession in the early seventies that revealed years of mismanagement. In a futile move to remain solvent and retain control, the family had offered a limited number of shares to the public, at just about the same time oil and natural gas were discovered under the fertile, when watered, ground. The company boomed again but now that only made it more attractive to outsiders, who made irresistible offers to restless descendants. Arzell was the most recent in a line of raiders to get control of the prize. He had plans for subdivisions and schools, an industrial park, and two shopping centers. That would still leave more than three quarters of the Tejilda land waiting, available for farming and cattle. Needless to say, Arzell would retain the oil and mineral rights to all of it.

It was the perfect setup for Paul. Tejilda would give him an entry into agribusiness farming and cattle. Plus oil and natural gas; on the drive up, he explained a scheme he'd already worked out for oil leases through which he could funnel millions of dollars. It could be done, like almost all of his business, on a laptop he could carry with him; his modem let him ride the electronic highway, stopping off wherever he wanted to set up his paper world. He would let Arzell stay on as the major stockholder of record; Tejilda was going to be a fabulous front.

"You're talking as if it's already happened," I said. "As if Arzell has already gone under."

"He has," Paul said. "He just doesn't know it yet."

Arzell had wanted to meet in a conference room at his hotel but Paul convinced him to drive out to the land. We took a county road that quickly left the suburbs behind and cut through fields still being farmed. We passed groups of twenty or thirty pickers, whole families bent over what looked like broccoli and kale. It was flat and hot and dry. Sun was reflecting off the miles of pipeline that brought the water in.

Paul slowed down about a mile past the last cultivated

fields. There was a car parked at the side of the road and we pulled to a stop behind it. Two men were leaning against it.

"Wait here," Paul said as he opened his door and got out.

It wasn't Arzell; these men were Paul's. If I'd had to choose between brains and muscle, I'd say they were muscle; even in their dark suits, I could see both had the rounded wide shoulders and upper arms of bodybuilders. I saw I'd been foolish; the scenario I'd written for this day was pulled out from under me. A polished table, the sound of pencils and computer keys, a civilized handshake—it didn't look as if there was going to be any of that. And even though I wanted Paul to show me what he did, to see how he did it, I felt fear of what might be coming now.

Something moved against my cheek. A fly had gotten trapped inside the car; I heard its droning as it flew against the windshield. I closed my eyes. My feet were pressing against the floor of the car as if there were brakes I could apply, but it was too late. I was already here, had wanted to come this far. I opened my eyes and looked across the road at the miles of flat and dusty land stretching out into the haze. I was moving and there was no way now to stop it.

Paul and the men turned; another car was pulling in. It parked behind me. I didn't look around. I heard the doors opening and closing, then footsteps crunching on the blacktop. The man I took to be Arzell went by; he was short and beefy and looked like someone who had come up from the building trades. Another man followed him and they both looked in at me, surprised, I think, to see me there. They went over to Paul and the others. Paul held out his hand and smiled; he was completely at ease.

I rolled down the window. They were too far away for me to hear anything except the wind, which was blowing steadily. There were no signs of it across the naked landscape; I could only hear it, although after a while I picked out the sharp creak of metal, a strip of fencing rubbing back and forth. Through the windshield I watched Arzell; he was shaking his head, gesturing, his face red with anger. I heard the trapped and buzzing fly. I had a sudden need to free it and I clumsily pushed it toward the window. It tried to evade my hand which must have seemed a shadow of catastrophe. But it finally found the current to the window and in an instant was gone.

I looked back toward the men. They were moving off into the fields through a gap in the fencing. Arzell was protesting. Paul was silent, shaking his head. His men were shepherding Arzell and the other man farther from the road; they were like old and trusted dogs, almost gentle, but determined.

The flatness of the fields was an illusion. Wind erosion had cut out countless gullies, and as I watched, Paul and the others disappeared behind a wall of dirt. I sat alone and heard the wind. Sun was beating down on the car; I was suddenly very hot. I opened the door and got out; the sound of the car door closing cut across the wind. I couldn't see Paul. My heart was beating faster; I felt that I was in a chute, a tunneling passageway, and being drawn ahead. Hesitantly, slowly, I made my way toward the gap in the fencing. The wind whipped my hair across my face; the fabric of my shirt and pants snapped against my skin. I kept looking around as if a thousand hidden eyes were watching me from that broad expanse. I turned in the direction the men had gone; in the glare of the sun I had to shade my eyes. I couldn't see anything. Then, as if in slow motion, not quite willing it but not resisting either, I moved off the road, and went after Paul.

I came up a rise. They were yards away. Arzell was down on one knee, his face bloody, his eyes dazed. Paul was saying something; Arzell shook his head. Then one of Paul's men swung and caught Arzell on the chin; his arms flew out as he went sprawling back. I gasped and maybe Paul heard; he turned and saw me. His jaw was set, and even at a distance I could see the tension crackling through him. His eyes zoomed into mine and held me; I couldn't look away. Look, he seemed to be saying, *Look!* This is what it is. Nothing prettier. Can you stand to see it? *Can you?* I didn't look away.

He turned back and the spell was broken. One of Paul's men was pulling Arzell's companion away as the other went after Arzell again. Paul was shouting something to him; Arzell looked so dazed I didn't know if he could hear or understand. I'd seen enough. I turned and stumbled down the rise.

I went to the car and leaned against it. I was panting, hungering for air. I saw Paul's eyes, the challenge and intensity. I saw the blood. It was behind all Paul's self-containment, his elegance. This explosive and erupting force was what coursed beneath it. I knew I should be horrified, but I didn't want pretense, layers of disguise. Some part of me welcomed such a graphic view.

I heard footsteps in the dirt, and Paul reappeared. He was alone. He came toward the car, stopped when he looked up and saw me, then stood at ease, his arms resting at his side. I knew that he was waiting. I moved toward him as if in a dream, only the wind between us and the sudden cries of birds. I stood before him, stood still in the center of his brown-eyed gaze, and then I reached up and smoothed his windblown hair. At the feel of him, I was released and felt myself flowing toward him, wanting his touch, his lips, his galvanizing embrace. But I held back and simply looked at him. What was he thinking then? Did he know that I had made a choice? Did he think that it was about him?

"It will be fine now," he said.

I nodded and followed him to the car.

He didn't turn back to Bakersfield but surprised me by heading in the other direction, deeper into the Valley.

"Where are we going?" I asked.

"Just up the road. There's something I may as well see."

I didn't say anything else; there were no other questions I needed to ask. I looked at Paul, but it wasn't him I saw; it was me, my deepening commitment. I sat back and let the land roll by. With every breath, I felt myself expanding.

After a while we came to a town called Cromwells Corners; someone with a sense of humor had printed the name on a water tank along with "The World's Largest Parking Lot." There were two intersecting streets lined with one-story stucco buildings that must have dated from the twenties. It was what had passed for a business district, and now most of the stores were boarded up. We pulled up in front of one of them. Paul sat staring out. He was very quiet.

"Where are we?" I asked.

"I grew up around here," he said, the wind biting off his words.

I was surprised. "I thought you were from New York."

He went on as if I hadn't spoken.

"Not much, huh?" he said.

There was a trace, but only a trace, of something I'd never heard in him before, an ordinary apologetic self-consciousness. I knew instinctively it wasn't only in front of me; he wasn't so much showing me this hidden part of his history as allowing himself to see it, permitting himself to look fully at what he usually kept hidden.

There was a faded sign on one of the stores; I could still read "Hardware—Lattimer's." I tried to picture him, at fourteen maybe, working in the store, but I couldn't put him together with any hayseed image of a Valley boy. He got out of the car, and I watched him through the windshield as he peered inside the darkened window. Nothing about him remotely suggested that he was the son of a man who had owned a hardware store in this tiny Valley town. What had inspired him to make the leap and get himself out? And what had it cost him to do it?

He got back in the car. We drove down the street and made a left. There were a few blocks of houses and then open land. At a dirt road marked with a rusted mailbox, we turned right and pulled up to a plain stucco house. It was unoccupied. I didn't need to be told it was the house he had grown up in. Small. Dusty. Nondescript. I could have described its interior from my own memories—the bare floors and unmatched furniture from the local thrift store, cracked dishes collected piece by piece in a supermarket giveaway. Nothing, absolutely nothing, to do with him, with who he was now. Or with me.

"Where are they now—your parents?" I asked.

"Gone. Gone."

I wasn't sure if that meant they were dead, but something told me not to ask. He had shown me this much; I wouldn't press for anything more. He hadn't turned off the engine and now he gunned it as we pulled away.

I left him to his silence. The surprise I felt at where he came from disappeared, replaced now by a recognition of how much we were alike. We had shaken off the same stultifying dust. Maybe after all it wasn't a surprise; maybe this was just one more piece of a basic recognition. I looked over at him. Somewhere along the line, and very early, I guessed, he'd had another vision, could see the particulars of another kind of life. I knew I wouldn't learn why that had happened, if there was someone who had inspired it, but I knew that in that vision he found the energy he needed to strike out into unknown territory, the means to make it real. Don and I had done that; we had gotten ourselves out. But I had needed Paul to show me how much farther I could go. I was the student and my teacher had appeared.

We wound down on a back road through the mountains and spent the night in Ojai, in a hotel cottage with a view of scrub oaks dotting the hillsides and a fireplace built of native stone. We made love in front of it, both of us stretching ourselves out, watching the glow on each other's skin, running our hands down each other's lengths as if we could feel and capture that warm and fluid light. I heard him sigh, saw the orange glow on his thinly veined eyelids closing now as his fingers slid between my legs. I watched his mouth, his lips slightly open, moving in time to his fingers and my answering hips. I was wet, pliant, as liquid as the light, but I was also watching, holding something back. I closed my eyes and let myself flow toward the center of his touch, arched my body at each slow and steady stroke as if his hand were the moon and there were ocean waves surging under me, longing to connect. But I still watched from behind my eyes. I was aware of pleasure, I was giving myself up to it, to the exquisite and precise intensity of touch. But in that very awareness, in that heightened consciousness I knew I stood alone.

After, I watched him as he slept in the dying firelight. Would he dream about that dusty town? Was he, like me, haunted by bare-floored and barren rooms?

He turned and I pulled the blanket up. His confidence: he held out an unshakable kind of power and it kept seducing me, a beckoning hand pointing to an easy track for me to slide onto, lubricated by desire and my awakened capacity to push beyond my fear. But the same unbending mask that attracted me also made me feel a stinging resentment. His ease, that comfort in his skin, the way he resided inside himself in a still and silent meshing—it challenged me, called out something that wanted to chip away and rattle him, to see his eyes flicker and hesitate in doubt. I wanted to find a way in, penetrate him, nail him to the ground. I wanted what he had. It was very strange, that the more he inspired me, the more detached from him I became. The more he set me free, the more distant I became.

I turned and stared at the red glowing embers. I

thought about Bobby; what I'd done to him wasn't so different from what Paul had done to Arzell. Only more polite. And Carland: I saw his photograph, his innocent smile. . . . I did want that prize, wanted to leave him—in my own way—bloody on the ground. And not so I could bring him back to Paul, or because of the cash that would move through him, or even the fact that he deserved it, but because he was a rung on the ladder I was climbing up and out of my past, a necessary step toward the freedom I knew Paul had, the freedom to create myself and stand on my own.

For a moment I felt I was in over my head. I saw Arzell, the fingers of his hands grasping at empty air as he went flying back. Something in that gesture terrified me. But I didn't look away. I stayed still and let it soak through me, let myself feel the woman I had been, so uncertain that there was something to hold on to. I felt her until I no longer felt the fear, and that digestion and expelling only strengthened me. My skin was cooling in the dying light; I pressed myself against Paul and took his warmth. I was ready to sleep. I closed my eyes and saw Arzell again, but he no longer frightened me. I knew now I would no longer be the woman who was afraid she was grasping at empty air.

Chapter Sixteen

Two days later, I called Carland and insisted that we meet. Bobby had already paved the way, but I'd told him to be vague about what it was I wanted.

Carland impatiently asked for particulars. "My schedule's very tight," he said.

I heard the irritation in his voice and realized that coming to him through Bobby put me in a weakened position; I came trailing all the associations Bobby always kicked up. I wondered if Carland could compartmentalize so that those associations stopped at an unwanted sense of obligation, before a conscious thought, a particular image of that rainy night. In any case, it didn't matter. Once I was in front of Carland and he'd heard what I had to say, I'd take on a meaning all my own.

"I'm bringing you an offer," I said. "It's something I think you'll be interested in. Very interested."

I had lowered my voice and put a certain breathiness

into it. Not enough to be blatant but enough, I hoped, to make him curious, to heighten his senses in the way a subtle breeze barely lifts a few stray hairs. I was having fun, playing on that blurry line between presenting myself as a professional woman and coming on overtly. I was cutting through the complications, the need a businesswoman has to show she can be tough, sometimes even cutthroat, in order to measure up, even though she's not supposed to use her femininity because that would be to take unfair advantage. But I saw it another way. It wasn't my femininity I was taking advantage of; it was most men's so easily aroused lust. Every woman knows that men always rise to the bait. I didn't think Carland would be an exception. We made an appointment for a meeting at his office.

I gave myself plenty of time to dress; I wanted to enjoy playing some more on that blurry line. I had splurged and bought a jet black designer suit with my own money, rather than NIGHT's. The jacket was cut tight with a narrow waist accentuated by padded shoulders and slim lapels; it flared out softly over my hips. The skirt was short and tight enough to show the roundness of my bottom below the jacket line. I wore a thin silk camisole under it, with just a touch of its ecru lace showing, dark stockings, and shoes with three-inch heels. The look had an edge, tough and sexy, and it worked because it challenged men, not to come on, but to ignore the sexiness. And that cost them precious energy; their attention was deflected, they lost ground as they struggled to keep things down. Tricky, but who could blame us? In a competitive society, it only made sense to exploit all your capital. And I knew it worked because, after all, the only women who could afford to dress this way were the most successful.

Carland's office was downtown. I took the freeway and thought about him moving through his day with no idea what was coming, that his life was about to be altered, veer off in a new direction. I alone knew what had already been set in motion and I alone was the one who could stop it, who had any kind of choice. I was the one with the power. I thought about what I'd say, how to handle him, but my mind didn't want to move beyond shadowy images of my own ascendancy. It didn't matter; I was feeling strong, strong enough to play it by ear. My instinct would prevail.

Carland's building was almost directly across the street from Nathan's and had the same kind of impersonal posh, a mix of marble floors and thick carpets leading across a soaring atrium to polished brass elevator doors. The offices of Carland's bank were more of the same, the usual attempt at a tasteful but rich blandness that could never give offense.

He kept me waiting in the reception area but I had expected that and actually enjoyed it. I was alert but not worried; I felt excitement, what a seasoned performer must feel just before going on. I could tell it made me appear very calm; containing the excitement slowed my movements, made me seem deliberate, confident. I wondered if it was what Paul felt. I pictured him, the straight back as he turned toward me, the press of his calves against the fabric of his slacks as he stood at ease, his slow hand as it leisurely brushed his dark hair back off his shaven cheek. Was all that the smooth shell around this animating energy?

A secretary appeared and led me down a long and narrow corridor ending at high double doors that opened into an enclosed executive suite. It was done up like an English hunting club, with prints of racehorses on the walls, forest green leather chairs, and Chippendale desks. The door was open at the far end, and the secretary indicated I should go through. It was Carland's office.

He was behind the desk and looked up when he heard me. I saw at once that he was very polished; he smiled automatically but his eyes remained unmoved. I think he was surprised by what I looked like, but he showed no more than a flicker, the kind of flicker I myself felt whenever in the course of business I came across someone physically attractive. I paused in the doorway. I wanted him to have the full effect, to notice and respond, and then to put it aside.

He got up and came toward me. He was wearing an Italian suit that very subtly accentuated the leanness of his body. He was taller than I'd thought from the photographs, with lighter hair, almost blond, very thick and cut short, and blue eyes surrounded by thick, dark lashes. Carland had been in the movie business, which was a magnet for men, including nonactors, who wanted to be gorgeous, but now he was another example of something I'd noticed through my dealings with Nathan: the most attractive men, with the best haircuts and in the best suits, weren't in the movie business at all but in the financial world, here in its highest reaches.

We shook hands, and he led me to a sofa grouped with two easy chairs. He took one of the chairs and I sat on the couch at the end nearest him. I didn't like the empty expanse opening out to its other end; all that blank space could only make me look smaller. But, with a new clarity,

I saw I had a choice, even over something as innocuous as this: I could step into that smallness and put myself at a disadvantage, or I could ignore it and work some other line. I crossed my legs, slowly, allowed my stockings to slide against each other with an extended silky sound. Carland, of course, didn't react. But I knew he heard it.

"How do you know Bobby?" he asked.

"I handle most of his financial affairs. Stocks, bonds—and general managing."

He nodded. If he felt the usual surprise, or skepticism, that someone who looked like me could be good with numbers, he didn't betray it in any way.

"Well, what have you brought me?"

There was a brusqueness in his voice. For a moment, I thought it was directed solely at me but then I realized it was probably the way he always spoke. The tempo of his business life kept him moving fast, but he also had the inner snapping-finger impatience of someone simply smarter than most of the people he dealt with. I guessed he was always quicker than anyone else, always there first, and that he spent a lot of time idling, annoyed at wasting energy, waiting for others to catch up. I didn't fool myself that I wouldn't be one of them. But so what if Carland was smarter than I was? The game we were playing wasn't about intelligence; it didn't depend upon smarts at all. It was about gambling, about pushing to the brink and going for broke. It was about balls.

I took out a Xerox of an old news story and laid it on the coffee table in front of us. One look and he stiffened; he recognized it instantly. It was the story about the police finding Beth's body and overturned car. I had gone to the library myself and tracked it down on microfiche. No one, not even Holly, had seen it. Carland didn't reach for it but sat quietly.

"Who are you?" he finally said.

"You know who I am."

"Did Bobby put you up to this?"

"Do you mean is he behind it?" I laughed. "Do you really think he could be?"

He fell silent again.

"If you're wondering how much I know—I know everything. Bobby can be surprisingly detailed when he's . . . encouraged."

Carland nodded, but I doubted that he fully believed me. Because if he did, an iron door would have clanged shut, he'd have no chance, and I knew, despite how still he sat, he was working hard inside, looking for that chance, searching for the out. It was silent in the office, the insulated city silence only money buys.

"I don't know what Bobby told you, and I don't want to know." He gestured toward the Xerox. "It was an accident. The police said so."

"They didn't have all the facts. But they could now. And I think they'd look again."

I paused, long enough to make him look at me.

"And you know Bobby," I went on. "It goes without saying he'd make a deal and testify."

The color that had drained from Carland's face when I'd put the news story on the table was quickly returning. Now his cheeks were flushed.

"How much do you want?" Carland finally asked. There wasn't even a quiver in his voice. I had to admire him; he was very tightly wrapped.

I sat back and looked at him. "Quite a lot, actually," I said.

"How much?"

I got up and walked slowly toward the wide windows facing west. I knew that despite everything—his fear and buried anger, the hate for me he must now feel—he would notice the fullness of my hips, the curve of my ass, the length of my legs in dark stockings and high heels. I paused in passing his desk and let my fingers trail along its highly polished length. I could feel him watching, waiting as I looked out toward the haze on the horizon.

"We—"

"Who's we?" he quickly interrupted.

I turned and started back toward him. "I and my—associates. I'm not alone in this."

"Who are they?"

I sat down again. "You don't need to know."

My voice was as hard and steely as I could make it. I saw his eyes flare in surprise and I hoped my tone had hit him like a whiplash, or a sudden blow to the belly. Of course, he wasn't used to being talked to in this way. It wasn't only that his success in business made him the one in authority; his innate talents and three hundred years of family history made him unused to insolence.

"I could go to the police right now," he said. "I'd be ruined. But so would you."

He had a point. For a moment, I felt a flicker of doubt: such a stupid thing, not to have foreseen that of course he had that option. I didn't believe he'd take it, but it served to show me what a dangerous game I was playing. The ground under me was full of deep and widening cracks. What else hadn't I prepared for? I began to wonder, when suddenly it came to me that this wondering would weaken me. Fear could stop me, unless I simply closed the door upon it, accepted it as part of the game, even embraced it and played with it, walked along its needle edge. Carland was waiting, his hands still and resting on the arms of his chair, playing his very thin bluff to measure my response. Everything about him should have threatened me—his power, his history, his physical attractiveness—but I didn't feel threatened at all. And not because I thought I held the upper hand but because I had stepped fully onto the playing field and into the game. I was committed, fully committed, to going on. It stoked me to a higher, more intense flame, made me feel more alive and present in my own skin than I had ever been. I was smiling when I turned to him.

"Why would you go to the police? You don't want to risk going to jail. Not to mention losing everything you've worked for. And your good name."

He was staring down at the table, and I hoped he could see the receding corridor of all that history, those proud and upright ancestors, an American heritage.

"What do you want?" he asked again.

"We need a conduit for cash."

"Jesus," he said. I could see he hadn't expected anything like that and I knew he saw it instantly, the ongoing imprisonment.

"No way." He shook his head. "Impossible. No way."

"Oh yes," I said. "Very possible indeed."

I leaned forward. "Look, you're a very smart man." I sounded friendly, open. "You can see what your options are—I must say you don't have many. The best one is to cooperate."

He was quiet, unable to look at me. I thought I could guess what was happening inside him, the realization that was spreading through him that he had a new and very big problem and it wasn't going to go away. I could sense him calculating. He was still struggling to find a way around that iron door; he still thought there was a way out. That was good. I liked the idea of his scrambling, frantic in the dark; Carland stymied was an intensely interesting idea. I suddenly wanted to keep it going. On impulse, I picked up the Xerox and put it back in my case.

"I know you're in shock," I said. "You need some time to digest what's happened. Why don't you take the afternoon? We can talk again later."

He looked over at me.

"Over drinks," I said, and crossed my legs again and made that silky sound. "I'm not unreasonable. And we should get to know each other. We're going to be in business a long, long time."

He heard the suggestiveness in my voice and I could see he was surprised. I knew that wheels were turning now: Was this the opening he'd been looking for? Could he get to me on that level; could he trade on sex? I wanted him to think so, to try to save himself through a woman's wiles. To make himself a Delilah to my Samson and think he could seduce me, disarm me, strip me of my power by stripping me of my clothes.

I was smiling when I left. I felt very generous. I wanted him to have a few hours of hope.

• • •

I decided we should have that drink at his house. I knew I was pushing it, playing with fire, that in the intervening hours Carland might plan any number of traps for me, but I was willing to take my chances. Something had taken over, an unassailable certainty that may have been arrogance, but I read it as momentum, a swelling tide I was simply catching. I was being borne up, rising; I wanted to leap from crest to crest.

I wore black, a heavy metallic knit cut very tight, with a high neck and long sleeves like a dancer's leotard, as tight as skin and easily peeled off. It ended above the knee and showed a lot of leg; I wore flesh-colored stockings and delicate black silk high-heeled sandals, the sort that needed nothing more than a single finger to flick off. My hair was down and intentionally wild; its dark tangles were an advertisement, an invitation to touch.

It was dusk when I found his house, an old Spanish mansion on a curving tree-lined street in South Pasadena, the kind of rich neighborhood with very plain front yards because a showy display of any kind is considered ostentatious. Carland's house was set back, and its front door, illuminated now by the yellow light from an antique wrought iron lantern, was shaded by the branches of a very old and thick lantana. I heard my heels echoing in the twilight stillness as I made my way across the intricate pattern of the brick drive, and I liked the staccato crispness, this sharp and spiky way of announcing myself.

Carland opened the door and held his eyes steady, not allowing them to look me up and down. I smiled to myself; he was very cool, a worthy adversary. His mouth hesitated, unable to smile in an ordinary greeting.

"You're right on time," he said.

"Yes," I said. "I always am."

I easily met his gaze. Only a few months ago, I would have been eager to be here with Jonathan Carland. I would have dressed in the same way I had tonight, with the same care and the same object—to make him want me. But the underlying terms would have been very different. I'd have been waiting, taking my cues from his response. How he felt, what he wanted—did he want me?—that's what would have set the agenda. So much of my past had been spent in a passive mode, waiting to see what the other thought. Not tonight. Tonight it was what I thought that mattered. Any agendas were my own.

He had changed into slacks and a soft blue turtleneck sweater that matched his eyes and set off his thick blond hair. He was the sort of man who had been raised never to betray a hint of personal vanity, but you couldn't spend a lifetime looking like Carland and not be aware of your appeal. It was easy to imagine the long line of women who had thrown themselves at him. As I followed him down a tiled corridor toward the rear of the house, through pools of light from copper-shaded lamps, I wondered if he had dressed tonight with as much care as I had, given real thought to his own embellishment. I pictured him preparing: under a warm and steaming shower with soap gliding down his skin, stretching as he toweled himself dry, running the towel through his hair, shaving with long and steady strokes, the razor cutting through thick, foaming cream, his fingers unfolding up his throat as he checked to see how smooth it might feel. Was he thinking of me in that moment? Had he tried on a half-dozen things, assessing each for how it would appear to me, trying to gauge what I might or might not like? And even though it was all calculation, did it arouse him nonetheless? Could he make those preparations and still be immune to their implications? For that matter, could I?

The room he led me into was partially screened, with floor-to-ceiling glass panels giving out onto a terrace. I could just make out a pool, gardens and a formal fountain at the end of a long path in the dimming light. The room was large, with beams across the ceiling and stucco walls that had been glazed a rough mustard color. Deeply upholstered furniture was covered in a light brown tweed and had a custom-made look. A professional eye had created the lighting; unobtrusive sources illuminated old dark paintings in ornate gold frames and a collection of Mexican retablos. It was all very solid, very tasteful, the well-furnished home of a man who expected to be on his own.

He offered me a drink. I took white wine and he poured himself a Scotch. I sat and calmly waited for him. I didn't know exactly how the scene was going to go but I was completely ready to play it out.

He sat down and faced me. "You realize there's no way I can do it. I just can't do it to the bank."

I took a sip of wine. "But that's exactly what you will do. You have no choice."

I didn't blink or look away. But he did. It wasn't a surrender; he was hiding the hate in his eyes. I wondered if that was a remnant of his breeding, an involuntary show of manners, even now when manners were the last thing either of us needed. But he might have looked away so quickly because to show me anything, anything real, could give me ammunition and put him at an even greater disadvantage.

He took a big swallow of his drink and got up again. He poured more Scotch, then stood facing me and leaned against the edge of a dark library table which held a stack of expensive art books about the West. His position showed off his long legs and thrust his pelvis forward. I had no doubt it was done intentionally and I wanted that, wanted him to be working a slow and deliberate seduction. He leveled his eyes at me and smiled.

"You know I did a lot of investigating this afternoon. About you."

"Oh yes?"

"You've done well for yourself. A woman in your field—that's unusual—"

"But getting less so."

"—especially one—who looks like you."

Those last words were a precise and high-pitched bell, calling us to another order. He was smiling, open and very, very cool. It was arousing, that frank approach to sex.

"And how is that? How do I look?"

"You must know. Beautiful."

There it was. I smiled, a parading female, ready to sashay down that inviting street, swishing my hips from side to side.

"How nice you think so," I said, and looked at him fully over the rim of my glass. His voice had been husky, full. He was leaning back, showing off the full line of his elegant frame. His eyes were very blue. My breathing suddenly deepened and for the first time I felt an edge of fear. Where were the boundaries of this game? What was I prepared to do; what would be required? As I looked, it was as if he began to wobble, to snap back and forth between the Carland I had come to turn and the Carland who was so much what I'd always wanted—rich, attractive, confident. I had wanted to be the woman wanted by such a man. Even now I wanted it, but I knew that desire weakened me.

He came to sit beside me and put his arm across the back of the sofa. With just a bit more effort, his fingers could touch me and carry us still farther.

"There must be some way we can work this out," he said and now his voice was soft and intimate. It raised me up and made me want to meet him there.

"How do you think?" I almost purred.

"I don't know," he said. He looked earnest, almost humble. "But I can't help thinking there must be a way, some way for us to work together, to . . . collaborate."

I could see where he was going.

"A kind of partnership?" I asked.

"Well, yes." His fingers played lightly over the inch of fabric between us. "Are you really in this with someone else?" he asked. "Or are you smart enough to do this on your own? Not just smart. Gutsy. Very gutsy. Are you?"

"Of course you don't know."

I knew he expected me to say something more but I let my silence hang between us, a swaying bridge leading to suggestion. He caught the scent and his smile deepened.

"You're right, I don't know," he said. "But it's very appealing, that kind of daring. Especially in a woman. In a beautiful woman . . ."

He leaned closer, slicing off a bit more of the shaft of space between us. His eyes were sparkling; through them he was saying he was more than ready and completely comfortable, at ease, and very welcoming. *Come up here,* he seemed to be saying, *up here with me in this seductive space.*

It would be so easy to lean toward him, to let go and reach for that welcoming hand. I knew he was full of calculation behind those vivid eyes, and yet the body overrides; I didn't doubt the desire I felt between us was real, immediate and had its own demands. For a moment, I saw an entirely new vista, one that was about Carland and me. He needed me as he'd never needed any other woman; I held the key and not only out of his current dilemma, but also out of what I knew were years of isolation. I knew his secret; he didn't have to hide the truth from me. There was no mistaking the appeal that must have. For me, as well—to be crucial to a man like Carland . . . I shifted my hips. With his arm thrown back over the sofa, I was aware of the width of his shoulders; I could trace the outline of his torso under his soft sweater. His body was an insistent whisper: *Share what I am and have, the wealth and history, the confidence and solidity. I can free you of everything that's barren and ramshackle, all that colorless and makeshift past. Let me free you . . . leave everything to me.*

Leave everything to me . . . something in me snapped back, pulled me back from a rocky edge. I was past the point where I could ever leave the crucial things to someone else. And I no longer wanted to hook in to anyone else's orbit. I was here with Carland because I'd already come far enough to dare to seize what I wanted. I no longer needed him, or anyone else, to want me and tell me who I was; I didn't need anyone outside. I was strong enough to create myself.

I looked at him and smiled. I moistened my lips with my tongue. "You certainly are . . . attractive," I said.

His eyes shone even more. I shifted my hips again, but this time moved a bit farther away. "Which is why I have so much trouble understanding"—I paused—"why you need to resort to violence."

I had flicked the whip. He pulled back in surprise, as though he felt its snap. Maybe he'd thought there was some way we weren't going to talk about it. Maybe he himself was so cut off he could skirt the one truth there was between us, the truth that had brought us together. I watched him calculating: what was the best tack to take? I hoped he saw that wherever he turned, he was facing a kind of betrayal, the double betrayal of talking about it at all and then of using it, of risking telling in the hope of getting himself off the hook.

He made a choice and faced me now, an errant child, an honestly perplexed human being. "I don't know how to explain it. But don't you think it's tormented me? It has, it has. I don't know what comes over me—I meet someone, and she does something—I don't even know what—moves in a certain way—I don't know—and suddenly out of nowhere it's there, not even slowly—but there, already on me before I even sense it building. By the time I know it's happening, I'm already in it, powerless. . . ."

He looked at me directly. "Do you know what that feels like? To be so helpless, unable to stop? I hate it, hate it."

His face was agonized. I could see I was supposed to pity him, and in some way I did. I knew that he was telling me the truth, that for all his surface suave authority, he lived every moment in terror of a part of himself he hated, and he was helpless before it. I could guess at what that must be like for a man like Carland. It might not be all the punishment he deserved, but it was harsh that the one thing in the world he couldn't dominate was deep inside him, uncontrollable.

"After that night, that thing with—with her—I went to a shrink. He started talking about sex offenders and the minute he used those words I knew he didn't understand, that he couldn't help. I'm not a sex offender, some pervert on the street. No, no, that isn't me. But I don't want to be this way. You've got to believe me—I don't want to be this way!"

I knew that was true, but not true enough for him to do whatever it took for him to stop. He was being frank, but his frankness still had a use; he was allowing it out in the hope of manipulating me. And it came to me now what it was I could do to him, aside from turning him at the bank, how to defeat him in an even more crushing way. I could strip him of all his defendedness, force him to his knees in genuine unguarded emotion, make him relinquish every self-conscious calculation. That would be for him complete humiliation. I could rape him in my own way, rob him of facade.

I leaned toward him and watched his face intently. "But tell me what it's like—what gets you going. Is it someone strong who can put up a fight?"

He got up. He was fighting to restrain himself. He wanted to shut me up, but he knew he couldn't. Everything he said had to be measured and weighed, evaluated for its usefulness in getting him out of this hole. The lid was off, his secret was out and, if he'd ever been afraid of that, his worst nightmares had come true.

I went on. "Because you can pay, can't you? Pay cash to rough someone up." He turned away. "Or find someone who likes it like that." My voice was gathering strength. "Did your wives? Did they like you to beat them up? Or is that why they left?"

I stood up and faced him.

"But maybe you need someone who doesn't like it—is that what gets you off?—forcing yourself on someone who really wants to get away?"

He turned back to me and I could see that rage was coursing through him. It was aimed at me, a fury that wanted to roll over me and lay me out. A moment more and he'd explode.

"Come on, come on." The words spilled out of me. "Come on," I whispered again. "Is that what you want to do to me? Maybe I should run. Or scream. What will make you feel good? To beat me up? Is that how you get off?"

I wasn't playing. I knew what he was capable of. But I wasn't afraid to face it down. Something in me went out to meet his rage, took it in, fed on it and was enlarged. I wasn't intimidated; I was going to stand my ground.

"Come on, come on." I was shouting. "Let me see it, the real Jonathan Carland! Come on. Show me who you are!"

Those words froze him.

"Show me who you are, who you really are!" I said again.

For a moment, there was only the sound of our breathing, the both of us at fever pitch. I wanted to turn, to see what was behind me, what I could use if he came at me. But I didn't flinch, and then, as I held him in my gaze, something in him gave way. It was visible for only a moment, but I saw it clearly: anger collapsed inward, down to the layers beneath of conflict, pain, and a terrible shame. He quickly turned his face away, but I had seen the look I wanted and I knew it was genuine.

When he turned back, he was again the Carland who was in control. He really was an expert at disguise. "All right," he said. "I know how to cut my losses. When do you want me to start?"

He was smiling. I hesitated before answering. The adrenaline coursing through my body wanted more, wanted a Carland groveling, his face frozen in all that shame and fear. But I took a breath; it was in my own interest to restrain myself. I had held my ground and forced him to the truth and the glimpse I'd had of that was victory enough.

"As soon as we can get the systems in place. I'll let you know."

He nodded, then took our glasses and refilled them. His fingers brushed mine as he handed me my wine and when I looked up he made sure I saw his eyes rake over me.

"Who knows? Maybe this is the start of a beautiful friendship," he said, his tongue circling the rim of his glass. "Maybe this is a very good thing that's happened to me. For all I know, you'll lead me places I've always wanted to go."

"Maybe," I said, as I got up to go. I wanted to encourage him; it might be useful somewhere down the line for him to think he still might get to me in that way. He followed me to the door and I felt him watching me, wondering. I knew he'd spend a sleepless night, scheming, trying futilely to find a way out. I liked it. I knew he'd be thinking about me, that for a long time to come I'd be very much and constantly at the center of his thoughts. It was ironic, because by the time I got to my car, having gotten what I wanted, Carland had definitely ceased to interest me. And I doubted a time would ever come when he would again.

Part FOUR

Chapter Seventeen

When I told Paul that Carland was in, he laughed and kissed me, but I didn't need him to tell me I'd landed a rainbow trout. I had faced down something through Carland that left me strong and free, ready for adventure, as if *I* were the rainbow trout, swimming at last through my own native waters.

I was bubbling and wanted only to talk about work. I persuaded Paul to give me time in front of the computer and carefully made notes on the roadways I'd have to learn. He let me inch my way through a possible way to funnel cash through Carland's bank and, when I thought I had it, he smiled and said it was good for a beginner, but not nearly good enough. I didn't mind. My ego no longer needed superficial strokes; I simply wanted to learn everything I could.

I watched as Paul set up an initial spread sheet and worked out a half-dozen passwords to be used up and down the layered lines of international communication. It was intricate, but he was a good teacher and I followed easily, as he took a hypothetical cash deposit, made to a bank in Panama under a dummy corporate name, through a currency buy in Deutsche marks, then plowed the initial amount and its now accumulating profits into a transfer to three separate accounts in a bank in Dubai, then sent half of it to a brokerage account in Tokyo and half to New York for shares in a real estate investment trust. From there, along with even more profits, it went to a number of accounts we set up at Carland's bank, all of them moving directly through Carland so that the only paper trail would be exactly what we wanted it to be.

As we worked I watched Paul refining, streamlining his ideas, looking for ways to keep the layers of concealment at a minimum and still do the job. I realized he was a kind of artist, interested not only in making it work, but in doing it with a certain style and elegance. Elegant, in this case, meant as slim as possible but ironclad, untraceable. It was very sexy, his complete absorption in a task he did so well.

I was a hungry woman when we made love. I put a pillow under my hips and raised myself up; I wrapped my legs around him and held him tight to me. I released myself, let go inside, felt myself opening, widening, giving out to borderless space. My fingers played up and down the smooth skin of his back, cupped his ass and pulled him in, pressed him to me as we moved in a deepening steady rhythm. Then I forgot about him and expanded out, moving to a hard and full throttle, a splayed female driving toward relief. I used him and I let him use me, and together we rode, stoking ourselves high.

After, when I heard Paul breathing evenly, I got up and

went out onto the terrace. The night had a desert chill and I put a throw over my naked shoulders. Somewhere far to the east a coyote cried and then another; their howls were a long way off, muffled by the night. The moon had risen and was almost full, and in its light I could see the hillside falling away to the streets below. I heard the dull vibration of traffic; straight lines of light, the main veins and arteries, ran out flat to the invisible sea. I breathed deeply. For a moment, I thought I could smell deep, dark, and salty water.

I thought about Carland. I saw again the rage in his eyes and I understood that in a split second, somewhere deep inside me, a choice had been made: I had stood my ground. And not only against Carland but against something even more deadly—my own fear. I had felt my heart racing and a vibrating tremble had rolled through me, but even so I didn't cut and run. I stood my ground. Now in the night wind, I felt a tide of gratitude surging in to wash away the fear. All my life I'd been looking for a way out, the way around whatever was imprisoning me. Now here it was, as straight as a knife edge and as sharp and true: stand still for the fear and see it through.

I heard an owl hooting from somewhere up above me and drew the throw closer, but I didn't feel a chill. I felt my power and I knew it wasn't any fluke. It was mine now, permanently. And I could see that, like the city below me, whatever I wanted was spread out before me, shimmering and possible. I couldn't see all the outlines, the labels and specifics, but I didn't need to. All I had to do was keep walking. The path was waiting, ready. Mine for the taking.

• • •

I called Gaby and said I wanted to see her.

"Of course, darling, anytime. Lunch? Dinner? Or a shopping binge, totally decadent?"

I laughed and said that lunch was fine. Both of us mentioned several places but nothing seemed right. Finally, I took the plunge.

"What about your house? I'd love to see it in the light."

She didn't hesitate. "Wonderful," she said. "We'll eat on the terrace. Shrimp and white wine."

The house was even larger than I remembered, its modern horizontal lines held up by a wide expanse of glass. At the rear, it faced out on an extended garden below the terrace, where we sat. There were lush plantings of day lilies and agapanthus scattered among symmetrical beds of roses and perennials; they ended at a hillside intentionally obscured by banana trees and eucalyptus. It had the kind of opulent perfection that could only result from a sophisticated eye, an encouraging climate, and wads of cash. When I expressed my admiration, Gaby said it was all Charles's doing, that he was the one with the green thumb. It was peaceful. Sunlight was reflecting off the pool. I knew the rest of the city was humming around us and that there were other houses close by but it was all invisible, very far away; we were in a private world, fertile and blossoming.

She was wearing a caftan, a loose gown of thin white linen, with flat gold sandals on her feet. She had no jewelry except a thin gold necklace, and her nails were red; they shone out against the white, stark signals in the sun. Her hair was down and shone in reddish highlights darker than her nails. When she got up to pour more wine, I could see the outline of her body through the thin fabric of her gown, her breasts and buttocks, the flatness of her belly. I stared; it seemed to me she wasn't wearing any underwear. She saw me looking and I didn't look away. I met her eyes. She smiled and as she sat down her hand drifted lightly across my shoulders. For only a moment, I felt her fingers deep in my hair. I realized she knew what I had come for and it was all right, and that knowing gave me patience. I began to relax into the light and the wine, the buzzing of bees deep in the flowers, the sound of her voice.

"I hoped you'd come," she said. "I thought you would, but I wasn't absolutely sure. Sometimes, a person is interested but then decides to turn away."

"I don't want that anymore—to turn away."

"From—this? From me?"

"From anything."

A flicker of disappointment crossed her face but I couldn't embroider on my being here, on what it meant. The truth was I didn't know. And that was the change, that I didn't know but was here anyway. I listened for a moment to a mockingbird trilling in one of the trees.

"I just want to be—brave," I said, turning back. "To not be afraid of what's inside. Whatever it is."

She nodded. "It was such a relief when I accepted what I wanted." She was playing with the rind of an orange she'd had for dessert. She had peeled it perfectly, a skill I doubted I would ever acquire. She turned to me.

"It was long before Charles. I always knew. But my family—it was hopeless—I knew instinctively I must never tell them. There was no way for them ever to understand. For a while, I pretended to myself as well. Forced myself to be with men. I slept with many of them, many, but only because I thought I had to. I accepted it, used it as a means to other things, made no sign of how I really felt."

She looked off down the garden, her eyes unfocused on the color there. "A few times, though, an enormous rage welled up in me, overwhelmed me, descended on me as completely as my skin. But I buried it, or tried to. I didn't scream or even murmur. It was as if that rage made me dead, blank. An old shoe acquiescing to a bony foot."

She looked back at me. "In those years, mute screams were always my milieu." She paused for a moment and then went on. "I saw a doll once, a clown with a plastic head. The mouth was shaped into the plastic itself, not simply painted on. A dull red circle, open, forever making no sound. That was me, an open red mouth from which no sound ever came."

She sipped her wine. "You see, I lacked your bravery."

"But something changed."

She shrugged. "Time passed, and brought its own insistence. I came to see I couldn't pretend to myself any longer, that I had to find a way. . . . It's strange, but sometimes to accept a secret, to accept that it must be kept, is the way to come out from under all its terrible anxieties. What I mean is, I decided I had to be what I was, but that I didn't want to run away from my family and the world they wanted for me. I went looking for a compromise . . . and then I met Charles. Who, in fact, thank God, was just like me."

"I wasn't sure you knew."

She laughed. "Darling, of course. And I knew that you did, too. He saw you that night."

I was suddenly very red.

"It's all right," she said.

"Awful," I said, but I was smiling. "Not just a spy but a very bad one."

"Oh, I was glad. I wanted you to see. That there was—how to put it?—latitude. That there might be an open door."

She put down her glass and took my hand. I knew that if I pulled away Gaby would be gracious, not insist or make a scene. I liked that, that for her, too, the choice was mine. I watched as she slowly traced circles on my skin with a polished fingernail, moved across my palm, down my wrist and along my fingers. She had the power of experience, of the seducer; I had the power of the virgin, the possibility of saying no. I sat still, hardly breathing; I felt the stirring of desire but also of fear. I had no idea what I wanted from her, beyond this present moment. This was different from being with a whore and in Paul's intervening presence; this was direct, one on one, and with someone who could stay in my life. I took a breath, trying to make that all right. My eyes moved from my hand to the outline of her breasts, breasts just like mine and I saw the irony, that what was same was so forbidden, frightening.

She pulled me up and put her arms around me. I let myself be drawn into her embrace. I felt her lips along my neck and throat. I was taller than she and felt her stretching up; her body was pressing into me, the full softness, her breasts just below mine. Slowly, irresistibly, I felt myself sliding down into that softness, pushing off as if it were an atmosphere, a silent pool of silver light flowing all around me. My heart was racing. *What does this mean? What do I want?* I didn't know—and then it came to me it was all right, I didn't have to be stopped by not knowing, that, in fact, I could be emboldened by it. Gaby found my lips and her tongue pressed in. I tasted her, took an inward breath and I crossed a line: on one side, the unknown set off red lights and raised brick walls, but on the other, the side I'd been crossing to, the unknown was a beacon and opened widening vistas urging me on. Gaby's breasts moved against me and my hands were suddenly alive, eager. I pulled her closer. All fear was gone, all restraint, and I only wanted more.

"Darling, darling," she whispered, and her hands were on me. I felt her fingers as they moved in exploration on my breasts and I shifted so that she could cup them fully. She leaned down and I spread my fingers through her hair as she buried her face in my soft chest. Her hand slipped down past my waist, down my thigh, across my ass. Both of us were moving, pressing in, already searching for a single rhythm, our hands and lips thirsty, unable to get enough.

I followed her down a carpeted corridor into her bedroom. My hands and mouth had a life of their own; I couldn't keep from touching, stroking, licking. At the entrance to the room, I pulled her back; I raised her thick hair off her neck and pressed my lips against it. I needed that moment, an island of infinitely tender stillness in the midst of all that passion. She seemed to know and let me hold her steady. I felt her hand reach up and hold my breast even as her cheek pressed into it. She was murmuring, a steady sound of welcoming, encouraging me, inspiring herself.

I didn't know if Charles had a separate room, but her bedroom seemed to me a woman's room and, like her, very light, all antique white linen and lace, silk and polished crystal. I held her hand and pulled her to me. I cupped her ass under the smooth linen; it was soft and rounded like my own.

I moved to help her out of the caftan but she pulled me down so I was sitting on the bed. She wanted to undress me. I watched as she knelt and undid the clasps of my sandals; I heard myself moan when she raised my foot and ran her tongue across my toes. I could see the outline of her breasts as she leaned in and the fabric fell away and I held my hand just beneath one's heavy point and watched her as she moved so that her nipple grazed my open palm. Her eyes were closed and I knew what she was feeling, all intensity narrowed down to that teasing delicate touch. I could feel myself opening, becoming wet, already longing, arching for the pressure of her hand.

She stood and pushed my legs open. I pulled her to me, my face pressed against her belly, my hands firmly on her ass. I raised myself up and buried my face in her breasts; I found a nipple through the fabric and began to kiss and suck. Suddenly, I felt a sob, a sudden intake to span a sudden chasm, into which I fell in a reckless tumble, out of which I began to soar. Something deep inside gave way and my thirst, my hunger was upon me; again, I couldn't get enough. I stood and kissed her, my tongue on hers and on her lips, and she quickly pulled off my blouse and bra and skirt. Her hands roamed over me as I lifted the caftan over her head and moved back to look at her. She was murmuring, wanting to show me, wanting my eyes running over her body; her hands were tracing paths for my eyes to follow, down her throat, over her lush breasts again and again, down her belly and between her legs. She wanted me to watch her taking pleasure, and in a body so like my own, the same curves and indentations but now mysterious, compelling, infinitely other.

I leaned in and ran my own hands, my tongue over where her fingers traced. Then I turned her and stood behind, pressing myself close. My arms encircled her, one hand playing over her breasts and teasing at her nipples, the other moving through her pubic hair to the split between her legs. I felt the tension in her body, a tension she could play in and I could play upon, as she both leaned back against me and the pressure of my body, and moved forward toward my restless teasing hands. Her head was thrown back and I buried my face in her hair. I knew she could feel my breath, my lips, my tongue on her neck, licking at her ears.

She moved onto the bed. I lay beside her and she pushed me on my back and rolled on top. I felt her knee and thigh between my legs and I lay back and gave myself up to her female embrace. She moved down my body and with her fingers spread my thighs. I felt her tongue as it licked at me, long and slow; I arched up to it as it burrowed in, found every crevice and wet glistening fold.

She raised her head and I kissed my moisture off her chin. My hands, my fingers were avid for her roundness, her fullness, at once so strange and so familiar. I sucked at her nipples, a sexy baby, hungering. Her smell and taste inflamed me and I freely offered up my own. Her fingers plunged inside me and her palm pressed on my clitoris. I rocked back and forth, taking her in deeper, pressing harder against her stable hand. I knew she wanted that as well. My fingers found her center and moved inside; I felt that slippery tunnel relax out in a widening welcoming, holding nothing back. I played in the sharpness of that penetration, testing, teasing, pressing in. "Yes," she was whispering, "yes," and I saw her eyes were closed in exquisite concentration and I knew what she was feeling, that simultaneous giving out and taking in. I closed my eyes, too, and felt her in me, moved along the shaft of her narrowed hand. My other hand was anchored on her breasts as hers was on mine, and pressing closer, we moved together, locking together in a rocking rhythm, pressing closer, closer, arching up and forward, our thighs together, moving ourselves higher, climbing toward that sharpening goad, the deepening thrust, that riveting button of intensity, and then we arched impossibly high, surged through again and again, until we came, like shimmering water erupting, spilling into thin clear air.

After I lay on the bed and watched her getting dressed.

"You always look so feminine," I said, as she stepped into the skirt of a tan silk dress.

She smiled. "Why not? I love being female."

She came to me and turned her back. I sat up to pull the dress's zipper closed.

"Besides," she continued, smoothing the tan lace bodice, "so much of our social life is actually about business and I mostly deal with men."

She was now searching for something in the drawers of

a burled walnut dresser. "And men are so easily threatened by a powerful woman. Which of course I am. So much so I see no need to flaunt it."

She laughed, then came back and sat beside me as she put on two small diamond earrings. I reached up and smoothed back her hair. She caught my hand and brought it to her lips.

"Will you stay?" she asked.

I shook my head. "I'm due to meet Paul."

She nodded. "Of course."

She hesitated, wanting, I think, to ask about Paul and me, to learn specifics. But she was very tactful.

"Well, you know I will be jealous now."

After I took a shower and got dressed, she walked me to my car.

"When will I see you again?" she asked.

"I don't know."

"But there will be a next time . . . won't there?"

I looked at her. "I don't know. Really. I don't know."

She hugged me quickly as we said goodbye.

I turned the car toward home. Breathing in and even after a shower, I could still smell Gaby on my fingertips, that unmistakable secret smell. Unexpectedly, I felt a stab of shame, as if I'd stumbled on a terrible secret: that odor, so much my own. I tried to take an even breath, and it came to me that hidden, deep inside, I'd been afraid, ashamed of my own smell, of my own body, had a secret behind the smell, a revulsion for my own skin. An image dropped into place, an old and faded towel, rust-stained and threadbare, and my mother quickly pulling it in front of her nakedness, so quickly I knew I had done something wrong. I could still hear the towel snapping and that sound was like a slap, a summons to a suddenly strange and frightening world with secret rules and hidden codes that could trip me up at any time. I saw a bathroom door, rough coats of paint chipped off its lower edge, always closing just as I wanted in, and the universe zoomed out into Right and Wrong and I had no idea which was which, or why. I saw the hand that sharply and angrily pushed my own small hand away from what was only me—was there some badness in my body, in my very own flesh? For the first time, I realized the world had hidden things, things hidden from me and things that I must hide and suddenly I was standing silently in a ring of shame, suffused with it, like a desolate Eve banished forever from the light of the garden.

But now here in the car and with another breath, those images faded as quickly as they'd come. I knew I was no longer afraid or ashamed of what was inside. In the way that the tipping of a single domino begins a chain event, barriers inside me had been falling, and each one falling was feeding my momentum, making me insatiable, a streaking Jaguar eating up the road. That road wasn't leading me to a single destination, one particular and final revelation of self; that road *was* myself, and its course, with a thousand twists and turns, switchbacks and straightaways, would go on as long as I did. It came to me that there was something deeper than Gaby I'd been after today: the part of me that had been afraid to go toward what I wanted. I had come to claim her, to claim my desire for her, because in doing so I claimed and accepted another piece of myself.

I saw her again, with her head thrown back, her breasts round and soft, responsive to my touch. For a moment, I froze, a suddenly alert animal scenting impending imprisonment, a just-taken prisoner whirling at the sound of the closing iron door. Was Gaby, or even someone like her, to be my fate? Something in me rose up in protest. It couldn't be right that in following attraction I would be led into a box canyon from which there was no escape. No, I didn't have to choose—between her and Paul, between men and women, between any one thing or another. I had come too far to limit myself; I no longer had any interest in ruling things out. I felt released from implications.

I understood now why some people keep pushing, go farther, don't stop eating up that wild tail of road. I thought about Nathan; for the first time I knew why he hadn't been content to own only one store, why he'd kept expanding, taking on more, creating a wider and wider arena in which to operate. For some people, putting out energy breeds energy; it doesn't deplete. To act isn't only to do; it's also to expand. I saw my eyes in the rearview mirror; I felt that I was one of those people. I could feel it, the expanding power flowing through me, and it was energy that needed a task. It was crying out to do more.

Thinking of Nathan gave me an idea. I knew I was strong enough now to protect him. It didn't take much to see that in one way or another, Peter was behind Nathan's most serious troubles, and Peter was the one issue Nathan couldn't objectively deal with himself. But I could. I had the distance and the strength now to force

Peter into line. I didn't know exactly what I would need to do it, but there was no question that the time had come. And I could start where I'd left off, following the trail. I headed the car over the hills to the Valley. I laughed with the energy spilling out of me. I had an assignment, a worthy task, and it was all still percolating.

Chapter Eighteen

I parked a half block down from Stella Jordan's house. I didn't doubt she was a dealer, so I knew a stranger knocking at her door wouldn't be exactly welcome. While I'd bought drugs before, it was only from friends, never directly, and I had the not-quite-irrational fear I'd be caught in a police raid, or more likely, Stella would mistake me for a narc and take a terrible revenge, lock me in the basement, which most Valley houses don't even have, and leave me to die of starvation. I wasn't even certain why I was here; "finding out what I can" seemed a flimsy reason for risking what I knew was real danger. Ten minutes passed as I worked up the courage to knock anyway and use Judd Mallory's name, or even Peter's, and go through the motions of making a buy—if she would let me in at all. Finally, I knew there was only one way to see, so I stopped thinking and got out of the car, walked to Stella's door and rang the bell.

I was startled when a teenage boy answered.

"Yeah?" he said, staring at me with so little interest I wondered if he thought I was the Avon Lady.

"Is your mother home?" Now I *felt* like the Avon Lady.

The boy turned and started down the hall, leaving the door open. I guessed I was supposed to follow. His complete lack of concern made me wonder if I'd been wrong: maybe Stella wasn't a dealer after all.

There were a half-dozen people in the living room, in a circle around a coffee table loaded with coke and grass and all the attendant paraphernalia. So Stella was dealing but security wasn't an issue. No one even looked at me as I stood in the doorway. I didn't get it.

They were all concentrating on the woman I took to be Stella, the only one sitting in an upholstered chair, who was in the middle of scooping a huge pile of white powder into the cradle of a metric scale. She was somewhere in her forties, with straight dark hair parted in the middle, a tie-dyed blouse, Gypsy skirt, and cowboy boots. Music was playing, twenty-year-old rock 'n' roll, and you could hear it in the concentrated silence, as everyone watched the white powder. Two of the men pulled their chairs closer; the scraping sound of their movement on the uncarpeted floor hung in the air. One of them took out his own mirror and razor blade when Stella finished weighing what looked to be at least eight ounces and pushed the mound toward him. He sliced and diced the coke, then drew out a plastic straw and snorted up a long, thick line. He breathed in deeply and held it in as if it were smoke, then relaxed as a broad smile crossed his face. Everyone else eased up, too.

Stella looked up and saw me.

"Yeah?" she said with just a trace of wariness. It was

strange—all that coke and so little sense of threat.

"Judd Mallory sent me," I said, and hoped I didn't look as nervous as I felt.

At the name, Stella burst into raucous laughter. "Damn that guy," she managed to say. "Damn his beautiful hide all to hell!" She turned to me. "You fucking him?"

"Used to," I shot back, without even thinking. I smiled conspiratorially, just us girls together, and forced my eyes to stay on Stella's. I knew the question was some kind of test.

Stella laughed again. "Shit, he couldn't get it up now for a fucking Miss America. Honey, I like 'em pretty, but they got to be ready—know what I mean?"

The others were smiling and nodding as more coke and a joint went around. Stella waved me toward an empty chair so it seemed to be all right. She didn't ask me how much coke I wanted and I didn't say; it looked as if I was expected to sit around and socialize. A couple of mirrors were being passed around and I did some lines. It had been a very long time, but when the coke kicked in I felt the high as if it were an old familiar friend, welcomed that particular increased light, a new brilliance to the world, clear energy, even the pharmaceutical taste in the back of my throat. I knew it was the drug, but everyone looked a little more vivid, livelier, and attractive. My foot started tapping in time to the music, and I was smiling, nodding like the others, feeling the peaceful, easy feeling the band on the stereo was singing about.

Then something crashed. My head swiveled in time to see an overturning chair rattling back against the wall as one of the men leaped up and away from Stella. It took me a moment to realize she had pulled a knife out of her cowboy boot and taken a swipe at him. I looked down and saw blood; the man's hand was cut but it didn't look very deep.

"Bitch!" he hissed. "That's my fingering hand!"

"I don't care if it's your goddam balls. You want to buy what I have, you don't question my integrity. No one does. Not ever."

"Well, fuck you," the guy spat out, but I could see he was afraid of her. The other man got up and for a tense moment they all stared at each other, like animals parading and puffing themselves up.

"Fuck you," the man with the cut hand said again, but it was his way of retreating and, without another word, he and his friend turned and walked out. Stella's laughter boomed out behind them.

"Don't take it personal," she called out, "come by anytime."

I suddenly understood. Stella was working out of some idea about dealing, a late-sixties counterculture thing, when drugs were supposed to be the solution rather than the problem, and everyone shared and wanted to turn each other on. But under the retro style, her booming laughter had a hollow ring; it was cold, like her eyes. I don't know how I knew it but I did, that she wasn't an old hippie who had turned pro, but a pro who had put on a hippie gloss.

I felt the ground sway as it hit me: Stella and I had a lot in common. Wasn't I, too, a criminal, operating on the other side of the law? I stared at her, a woman who could pull a knife and without fear—but with cold, cold eyes. Was that where I was heading? Maybe it went with the territory; maybe Stella's coldness was the price of fearlessness. I thought about Paul and the steeliness that always aroused me, the things he was willing to do to get what he wanted. Were his silk shirts the same artificial covering as Stella's tie-dyed blouse, a pretty show to mask the ugliness within? And what about me? Where were my denial and pretense? Just what was I becoming? For a moment, I felt like a spinning top suddenly locked in place, twisting deeper and deeper into disappearing sand.

I was half-rising from my chair, uncertain what to do, when there was a noise in the doorway and a new person appeared. It was Don. I shook my head as if to clear it; I couldn't understand what he was doing at Stella's. I had the crazy thought that he'd been following me. But then I saw his own surprise as he slowly registered me. He had trouble putting it together, too, but as he did, a shudder rumbled through him and panic filled his eyes. He hesitated only a split second, then turned on his heel and was gone.

"Don!"

I jumped up, but he didn't stop. The front door slammed, and I raced after him. Stella turned to look after me, like a lizard momentarily distracted by a shadow, but no one else moved. Ten minutes from now they'd have to be reminded about the woman who'd jumped up and rushed out.

Don was already in his car when I came out of the house.

"Wait!" I shouted. "I just want to talk to you!"

But he pulled out and sped away. Without thinking, I ran to my car and went after him.

He headed for the freeway and I almost lost him across

the lanes of traffic. My heart was pounding, but I was thinking very clearly. I saw I'd been stupid not to guess about Don and drugs; I understood now why he looked so bad and why he was desperate for money. It all made sense. But I didn't judge him. My heart went out to him. I wanted to help.

It also came to me that it might not be coincidence that Don shared a dealer with Peter Broadman; they might very well be mixed up with each other. Maybe that flash I'd had that Don and his friend Nate and Judd and others were part of some conspiracy against Nathan orchestrated by Peter was actually right. I had to find out.

Don turned off the freeway and when he stopped at a red light at the bottom of the ramp I was right behind him. He saw me in his rearview mirror. His body slumped, but the light changed before I could get out of my car, and he pulled away. I followed and then realized we were in his neighborhood. He was heading home.

He lived in a rented townhouse farther out in the Valley, in Sherman Oaks. He was already unlocking his front door when I pulled up. I called his name. He didn't turn and went inside, but he didn't close the door and I followed him in.

"I'm not going to tell you anything," he said, uncapping a bottle of booze and pouring himself a shot. He didn't offer me any. Sweat was glistening on his face. I could see the fear propelling him as he paced around the narrow room.

"You don't have to," I said. "I can see. Is that what it's all been about—drugs? Because you can quit, get help, there are all kinds of programs."

He looked at me with an odd mocking expression as if

I were incredibly naive. And I felt that I was, because the dark energy coming from him suddenly seemed huge, monumental, needing something greater than a few days of rehab.

"Is it something else?" I asked. "Something with Peter Broadman?"

He didn't react but sank down in a chair. He looked up at me, but I couldn't read his expression; I had the eerie feeling I wasn't talking to Don but to a man who had short-circuited and now was going through the motions of being in this room, in his own skin.

"I know you own NNE stock," I said.

"You mean it's in my name."

I saw the self-loathing on his face and immediately I understood.

"That's it . . . you've been buying the stock in your name for Peter, parking it for him so no one will know he's the one who really owns it. And Judd and Stella—he's gotten them to do it, too, hasn't he? He's trying to buy up enough shares to outvote Nathan, to get rid of him—that's it, isn't it?"

He was looking at the floor, but I knew it was the truth.

"You never liked him," I said. "Why are you doing it?"

Don laughed, a strangled sound that died in his throat.

"Has he got something on you? Because of the drugs? Something through Stella?"

He made a sound of contempt. "Stella? She's my bonus. All that great coke—a real rich vein, baby. Look how great it makes me feel."

"What do you mean? Bonus for what?"

He was rubbing his forehead, his head down. I couldn't see his eyes.

"Tell me," I said, my voice softening. "You don't have to be alone—maybe I can help. What's Peter got on you? What?"

He looked up at me, but his eyes were devoid of any appeal for help. They had gone dead. Suddenly, he raised his arm and brought it down in a pantomime of disgust. It was the gesture of someone who didn't care anymore, who had just made a decision to throw it all away.

"What do I care?" he said, but he was talking to himself. "I'm going down anyway—what the hell do I care?"

He got up and went to a small bookcase and pushed some books aside. When they fell off the shelf and thudded on the floor, he kicked at them, searching on the shelf until he found an envelope and tossed it over to me.

"Here," he said, his voice flat and cold. "Here."

There were photographs in the envelope, of a woman stretched out on a bed. I shuffled through them but didn't understand. I looked over at Don.

"Who is she?"

"Look again," he said as he poured himself another shot.

I took the pictures over to the light of a lamp and went through them again more slowly. They had been taken in a bedroom; the woman was in three or four different outfits. I didn't know what I was supposed to see, but then I caught something familiar. It took me a minute—maybe I didn't want to see—but then I realized who it was. Don.

I looked over at him, but he was staring into his drink. I looked again at the picture in my hand. He was wearing some kind of long nightgown and was leaning back suggestively, in a come-and-get-it pose, with large, obviously fake, breasts pointing at the camera. His face was disguised behind full makeup and half hidden by the long red hair of a wig; nonetheless, I could see huge, gaudy pearl earrings dangling from his ears. I thought at first he was dressed for a costume party or Halloween, but then I realized it was something else: in one of the pictures, I could clearly see his erection jutting up under the thin shiny fabric of the black negligee.

I turned to him. He glanced at me and then looked away.

"Who took these?" I finally asked.

"A hooker I hired. She turned out to be very enterprising—and to know Peter Broadman. Nathan's little boy."

I nodded. I felt disgust, but not at Don. It was Peter who made my stomach cringe.

Don got up and stood near me as I looked through the pictures again. I could feel what it was costing him to show these things to me. I looked up at him.

"But if this is what you like, why do you pretend and go after women?"

"You think it means I'm gay? I'm not. I've never been attracted to men. Only women."

He laughed but I could hear the bitterness.

"Not that that makes it any easier. There are a million men out there who'd probably be thrilled to be with me like that. But I don't want them. I'm a rare breed—a heterosexual transvestite. A real freak."

I shook my head. I had thought I knew him so well, but it turned out I didn't know very much at all.

"Did you do this when we were married?" I asked.

"Yes."

He hesitated, even now unsure if he should open up completely.

"Ever since I can remember."

"I can't quite take it in . . . that we lived together and you had this secret life. Did you look forward to my leaving the house?"

"Sometimes."

"And where did you keep the clothes? It seems so awful—that you had to keep it hidden."

"What if I hadn't? You would have thrown me out."

"Not necessarily."

I was looking through the pictures. In one, he was kneeling on the bed, his back arched to show off his breasts, his mouth half open in what was almost a parody of a sexpot pose. Something in me stirred, moved by how vulnerable he had made himself to the camera, to the viewer—to me. That vulnerability had a certain appeal.

"There must be women who would be turned on," I said.

He looked over at me. I had surprised him.

I thumbed through the pictures again.

"I mean, there's something very sexy in the way you're presenting yourself, how you're offering yourself. I like that, how much you want to be admired—"

I stopped. I realized I didn't want to hear exactly what it was all about for him. I was thinking for myself; I was already writing a scenario in which I was the one who must be pleased. I put down the pictures and sat back in my chair.

"I'd like to see you like that," I said.

His eyes widened; I had definitely taken him by surprise.

"No," he said, and laughed nervously.

"Why not? I think you want to show me."

"No."

I heard the waver in his voice, and he knew I heard it. I looked up at him and reached for his hand.

"You do want to. I can feel it. And you can trust me," I said, "you know you can."

"You'll laugh. Or something worse."

He was protesting but he had the giddy grin of someone ricocheting between an obligatory "No" and a deeply desired "Yes."

"I won't laugh. Look at me—can't you see it's got me going?"

It was the truth. That waver, his almost fawn-like trembling and my own confidence: I could already feel the excitement of coaxing him along. I stood up and when our eyes met we both knew we were already walking down the same street.

He got up and led the way upstairs to his bedroom. I sat on the bed as he opened a drawer and took out three or four boxes, the kind you get at department stores. His hands were shaking, and he was breathing in a rush. I thought it was from nervousness, but then he opened the first box and took out a black silk slip and suddenly crushed it to him. Rapidly, violently, he ran the silk over his chest, down his thighs and between his legs, and I realized it was lust I was seeing, pure, overpowering lust. Then he remembered me and laughed with embarrassment.

"Are you sure you want to see this?" he asked, half hoping I'd say no.

"Absolutely. I want to see you dressed. Please dress up for me." He began taking off his clothes.

"You won't laugh?"

"No, I won't laugh."

When he was naked, he opened the other boxes and took out an enormous black lace bra. I almost laughed then; it hadn't occurred to me that an actual bra was under the clothes I saw in the photos. But I kept silent, even when he rummaged around and came up with two foam rubber falsies and stuffed them in the cups. As he put the bra on and struggled with its closure, I saw his cock was already very hard.

"Come here," I said. "I'll do the snaps."

He came to the bed.

"Kneel down."

His back was to me, in between my legs. When he felt the snaps close he wanted to get up, but I held him back. I had seen that there was only one meaning to his putting on that bra—it was strictly about sex—and that utter directness inflamed me. I pulled his head back, ran my fingers along his upturned throat, kissed his mouth, responsive but impatient. I didn't care. I ran my hands down his shoulders and over his breasts, across the silk of the bra. He arched his back seductively.

"Are they pretty? Do you like them?" he asked shyly, and I suddenly saw what he wanted to be. Feminine. Submissive. Desired.

"They're beautiful. Show me what else you've got to put on."

I watched as he slowly unrolled black shiny stockings up the length of his legs and anchored them with a red silk and black lace garter belt. He stepped into a red satin bikini bottom, then put on a green silk camisole. I could see the fabric stretching tight across his chest as he leaned down to pull a black silk slip up over his hips. Again, I saw the lust as he ran his hands over the silk, across his breasts, down his legs, over his ass. His cock pushed against the slip. There was more he wanted to put on: a deep red satin blouse and a heavy black silk skirt. The blouse had long sleeves and a high rolled collar; I realized he wanted to feel encased, surrounded by silk.

"Do you like this color? Is it sexy?" he wanted to know.

"Incredibly. Come here."

"Wait."

He brought out a thick black leather belt and put on a pair of pointed black high-heeled shoes. He wanted me to do the buttons of the blouse, at the neck and sleeves, and to pull the belt tight, as tight as I could. Where had he gotten these things, and what had he felt as he bought them? Immediately, I could imagine taking him shopping, selecting things to please me, having him model them for my approval. Things that were tacky, vulgar, whorish. Things that could only be about sex. My hand moved to my groin. His need to have me approve of him, to think him attractive, was intoxicating. He posed for me, his hands linked behind his neck, his chest raised, completely offering himself to me. In that moment, as he showed himself to me, so avid for me to see him and think him beautiful in all his artifice, I knew we had never been closer.

"What do you think?" he asked. "Am I beautiful?"

"You want to be, don't you? Attractive for me."

"Yes. For you. Just for you."

I looked down at his feet and he immediately moved them and strained to point his toes. He bent his neck at a more graceful and submissive angle and lowered his eyes demurely. I looked at the skirt falling casually across the skin of his thighs. He saw and I could feel all his intensity on that band of fabric, its feel on his skin, the air that entered and moved below it. He could be fully exposed by the most casual gesture, taken so easily. He knew I saw it. I felt him wanting to spread his legs, to raise the fabric to show more of himself. A small sound escaped him, a moan, as he thrust into the air, again and again. He looked at my hands and his eyes were beseeching: if only I would touch him. He ran his tongue over his lips to moisten them and make them more appealing, then looked from my hands to my mouth, his tongue straining toward me, his back arching even more, his pelvis, too, straining for a touch. I went to him, ran my hand along the hem of his skirt, back and forth, and a sigh broke from him, unguarded, from the deepest part of him, his whole body became that sigh, completely submissive.

I slipped my hand under his skirt. He followed it as I clasped one thigh and then the other, played my fingers easily over the exposed skin, along the silk garters, teased the hair on his spreading thighs. I ran my finger under the elastic of his satin bikini; his cock had completely pushed it aside. He was moaning now and couldn't stop thrusting. He closed his eyes but I turned his face to me; he understood that I wanted his eyes open and looking at me, that he was no longer permitted anything hidden or private. He was moving more now, in larger and larger thrusts, his eyes on mine, holding nothing back, offering me his desire and his fear, creating himself, his most secret self, in the reflection of my gaze.

There was a full-length mirror on the door and I led him to it. I wanted him to see himself from every angle and I wanted to see him there as well. He reached out to me, but I didn't want to touch him yet, refused to, even though he rotated his hips in a way he hoped I'd find alluring, moistened his lips and showed me his tongue, pulled back his shoulders to show off his chest. His hands ran over his breasts, cupped them, pulled the fabric of the blouse taut to set them off. His fingers caressed the softness, played over the heaving softness, and he began swaying, his hands traveling across his chest and shoulders and arms and back once more to his chest. He couldn't stop moving, touching himself, the silk, his breasts, his hips flaring out beneath the tight belt, the shaft of his cock bulging against the skirt. There was a smile on his face I'd never seen, a serene wonder as his eyes met mine. He looked like a child playing in the water.

I forced him to his knees, then knelt beside him. He looked at me in the mirror, his eyes dark and intense, riveted on mine watching him. I encircled him with my arms and I could feel how much he wanted to take my hands in his and place them on his chest. We were so close I could feel the heat coming off him. Small cries escaped him; he wanted to fold himself against me, to press against me, to feel the pressure of my hand on his pulsing cock. I heard his breathing as I brought my hand down toward his skirt. Now he cared only about showing himself. He was thrusting forward as if each thrust could push away the skirt. I tapped him lightly at the knees and he slowly spread them. I wanted him to feel free and open, wide open. Then I lifted his skirt and pulled down the red satin bikini, pushed the yards of silk fabric into his belt so that his cock and his ass were revealed. I looked up at his eyes in the mirror; I could see the pain and the desire. He wanted to show me everything.

I looked at him in the mirror. An incredible creature with a hard, erect cock and huge breasts, all of it surrounded by silk. Suddenly, I crushed him to me, buried my head in his chest, allowed myself to be engulfed by those enormous breasts. They cradled me and I sucked, sucked as if they were my mother's. Something in me gave way and I was moaning with him, pressing myself against the side of his leg, one hand on his breasts, the other on his cock as we found a steady rhythm.

"Fuck me," he said, "fuck me."

I laughed as he sucked his fingers, leaned over and brought the moistness to his ass, spread his cheeks and rubbed the wetness around his hole. His hand stayed to hold his cheeks spread wide, to open himself and show himself completely, and I could feel his whole body straining to lift his asshole higher and offer it to me.

"Fuck me, baby, please."

I moved still closer to him, then pulled his head back so he could suck my fingers. He leaned over again and I took my moist fingers, warm from his mouth, and ran them around his hole, teasing it, pressing it open. He moaned again, that same soft moan of complete submission, and everything about him was open to me, soft and pliable, and with me pressed up against him and his cock thrusting deeply into my firm hand, I took the other and pressed into him, plunged into him, deep, deeper, deeper, and fucked him until we came.

Chapter Nineteen

"Don't go," Don was saying, "don't challenge Peter. He's bad, Vega . . . if he thinks you're a threat, that you'd tell Nathan, he could do something very bad to you."

I was watching him take off the layers of silk he had so impatiently put on. It struck me how ironic it was that he'd gotten dressed for sex, and in getting dressed he'd stripped himself bare; in putting on his secret clothes he'd made himself more naked to me than he ever had with skin. In stepping into what was artificial, he became his most real. It was such a mystery what people liked, what got them going, how much larger the arena was than I had ever thought. I felt no judgment of Don at all. All he wanted was to offer softness and when I remembered what I felt when I buried my head in those breasts I realized how much I, and probably everyone else, wanted that softness, too. If I felt bad about anything, it was only that he'd carried around what he thought was a shameful secret, and that he'd given himself up, to Peter Broadman and to coke.

He came and sat beside me, now his ordinary self in a faded cotton robe.

"Besides, I feel like shit already—you'll make it worse if you fight my battles," he said.

"It's not just your battle," I said. "It's about Nathan. Peter's trying to push him aside—I can't let that happen. I owe him too much."

I turned to him. "But you have to get off the coke. And figure out some way to get yourself together."

He was nodding. "Right, right. I will."

He said it in the same way you tell a casual acquaintance you'll be sure and call. He wanted to mean it, but that desire carried no weight; it didn't motivate. Something was missing. I could hear it in his voice, which sounded thin, like a wafer sliced in half.

"I will," he said again, with the well-meaning docility of someone used to failing. I left him pouring another drink and settling in for the long, dark night.

I drove directly to Peter Broadman's house. It was late, but I didn't want to wait. I was carried along by the momentum that had been building for days.

I took Coldwater Canyon across the hills and turned on to the sharp curves of Mulholland. The night was dark and I could see the lights of the Valley below me. I wasn't planning what to say; I felt sure of myself and knew the right words would come. I kept seeing Peter's face, his usual sneer, and that was enough to move me on.

I was thinking more of Paul, who actually seemed very

far away. He was the cornerstone of all that was happening to me but I'd been drifting far from him. For a moment I felt afraid that if I drifted too far I would find myself lost. But then I steadied myself and remembered I was walking my path, not his. It couldn't be Paul I believed in; it had to be me.

Peter's house was hard to find, marked only with a hastily painted number and a driveway that disappeared up a knoll over the road. I passed it once, then came back and turned in. A gate stopped me a few yards up. I rolled down my window and buzzed the intercom. After a long wait, a maid's voice came on and it took some wrangling to get to Peter directly.

"It's Vega," I said. "I need to see you. Now."

"Vega? Vega who?" I could almost hear the laugh.

"Come on, Peter, open up."

"Well, what brings you all the way up here? It's late, baby. You have something interesting in mind?"

"Open the gate, Peter. You want to hear what I have to say."

I heard him release the intercom and after a few seconds the gate swung open. Stucco lanterns lined the drive. It circled around a fountain at the front of the house, which was modern, a white box of glass and metal tubing cantilevered out over the hillside. I knew there would be a breathtaking view from inside, and I knew how much it had all cost; even though Peter held title to it, it was one of the properties in Nathan's private portfolio.

Peter was standing at the wide front door, leaning against it with a drink in his hand.

"Vega, Vega," he was saying as I got out of the car,

"such a long way to come. But I'm so glad you did."

He was almost smirking. I ignored it and moved past him into the house as if I were the one who owned it. "We have business to discuss."

"Business? And here I thought it was me you wanted to see."

I waited without saying anything. He politely bowed as if my silence was a gentle lob in his direction, then finally moved toward the back of the house and into the den. One wall was glass and I saw the river of lights stretching away to the limitless distance. Peter shuffled over to an Eames chair. I realized he'd been drinking for a while. He sat down heavily and swiveled around to face me.

"Now, have a drink. It's late. But it could be early. Know what I mean?"

It could have been funny, his overriding male vanity. Or maybe it was a kind of moral stupidity, a lack that made him oblivious to every obvious cause and effect.

"I want you to leave things at NNE alone," I said evenly.

"What do you mean, honey? I'm the president. How could I leave it alone?"

"Don't play innocent. I know you're trying to get rid of Nathan. I want you to stop."

He was smiling. Maybe he didn't yet realize how perfectly serious I was.

"Why, that's a terrible thing—a son plotting against his father."

"That's right, it is. And you're going to stop."

He squinted at me, assessing. I knew he had a shifty kind of intelligence, the kind it was easy to underestimate. He was looking for the angles now, for what he could play.

"You really think I'm trying to steal NNE? I'm flattered."

"I know you are. And I know about Don."

I could see he was surprised. But it didn't seem to throw him. He laughed instead.

"Just what do you know?"

"That you've blackmailed him into buying stock for you. And using Judd Mallory and Stella Jordan and I don't know how many others—getting them to buy stock so that you control it without Nathan knowing. Just when were you planning to tell him he's out?"

"Clever of me, isn't it? Don't you like that—how clever I am? Doesn't it turn you on?"

He laughed again. It was getting to me that he didn't seem at all threatened by my knowing about his plans. He wasn't scared. It didn't go with what I knew about him, the weak and slippery side. I didn't like it at all.

He got up and poured a drink. I shook my head when he offered one to me. He came toward me.

"It's touching, how much you care about Nathan. Very . . . female . . . you know, I always wondered what it would be like with you, Vega. From the first time I saw you. Know what I mean?"

He ran his fingers up my arm. I jerked away.

"Really, Peter, you're pathetic."

"Am I?"

He moved toward me again and I backed away. I'd been trying to maintain a kind of detachment, but despite myself, I was getting angry.

"Actually, you disgust me. You always have. From the first time I saw you—know what I mean?"

He laughed again. Something was wrong. I could feel

it, as if the well-marked road I'd been racing down had taken a sudden twist. If he wasn't afraid of me, it could only be because he felt secure. I needed to know why.

"Look," I said, "I told you what I'm here for."

"What you think you're here for."

"What do you mean?"

He didn't answer. I realized he was very drunk.

"You have no idea . . . such a smart little girl . . . you think you know, know all there is to know . . . and now you're going to play savior and make it all all right. . . ."

"Just lay off NNE."

"Or what?"

"I'll tell Nathan."

"But, baby, why would you do that? You know it'll kill him."

I hated him in that moment, that he had a hold on Nathan through love and that he knew it. "He'll survive. And you'll be out."

Again he laughed. "Oh, I'm scared, I'm so scared. . . ." He suddenly straightened up and his face was hard despite all the whisky. "Nathan—my father, my wonderful generous loving father—is the least of my worries."

"What do you mean?"

"Christ, Vega, you're such a fool, such a goddam fool . . ."

His voice trailed off until I could hear my own breathing.

"How? How am I a fool?"

"You want me to spell it out?"

The ground was shifting. Something was creeping up on me, as if a tide were actually rising through me, a flush, a sense of something about to fall. I knew in that moment I was going to hear something terrible but I was powerless to stop it.

"Spell what out?" I asked more quietly.

He shook his head and looked at me, full of pity. He smirked again.

"Spell what out?" I asked again.

"Why don't you ask your friend Paul?"

It was so unexpected I didn't understand.

"Paul? Paul who?"

Even as I asked again, I think now I knew, could see it all clearly, and irrevocably, behind the chaos Peter's words unleashed.

"You know Paul?" My voice betrayed me. It was as tentative and wispy as a little girl's.

"Honey, your friend Paul—your good friend Paul—he's the one behind the one—the top of the food chain."

I was staring at him helplessly. And he was smiling back with what I knew was pure contempt.

"You cunt. You goddam stupid cunt."

The tide was breaking all around me but I fought its bearing me away. Something was so wrong it couldn't be real; there had to be some mistake somewhere, some way I was misunderstanding reality. Peter was in front of me, that terrible smile twisting his mouth, but the room that contained us had sailed out into space and it was all I could do to remain upright.

"I don't understand. . . ." I managed to say.

"Come on, Vega, you're quicker than that. It's not me who's after NNE. It's Paul."

I stared at him blankly but he had turned away and was gazing at the darkness beyond the window.

"He met me, he hooked me . . . I needed money to cover some—unexpected expenditures. Someone introduced me to Paul—as a favor—and that's how it began. He loaned me the money but I got in deeper and deeper, and then, when I looked up, he was calling the shots. Ironic, huh? I didn't want my father to know about a little overextension, and now I'm the reason he's going to lose everything."

My heart was pounding, in flight, racing away from what I knew was coming. "How do you know I know Paul?"

He turned back to me. "Shit. Who do you think got Don to introduce you? Paul knew you handle Nathan's personal stuff—you were just one more base to cover."

I spun around as if I'd actually been slapped. I couldn't stand to hear another word. I had to get out of there, out into the clear night air. I stumbled toward the door.

Peter tried to stop me.

"Hey, stay," Peter called, coming after me. "We might as well enjoy it! Let's get it on—we're both fucked anyhow."

His laughter echoed after me.

My car careened down the drive and out onto Mulholland. I couldn't think; every thought led someplace I couldn't stand to go. I heard the brakes screeching around each curve but everything was too unreal, too disconnected; I was too numb to feel any danger. Paul and I were to meet at my house and I had to get there. That's all I knew: I had to get to Paul. The sight of him, his voice, would wipe out everything.

His car was already in my driveway. I flung open the door to the house and went through toward lights in the kitchen. He was there, making himself a sandwich. He looked up and smiled, that open smile that always pulled me in, and I stopped, completely helpless; like a drowning woman, I wanted to latch on to it, to make the welcoming curve of those lips the only reality and thus be saved. But the tide released by Peter kept pulling me down and, no matter how much I tried to shake it off, or shake myself awake, I couldn't make it go away.

Paul looked at me again.

"What is it?" he said. "Something wrong?"

"I just saw Peter Broadman."

He turned away from the counter and faced me. His eyes had widened but he didn't say anything.

"Is it true, that you got Peter to get Don to introduce us?"

He was looking at me.

"Have I just been part of the scheme? Because I work for Nathan? Just one of the angles you've been playing to get at him?"

I was desperate for him to deny it, because I was trying so hard to deny it to myself. I wanted him to shout, to protest, to say at the least that maybe things had begun that way but . . . Even now I was ready to flow toward him, so he could help me, take my hand as if I were a child, or an invalid, and show me how to reconstruct the world, to make it all okay again.

But he didn't.

"That's right," he said. And smiled. I made a noise but it died in my throat.

"Why are you so upset?" he asked. "We've been very clear about what's between us. You can't pretend you didn't enjoy it."

The unthreatened look in his eyes made me sick.

"And you're getting rich through me," he continued. "There's no reason why the business can't go on. I don't mind. In fact, I want it to. You have a knack for this kind of thing, Vega. Bringing me Bobby Melner and the others—even Carland—and all on your own. I have to say I was surprised, it was so much more than I'd expected. But then I've always been lucky."

His smile broadened. "Anyway, you'll be very useful and I'm willing to pay for what I use."

I didn't know which was worse, the truth or his complete indifference to my knowing it. That indifference left me no room. It completely silenced me.

"What is it, babe? The sex? Well, that's been great, too—truly an unexpected bonus. And we can keep it going. I'm willing to. When I have the time."

The cruelty of those last words was the final door clanging shut. I didn't doubt he'd said them purposely, to let me know the score.

"You bastard." My voice was very soft. "You bastard."

He nodded knowingly. "You're just surprised. You thought things were one way and now you see they're not exactly what you thought. I understand. But I'm betting you're too smart to walk away from a good setup. Especially since nothing has to change."

I looked at him. He was at the end of a very long tunnel and everything was changed.

"You need some time. I understand."

He moved past me, so close I could smell him. The air between us was barbed wire. If he had reached out to touch me, if I had felt his fingers on my skin, I would have been undone, would have screamed, cried, gone after him with my fists. But some sense, the same sense that made him so successful, must have cautioned him, and he didn't touch me before he went out the door. I stood unmoving and heard every sound with crystal clarity: the front door closing, his footsteps on the drive, his car door opening and closing, the engine coming to life, the turn of the tires as he drove away. I stood still until the sounds faded beyond my hearing. Then I became aware of my own breathing; I was panting, gasping in short gulps, could not get enough air.

I sank down into a chair. A voice was driving through me: a lie, lies, every moment with him had been a lie, part of his plan to use me. I saw all the smiles, the hand held out to me, the oh-so-caring voice. All of it a lie, every gesture, every intonation. His face when I brought him the check on Bobby's account, or first mentioned my other clients, and then when I brought him Carland, so proud of myself, so flushed with triumph, so confident about my own agenda. I was so stupid. *You stupid, stupid cunt!*

I spun out of my chair and stumbled through the house. Each image felt like a body blow, but I couldn't turn away. I threw myself down on my bed but then I saw myself lying back and spreading my legs, raising myself up to him, I saw him standing over me as I opened my mouth to take him in. The look in his eye, that lying look—my full humiliation broke over me. I cried then, sobs from the deepest part of me, shuddering with shame and self-loathing, a grotesque and floundering beached whale utterly helpless and defeated. I saw Don introducing us, and Peter as he looked at me in Nathan's office, all the time knowing, laughing at me, knowing. I thought of Gaby—was she part of it, did she know, too? I saw them all laughing, talking about me and laughing at how easily I'd been had. In every mortifying sense of the word.

I must have blacked out, but I came back and for an instant, but only instant, I was in the world I wanted. Then I remembered and, with that remembering, I felt the humiliation descend again, as if for the first time. Used, used, used. Why hadn't I screamed at Paul, hit out at him? The bastard, the bastard, the fucking, fucking bastard. I suddenly wanted to beat him with my fists, make him bloody, drive him to his knees and grind my black high heel into him. I could feel my jaw hardening as I imagined that, the steel-plated point of my stiletto shoe slicing into his chin, making his head snap back and snap back again, a passive punching bag. I wanted to grab his cock, twist it, my icy hand implacable as I made him writhe in helpless pain. I wanted—

I couldn't stand it. Whatever I imagined only made me feel more helpless, more impotent. And the desire for that kind of revenge, for blood, sickened me, made me feel that I had become like Paul, the worst part of him, that in buying into what I took to be his strength and freedom, in wanting it for myself, I had really been preparing the way for all this ugliness. And sealing my own terrible, terrible doom.

I jumped up; I had to do something. I couldn't let him get away with it. There had to be some way to stop him. I needed help, someone outside that horrible laughing circle . . . Nathan. Of course. Nathan had always been my inspiration and now he was my chance; he would help me. I had wanted to protect him, but now he and I would have to protect each other, against the same enemy. It was early, barely dawn but I didn't care. Somehow

Nathan and I would figure out how to stop Paul. I would tell him everything, not just about Peter, but about me, all the shameful things that I had done. And I knew it would be all right, that he would understand and know what to do. Nathan would save me.

I rang Nathan's doorbell three times before he answered it. He was in pajamas and a robe but I could see he'd already been up.

"Nathan, I need to talk to you! I—"

He held up a hand to stop me but words were tumbling out of me. He turned and as I followed him down the hall the whole story poured out, about Peter and NNE, about Paul and me. I kept trying to touch him, to hold his hand, to make him look at me so I would see myself in his eyes, as if his look could anchor me.

He went to the living room and sat down heavily. Someone else was there: it was Peter. I fell silent. I didn't understand.

"I told him, Vega," Peter said.

I looked at Nathan, but he didn't say anything. For the first time, I realized how crushed he looked, depleted.

"Nathan," I said. I went to him and sat down beside him. I took his hand; he didn't respond.

"We can stop Paul," I said. "I know things about him, how he set things up—we can find a way."

Peter moved toward us. "Leave him alone, Vega."

I ignored him. Nathan was shaking his head, an old man completely at sea. He was staring into the empty fireplace.

"Nothing is worth my son's life."

I looked at Peter. I didn't understand.

"Paul will kill me," he said in a tired voice, "if we don't give him what he wants."

"No!" I said, but I didn't doubt that Paul had already made the threat and that he meant it. I turned back to Nathan. "But you can't let him blackmail you like that—you'll lose everything."

"No, we won't," Peter said evenly. "On the surface, nothing will change."

I ignored him and tried to take Nathan's hand. "You have to fight back! Nathan, please, help me here, help me find a way."

He finally looked at me and there was nothing in his eyes, no feeling at all for me. He knew what I had done and I had lost him, finally and forever. "Don't you understand?" he asked. "Nothing is worth my son's life. Nothing."

I sputtered out another protest, but I knew there was nothing left to say. Nathan was helpless and not just against Paul. He was also helpless against Peter, against the fact of his love for him. For the first time, I realized that Nathan had no illusions about who Peter really was; he saw how weak he was. But that clarity didn't lead him to turn away from his son; instead, it called out all his love. I saw how deluded, how arrogant I'd been to ever think there was a time he'd choose me over Peter, a time when he'd let his only son go.

I stood up, but Nathan didn't notice. He was looking up at the painting over the fireplace. It was a large abstract, unexpected in this eighteenth-century room, with thick bands of vivid color.

"Your mother loved that painting so much, didn't she?" he said to Peter, as if I weren't there. "I always wondered what she saw in it. . . . What do you think she saw?"

He continued staring at it as Peter went to stand behind him and put one hand on his slumping shoulder. Peter turned to look at me and despite everything there was a kind of triumph in his eyes. I turned to leave. In the arched doorway of that beautifully furnished room, I looked back at them, father and son, both contemplating the mysterious painting, put there so long ago by Margaret's loving hand. And I shivered, because I saw there was in fact one way in which Peter did triumph over me: he had a kind of love and connection that I had never had, and maybe now never would.

I found myself driving to the beach. Humiliation mixed with anger and made me want to hurt myself, to punish myself for all my arrogance. I'd been so certain with Paul, so sure that I was in control, absurdly pleased that I'd withheld Nathan, kept my working for him clean. It was a terrible joke, how free I thought I'd been, when all the time I was as shackled as a draft horse made to go between the shafts. And I myself had added to my chains, furnished my own trap, actually helped Paul to even more control.

I parked the car and wandered out to the sand, my hair whipped loose by the steady wind. I felt as desolate as the sea churning now in front of me. Even now and despite everything, I felt a longing for Paul, the Paul I'd thought he was, and I wanted once more to be the woman I'd thought I was, to feel again the steady ground beneath me, the firm ascending path.

But that path was gone now; everything was changed.

And there was no way around it. Nothing was the same and it never would be; this terrible humiliation and anger, the deadening bondage, would always go on. Paul was right, there was nothing I could do. To accept that fact seemed like death, but to fight against its acceptance would be a living hell.

I took a breath of the moist salty air and forced myself to think. It couldn't be true that there was nothing I could do. Yes, I'd been very arrogant, completely blind to the fact that I'd had it all wrong. Once again, humiliation dragged me down: I saw myself lying back . . . spreading my legs . . . opening my mouth . . . No! I couldn't let myself go down that shameful, shaming street. I turned away, as if the physical gesture itself could cut the truth out of existence. I forced myself to begin again. Yes, I'd been used, made to play the fool, and the world I'd been living in had been an illusion, stage-managed by Paul—but did that mean that everything in it had been a dream? Wasn't there anything at all in what had happened that I could call my own? What about the strength I'd felt growing in me, the willingness to risk? Were they illusions too, only phantom aspects of fundamental lies? Or were they real, and could I use them now to find a way out?

I sat down on a wedge of rock and stared out to sea. Something was pushing up inside and I could almost taste it—and then I remembered. I must have been seven or eight and it must have been summer because I could see long slow twilights and the group of kids from the neighborhood who gathered after dinner. I wonder now what town that was and how long we were there. One evening, some of the older boys found an enormous metal hoop three or four feet across. They lined it with rags and doused the rags with kerosene; before I knew what was happening they'd set it on fire and everyone was lining up to race through the flaming circle. I was terrified but even more terrified to run away. The line surged forward. I could feel the kids behind me, their tension and fear, felt hands and bodies pushing me on, pressing me against those in front, heard their high shrieks and laughter. This was danger, real danger, a burning emblem of another world, the adult world, which was circled with mystery and deadly possibility. As my turn approached, I felt the heat, saw its waves distort the air above the hoop, heard flames snapping in an oxygen-eating wind. Then there was no one between me and it. The pushing behind me grew more determined; a face, one of the boys, loomed out at me, demanding that I leap. My terror was traveling inside me, an electric current racing down a fragile filament, propelling me, and I took a step, I thought to run away, but instead I went forward, I moved toward the flame, into the burning hoop, and suddenly everything went silent, was calm, and all sense of danger fell away. I felt the warmth of the flames on my skin, their vivid light a compelling illumination. There was nothing to fear. I was passing through and there was nothing at all to fear.

Now, on the beach, something in me was quickening, pushing me toward the next step. What if I bet that the changes in me, the growing strength and certainty, were real, what if I now planned and acted as if they were—what could I possibly lose? *There is no truth, only perspective. . . .* Then who's to say that Paul's perspective on how things now were had to be the right one, the last and final one? And maybe it didn't matter if the strength and freedom I'd thought I felt were real; who in any case could say? Here I was, so angry at myself, at what had been done to me, as if I had allowed it. Well, why not use that sword of self-loathing in another way, turn it on its head? If I had allowed my own imprisoning, I could *dis*allow it. I could act to change it. I could fight back.

I got up and started walking. The flame inside was growing and I needed to be in motion. I looked out to the horizon. Only a few moments ago, all I could see was imprisonment and Paul's lying smile closing me down. But now I could sense that there were other possibilities—if I could rouse myself to act. I saw myself rising up in front of what Paul had done, rising up like a determined seed through the center of my own life, refusing to accept what he was trying to impose. Why not? Why not bet on myself, on what *I* could do? Why not choose to believe, not in Paul's reality, but in my own, in one that I alone would create? What did I have to lose?

Nothing. I had nothing to lose, and for a moment that rocked me. There was nothing to lose because I was so alone. I'd run to Nathan like a helpless little girl wanting him to save me, but he couldn't help me. No one could. Even if Don had wanted to, even if Gaby didn't know how Paul had used me—it didn't matter—no one could help me now. I shuddered again. I had said I wanted the truth, but this truth was terrible to accept because this truth cast me out into the darkness. And if Paul had his way I would always be alone, trapped in my secrets, imprisoned in the dark. With a shuddering finality, I knew I was alone.

The tide was coming in and a flock of sandpipers was running across the sand, their long curved bills searching for food in the rushing tide. I watched a pelican out beyond the breakers flying straight and low. All right, I was alone, but was that really such recent news? I thought back to my stick-dry childhood in a prairie wind . . . to the years with Don . . . and the only-marking-time that came after. I saw my shadow in the California light. When really hadn't I been alone? And hadn't I always known it?

I stood still and listened to the wind. The pounding inside me stopped; I was calming down. I suddenly felt lighter, so much lighter I almost looked behind me as if I could see all that I had shed. Yes, I was alone. Now I knew it, and it was time to start living out of my true condition. I was going to bet on myself. I was going to take a chance. The thought of Paul's face, his seductive touch, only made me more determined, and not simply to be the author of my own life, but also to be the author of his.

Part

FIVE

Chapter Twenty

I needed time to make a plan, but meanwhile I had to stay close to Paul. I wanted him to think I was safe in his pocket so he would keep his attention on other things. I called him and said I understood now how it was between us but that I still wanted to play.

"You're right," I said, "I like the money. So I'll do whatever you want." I kept my voice as soft and smiling as I could make it. "I guess you won."

"Well, don't take this wrong," he said, "but I've been at it a long time and I usually do."

I flared at his condescension, but I couldn't let it show. Instead, I held on to my fury, stoked it, let it feed my contempt for the arrogance that made him oblivious to all that was seething in me.

"I know," I said. "It's part of what makes you so attractive. That power . . ." I was almost purring.

He didn't say anything and I hoped I'd surprised him

by moving right to sex. I wanted to throw him, even if it was just a fraction off center.

"How about if I come to your place?" I asked. "You want me to, don't you? Now?"

I heard him laughing, but he quickly responded. "Yes. Sure. Now."

I didn't know if I could pull it off. But he made it easy because he acted as if nothing had changed, and I suppose for him nothing had. He made us something to eat, veal with fresh tomatoes, and we sat at his dining table, clinked our glasses, and looked down at the city lights stretching out below. I smiled, my eyes clear and my face untroubled; I stared at him suggestively over my glass and I let him watch my tongue circle the rim. I didn't pull away when his fingers played across my arm and moved under the fabric of my long and silky sleeve. I shifted my hips and leaned closer to him, resting my breasts on the edge of the table as if unaware. He'd said I had a knack for the kind of business he did, and maybe this was part of it, the ability to play out this particular lie, and to do it not only effortlessly but with a certain pleasure. It was amusing in a certain way, that one set of lies in our relations had been revealed only to be replaced by another. His lies had given him the power, and he thought he still had it now, but I was watching from behind my smiling eyes, and that constant calculation gave me a surprising sense of strength. He thought he knew how things now stood, but only I did now: I had the power, the possibility, to take him by surprise.

• • •

I lay back and spread my legs. I moaned, and it wasn't a lie—I was very wet and fevered with desire. I watched, and avidly, as his fingers traced circles on my breasts, around my hardened nipples, and I arched up to feel the intensifying pressure of his emphatic touch. I ran my tongue over his lips and his outstretched neck; I played my hands over his ass, then parted him and found his hole. Once again, desire made me vigilant, but in a new way: as I felt my skin flame at the prospect of his touch, saw his mouth tease at my nipples, even felt his cock slide into me with deep and easy thrusts, I remained distant from him, unmoved and alert, calculating. Yet at the same time I gave myself up to desire, and it was genuine. Not desire for him, I'd been cut free of that, but desire for consuming pleasure, my own satisfaction. It was as if I'd separated into two different women, two levels of consciousness, and the splitting off didn't weaken either: it only made them more intense.

He fell asleep. I watched him breathing evenly, sprawled on his back, vulnerable and undefended. How many lovers had stared across the pillow as I was doing in the middle of the night, feeling hate and a thirst for revenge, icy insomniacs?

I got up and went to his computer, turned it on and sat in the dark, scrolling through his files. I had no trouble following the spreadsheets and pathways he'd designed. After a while, I got up and stood in the dark, looking out into the night. The lights of the city were reflecting off a thin marine mist drifting in from the sea, and the night seemed gray, a translucent shell set down over Los Angeles. I welcomed it, felt protected by constriction, sheltered from the dizziness of an infinite black sky. I saw that with no effort at all I could cause chaos in every one of Paul's systems and bring them all to a halt, at least temporarily. I was very good with numbers. But it wasn't enough. I didn't want to cause him problems; I wanted to stop him cold in his tracks. I wanted him unmasked, humiliated, afraid; I wanted him unmanned.

Still, I hesitated because it came to me there was another option: I could simply walk away. Accept that Paul had used me, swallow that humiliation, and resign myself to his owning Bobby and Carland and even Nathan, who in any case was lost to me. I could move on, go back to a semblance of my old life. Why not? All that would be different was that I had more money and had learned some hard lessons. A terrible despair suddenly opened up inside me, an intense longing to erase the past few months, to go back to living as if none of this had happened, to live once more in the free world that had ended without my knowing it in the moment I met Paul. But that world had ended and I saw with vivid clarity that I, too, was owned, would always be owned by Paul because of what he had on me. And I knew he wouldn't hesitate to use it, that there was no telling and no limit to what he would force me to do. There was only one way to be free and that was to ruin him. I had to be brave enough to do it.

I sat down at the computer again and began calling up file after file. A plan had begun to form: using Paul's sheets as a model, I'd plug in phony numbers, designing it to look as though he'd been skimming money from all his investors, had been doing it for years. It wouldn't be very difficult. Then I'd make sure the right people saw the phony numbers. It wouldn't take very much at all. I worked intently, the hum of the machine and the rasp of my pen on thin white paper smothered by the silence, and all the time he slept. If I had seen in that moment what was going to happen, all that I was setting in motion, I wonder now, would I have gone ahead? The truth is, I don't know. God help me, I don't know.

I called Gaby. I needed to know how much she knew.

"Darling!" she said at the sound of my voice. "I've been longing for you to call."

"I want to see you," I said.

"Of course. Come here. Anytime. Now."

I laughed. "How about lunch? At the Bistro—this time on me."

"But, darling, I have the best cook in town."

"Maybe so. But indulge me."

"All right," she said. "See you there." I could hear the disappointment in her voice.

She was waiting when I got there, her shoulders wrapped in an expensive velvet shawl painted in a swirl of colors. Her hand reached for mine as I sat down.

"I'm so glad," she said. "I was beginning to think you weren't interested."

I smiled but didn't say anything.

"I've thought about you," she said, her eyes unafraid to meet mine. "And wanted very much to see you."

The maître d' came to take our order. Afterward, I kept the conversation to small talk, what we'd been doing, and with whom. It felt strange to be surrounded by the elegance and civility of the restaurant and to feel how easily the reality of that pampered burrow could be torn apart by harsh, cold truths. Each time I mentioned Paul, Gaby gave no hint of knowing what he had done to me, but she might have been acting in the same way I now was. It wasn't until the plates were cleared that I finally took the risk.

"What's this?" Gaby asked.

I had placed a file on the table.

"Open it," I said.

She was puzzled but turned the cover and looked at the first sheet lying on top.

"I'm not sure I understand. What are you showing me?"

"It's a copy of the figures Paul kept on the projects you were in on with him, starting with Sea Horse Ranch."

She looked at them again. "I still don't understand."

"I believe they're very different from the figures he showed you."

"I see." She studied the spreadsheets in the file. "You're saying he lied to us."

"Yes. He cheated you."

That was the risk: if she knew how Paul had set me up, how I'd been used from the very first, she would guess now that I might be lying, looking for revenge. I had nothing more to go on than the look in her eyes, the way she touched me, my instinct that she hadn't been toying with me in that very tangled web. But I'd been so wrong about Paul; to trust my instinct now was to leap into the void.

I watched as she turned over the separate pages, her eyes moving quickly down columns of figures until she closed the file and rested her hands on top of it.

"How did you discover this?" she asked.

I couldn't read her voice.

"He was eager to show me. Arrogant. Like a little boy."

"And you've brought it to me."

I looked at her fully, and hoped she was finding in my look whatever she needed.

"You realize that, if what you've shown me is accurate, it could go very badly for Paul."

I nodded.

"And—your feelings for him—you wouldn't mind?"

"No, I wouldn't mind."

She smiled and put her hand on mine. It came to me she thought I was doing this out of my feeling for her, choosing her over Paul. I almost smiled at how all of us write our own scenarios, based entirely on our own need. It's what I had been doing. Gaby had no idea that now I felt nothing at all, for her or anyone else, only an overriding urge, a deepening need to make myself free. But her eyes told me I had been right to take the risk. Gaby was on my side.

"Of course, I must show this to Charles. Then we shall have to talk to one of Paul's main investors. A man named Gunther—"

"I've met him."

She nodded. "He's a man with a very broad reach. Very capable of doing whatever must be done."

"What exactly do you think that might be?"

"Oh, darling, I never ask about the details. It's the larger picture that satisfies me."

• • •

I drove back to the office and went through the motions of taking care of business. I knew that Gaby would show Charles and the others the figures I had cooked up and that they would be checking, trying to determine whether my numbers were the true ones. But I didn't think there was any way they could actually tell: the only numbers they had had been supplied by Paul, and now here I was with another set that certainly had the look of authenticity. I had made it appear that Paul hadn't skimmed large amounts from them but had done it steadily, cynically, with a kind of matter-of-factness that looked as though it came from a certainty he wouldn't be found out. They wouldn't like that, that he had discounted their intelligence, judged them to be such a small threat. I hoped that would make them feel some of my fury, and the same thirst for revenge.

Gaby finally called. "I'm at Gunther's," she said. "We'd like to talk to you."

At Gunther's house, I watched him running his forefinger down columns of numbers glowing on the screen of the laptop I'd brought with me. It had taken me hours to fabricate the spreadsheets he was looking at, but it was worth it; those numbers humming on a screen were very impressive. Gaby was beside him, going over the pages she had taken with her after lunch. When Gunther had seen enough, he got up and went to one of the heavily draped windows and stood looking out.

"Why have you brought us this?" he asked. "Why not ally yourself with Paul?"

Gaby started to speak, but he stopped her and waited for my answer.

I had prepared for that question but I hesitated and looked uncomfortable. It wasn't entirely an act. "Personal reasons," I said quietly, my voice soft, the words falling like petals in the velvet stillness of that insulated room. And then after a beat, "You aren't the only ones he's humiliated." I sat back and crossed my legs and saw Gunther's eyes move down their silky length. I knew he understood.

"But there's something more," I said, looking up. "I don't want you just to know about Paul—I want you to know about me as well."

"What do you mean?" Gaby asked.

"How capable I am. And trustworthy. I can be very useful to you in the future."

"I see," Gunther said, looking at me directly. "You mean this is a kind of job interview."

I smiled. "In a way. But more than a job. I have in mind a partnership."

"A partnership," he echoed, and I could see him wondering about me, how far I could go. Gaby looked very pleased.

"Yes," I said, "based on whatever I can bring you. I think you'll find I have an awful lot to offer."

I didn't need them to commit to anything specific. All I wanted was to make room for possibility; it was too soon for anything more. But I'd begun to see the particular delight of that particular possibility: not only to destroy Paul but also to replace him.

Gaby walked me to my car. I'd given her and Gunther

all they needed: the figures, my reason for contacting them, my desire to forge a more permanent alliance. Now it was up to them.

"When will I see you?" Gaby asked as we reached the car. "I don't want to wait very long."

She found my hand and raised my fingers to her lips. Her mouth was soft and warm; the ocean breeze enveloped me in her scent. I could imagine the softness of her body, its pliancy, the ease with which I could fold her in. But I was unmoved, focused only on the plan I'd set in motion, and I pulled back my hand.

"Soon," I said, "I'll call you very soon."

I kissed her cheek before I drove away. Watching her recede in my rearview mirror, I knew she thought there was a future in which we would be together in some way. It was a lie, and that made me feel bad. But I had to let it go. Besides, maybe there would be some way and some time when I could make it up to her.

I didn't know what would happen, or when, so I lived the next few days as if I had a life that would not change. I went to the office, saw clients for lunch, listened to Holly talking to Tom. And at night I wrapped myself in silk and stretched out fully, luxuriously, a generous lover, open, patient, with all the time in the world for the urgency of desire.

I wanted him to suck me. Lying back, I felt his tongue, slow and thick, lapping at my core. I needed to watch him. I raised myself on my elbows and looked down across my flushing skin. For a moment I lost my moorings, awash in contradiction: the intensity of his tongue, the fury deep inside. My thighs pressed against him and I suddenly felt that I could crush him, twist him in two. I reached down to him and pulled him up so he could enter me; I rammed myself onto him as deep as I could. I felt him gladly find my rhythm. He thought it was passion, and I suppose it was. But of another sort.

The call came in the middle of the night while we were at Paul's. He sat up and turned on the light.

"What do you mean?" he said, and listened silently to the answer. I knew it was trouble; I saw the muscles of his back rippling, tightening with tension.

"That can't be," he said. "No way."

He hung up.

"What is it?" I asked, but he ignored me and went into the living room. I heard the scrape of a chair as he sat down in front of the computer; I saw its gray cold light beyond the bedroom door. I lay back and waited; whatever was going to happen was happening now.

After a long while, I heard him dialing the phone.

"There's nothing wrong on my end—no, no, I don't know how—" he said. "But you're wrong—it's a mistake—"

He listened for a moment.

"No, you're wrong. Look, let me show you. Sure, now, if you want—I'll be there in an hour."

I had gotten up and was standing in the doorway, watching as he paced in a tight little circle, the robe he'd pulled around him open and flaring with each turn. Even now I could see how beautiful he was.

He tried to say something more but the line went dead. He replaced the receiver slowly.

"What is it?" I asked. "What's wrong?"

He looked up at me and for a moment I saw how puzzled he was, uncertain; something he didn't understand at all was happening and he was totally unprepared for it. He didn't answer me but went back to the computer and sat in front of it, reassuring himself from the numbers on his screen that someone had made a mistake and that's all it was, a mistake, that everything was fine. He didn't know it, but it was already too late for him. He could go to Gunther and Gaby and the others to show them, but it wouldn't make a difference; they had my facts and figures and there was too much money at stake, and too many reputations, for them to give Paul the benefit of the doubt.

I stood gazing at him and felt something unexpected, almost a tenderness, for his ignorance of the forces that were gathering around him. Is this what he had felt when he looked at me? Or had he been laughing, across the dinner table and across the sheets, laughing as I raised myself up to him, so he could tease me, stroke me, lick me, take me from behind?

Anger surged up in me, and I turned away so that I wouldn't speak. It was too tempting to tell him to stop looking for the problem, that it was standing in front of him, in a silk and lace black nightgown. I wanted him to know.

He left the house without saying where he was going, but of course I knew. He didn't look worried but rather especially intent, focused, absorbed by what he had to do. It was his talent, this full concentration, and it made me smile to think what he had taught me.

I got dressed and drove home, the sky lightening as I headed east. I wasn't tired, but I felt instead an unfamiliar lightness, a lack of gravity, as if I were slowly tumbling into another atmosphere. So much was at stake. I could see what the dangers were but nothing felt real, and I was curiously at peace. What would happen now was out of my hands.

By nine o'clock, I was in the office. Paul called sometime before noon.

"I need you to meet me," he said. It wasn't a question but an order. "With as much cash as you can get your hands on."

When I hung up, I wasn't sure what to do. For the first time, I'd heard real fear in his voice; Gunther and the others had obviously taken action, and now Paul was on the run. But why should I go meet him? It could be a trap; maybe he knew I was the one who had set it all in motion. And if he didn't know, why should I turn up and give him money, help him get away?

The obvious thing was not to meet him. I could call Gunther and tell him where Paul would be and when and keep myself out of it. I reached for the phone, but Paul's face was suddenly before me and I stopped. I realized I wasn't ready to turn it all over and let him go. I needed to see him with fear in his eyes, to see his look when he knew I was the one who'd set him up. It was dangerous, but all along I'd been walking up to danger—wasn't that the point?—and I felt how much I needed to do it now.

• • •

He said to meet him up at the top of Sunset Plaza Drive. It was high up in the hills, little more than a paved one-lane track butting up against the hill, lined on the other side with houses on stilts hanging out over a panoramic view. The higher you went, the smaller the houses and the more empty lots; there was a stretch of it, before it dipped down the next hill into Laurel Canyon, which was entirely deserted.

He was waiting for me at the top, parked in a turnout around a dusty curve. I pulled in and saw him sitting on the hood of his car, looking at the view, across the basin and the oil-derricked hills, out to the ocean beyond, which glinted like a silvered mirror in the sun and haze. He looked relaxed, almost as if he were posing for the cover of a slick magazine: the well-dressed, well-proportioned man. One more time, I felt that strange combination of anger and desire and the sudden need to smash, to destroy what attracted me.

I got out of my car and walked to him, a tightrope walker suddenly dizzy at the realization she hasn't any net. It had been so much what I had wanted, to be moving toward him and all that he seemed to hold out to me, but now, although the sun was shining, I felt I was in shadow, pinned beneath the outline of a diving predator about to pluck me up. Each step was dangerous. I must be walking into a trap. How could he not know already that it was me?

"How much did you bring?" he asked.

I'd thought it would be his first question and I came prepared. I reached into my purse for an envelope and handed it to him. I said nothing as he counted it.

"This is all?" he asked.

I nodded. It was only a couple of thousand and wouldn't get him very far.

"Jesus," he said and turned away, back toward the view. I realized that if he had set a trap for me, it would be sprung right now; his turning away told me he didn't know I was the one who'd put him where he was standing now. I was relieved but also irrationally miffed—didn't he think I had it in me? It was laughable, that question, but I felt again the need to have him know.

"What's happening?" I asked. "What's wrong?"

My fear had fallen away and I felt only an intense curiosity about what he would say.

"I have to get out of town."

I wasn't sure, but I thought I heard a tremor in his voice.

"Why?"

"You don't want to know."

"Yes, I do. I need to know everything about you."

He turned to me. He had needed me in one way, but now the script had changed and I could see him reassessing. Could he still use me now, use my desire for him? I realized how afraid he must be, how alone, to even be considering it.

"People are after me."

"Who? What did you do?"

"I didn't do anything! But they don't believe me."

"Who? Your investors?"

He nodded. "But they're not the worst of it—they've already told—"

He was hesitating.

"Who?"

"The guys I go to to get things done. You understand?"

I was beginning to. Paul was an independent contractor, the middleman who brought together the money from investors like Gaby and Gunther and the gangster muscle to get things done. If Gunther had found a way to show the other side of the equation my phony spreadsheets, no wonder Paul was afraid. People like Gunther and Gaby might be too clean, but these others wouldn't stop at putting him out of business. They would want him dead and have the means to make it so. No wonder he was scared.

"What can I do?" I asked. "How can I help?"

My voice was gentle, intimate, and he looked at me with a question in his eyes. I wanted him uncertain, wondering not how much he could trust me but how much he could use me. I didn't have a plan but I needed to keep it going.

"I've got to disappear," he said. "You've got to come up with more money, a lot of it."

"Sure. I can." He was getting off the hood of the car, opening the door. I realized he was leaving. I wanted to hold him back.

"How will I get it to you? Where are you going?"

"Just get as much as you can. I'll let you know."

He was in the car. I heard the ignition.

"When?" I was shouting. Suddenly, I couldn't stand that he was leaving, that he was driving off and I didn't know where and that I might never see him again. I tried to open the door.

"Where are you going?"

He grabbed the collar of my dress and pulled me to him roughly through the open window. I felt his mouth press hungrily on mine, his tongue hot and wet, as if he could devour me. I knew it wasn't me he was hungry for, but for safety, some way out of the box he was in. Then he pushed me back and I stumbled as the car screeched out to the road and disappeared down the hill. I ran to the edge of the turnout and looked over, down the dusty brown hillside to the curving track below, but I was helpless as Paul's car descended among the twists and turns until it disappeared in the maze of streets now hidden from my view.

I stood there until I became conscious of my own breathing. Then, not knowing what else to do, I got in my car. I turned out onto the road and headed down, but in the other direction, into Laurel Canyon. I needed time to think.

It wasn't played out and I knew it.

I bought a cup of coffee in a place on Ventura Boulevard. I was shaking, but by the time I asked for a refill my hands were steady and that steadiness was my only anchor; I knew where I was physically, in that immediate moment, but I had no idea where I stood in any other sense. I kept seeing Paul's car disappearing. He had vanished around a curve, and for all I knew, it could be forever. He could be anywhere. I assumed he must have access to credit cards, to whole identities I knew nothing about. He was too smart not to have prepared years ago for an emergency; he must have had his own NIGHT. But he'd said he needed more money from me. Maybe that meant he couldn't get at it, that there hadn't been time; maybe it was a sign of how afraid he was.

I had to move; I couldn't sit still. I got in my car in the

parking lot, unclear where to go next. I couldn't bear it. That he would get away. And be free to start all over again. To find other people to use. Other women. I couldn't stand it. There had to be something I could do. I had to stop him. I couldn't let him get away.

Suddenly, I remembered the house in the San Joaquin Valley. It was someplace he might go to bury himself while he bought some time. I shook my head—he was probably on a plane by now, flying to Europe or South America . . . but I kept seeing the town and followed the road out to the house. It wasn't likely he'd go there—but there was a chance, a very small chance. Besides, I couldn't think of any better possibility. And now that I'd thought of it, how could I turn away? If I didn't drive up there to check it out, I would never know, and the not knowing would eat away at me, like dark, destructive water rusting iron piers. I was a new person now with new clarity; I needed to push, to do that one last thing. The point wasn't whether Paul was there or not; it was about my willingness to make the effort to find out.

It was night when I got there. I parked my car in a grove of trees near the turnoff to the house. I wasn't sure what I would do, but if Paul was there I didn't want to give him any warning. My mind had been thick on the way up, suffocating all my attempts to make a plan, and so I'd given up, listened to the radio instead, blaring out rock 'n' roll at seventy miles an hour. It was all right. Something aside from my mind was carrying me and had been for days. A force greater than my own thinking was leading me on, as if I were simply an entranced spectator compelled to watch what would unfold. It was a paradox, because at the same I'd never felt more clear, and less afraid.

He was there.

His car was parked beside the house. I stopped and looked at its shadow looming in the night. It was dark and silent; only the wind made any sound. I took a step and heard the crunch of gravel. I took another and continued on. Then I saw him, crouched on the front steps. He had a gun and it was aimed at me.

I stopped again.

"It's Vega!" I shouted across the thin night air.

He didn't move. I heard a dove somewhere behind me; its lowing murmur was clear across the night.

"Vega," I said again. "I'm alone."

Slowly, he began to rise. I moved toward him, my body light now, an undefended presentation, steady and inevitable. I was not afraid. When I got close enough, I could see that he was smiling.

"I couldn't stay away," I said, and his smile broadened.

"I always said you were very smart." He lowered the gun and put it in his belt, reached out and ran his fingers across my cheek, down my neck. Then he turned into the house and gestured for me to follow.

There was no light. The electricity had been turned off years earlier but there was a fire going now in a potbelly stove. Paul had left its door open and the fiery glow threw sharp, steep shadows over the darkened walls. He went to it now and I watched him breaking twigs, a small branch, and pushing them inside.

I thought about his smile and wondered what was behind it. Was he playing with me now, as I was playing with him? Or did he really think it was love that had brought me to him? Could he be that arrogant? Surely by now, with time to think, he must realize that I was the one who set him up. That reality was pounding through me, roaring in my blood. How could he not hear it?

"I'm glad you came," he said, walking toward me. "I'm going to need you to do some things for me. Pick up some papers. And of course the money."

I nodded.

"You can't go now. But in the morning."

"Yes. Of course. Anything."

He took me in his arms and crushed me to him. I realized how tense he was, scared, and he was alone in it; my suddenly appearing must look like a lifeline to him. I felt his mouth hot on my neck and his hips pressing into me. I felt his cock and flashed on the first time I'd seen it erect, that first night, as he came down to the edge of my pool, silhouetted in the moonlight. Despite everything, I felt myself respond. But there was a different vibration in him now, a definite desperation; he was hungry and for something more than sex, for a kind of reassurance, an easing of the fear. I didn't want to give it to him. I didn't want to be used again. I stepped back. And as I did I pulled the gun with me. It came smoothly out of his belted waist, its barrel rustling against the silk of his shirt.

"I know why they're after you," I said.

I could see he didn't understand, why I'd pulled away and why I had the gun.

"Someone set me up," he said.

I nodded. I needed him to know. "That's right," I said. "Someone did."

As I watched, he got it. He shook his head in surprise and gave a single laugh, but without missing a beat he swung right in to calculating the new circumstances. My very cool lover; very, very slick.

"I deserved it," he said, with a grin designed to disarm me. "I used you, but I underestimated you. You're gorgeous, Vega, gorgeous."

He moved toward me but I signaled him to stop and he did. His eyes were laughing with that special glint that always drew me in.

"Okay," he said. "Now we're even. We can go on from here." His voice lowered and his whole body seemed to relax. "You wanted to be partners—well, we can do it now. Come with me. We'll go someplace new and start again. You and me." He was running his hand across his chest, letting me see his long and gentle fingers. He drew a long breath in and his chest expanded. I could see the silk of his shirt glowing in the light. "I can't imagine a better team."

I knew he was lying, but for a moment I thought about pretending I believed him to see what he would do. Would he come to me and gently cup my breasts, pull up my skirt, and slowly spread my thighs? Would he make love to me, glide into me with all the ease of familiarity and the thrust of urgency? And what would I feel if I let him, what new permutation on desire—before he pulled the trigger?

He moved, but I stopped him again.

"No," I said. "We're not going anywhere. "You're—"

I thought I hadn't seen his arm move, but I must have because I turned my head a split second before his fist connected. Even so, he sent me sprawling, but as I went I kicked out and caught him in the groin. He took a step back, clutching at himself. I heard the gun clattering somewhere to my right. That gun was all that mattered. I felt him pulling at me, and I kicked like a swimmer shaking free of undergrowth. I got to the gun and spun on my back, pointing it at him with both my hands. He saw it and froze; it gave me time to scramble to my feet. I was shaking and tears were pouring down my cheeks. My jaw had already begun to throb. But I was the one who had the gun.

He sat for a moment on the floor staring at me. Then he smiled and slowly started up. He was moving toward me again.

"No," he said, "you don't want to hurt me. You know you don't, baby. . . ."

His voice was mellow, as dark and seductive as the firelight. "Listen to me. You think I could have been in bed with you if I wasn't really turned on? I was using you, but not in that way. Never in that way. It's incredible between us, Vega. You know it is. I always want you, baby, you always make me ready, and you want me. We'd be crazy to throw it away. It can go on, honey . . . oh yes, so sweet . . ." His tongue was circling his lips. "Even now. Right here . . . I want you, baby . . . and you want me."

He was coming closer. I looked into his eyes. For a moment, they were as open and as welcoming as I'd ever seen them and I felt what I would give to know that it was real. But then his gaze shifted and, without following, I realized he was trying to herd me back, toward a wooden crate near the wall. He wanted me to stumble so he could push me over, keep me down.

"Stay where you are," I said, holding the gun closer.

He smiled, but now I knew the truth all over again. He had used me, always and only used me, and now he knew that I'd betrayed him. Here, tonight, he wouldn't stop until he killed me.

"I'll shoot," I said. "I don't want to, but I will."

This time I saw the fist the instant it moved. I looked into his eyes and we were locked together. I'd never felt more connected to him.

I pulled the trigger.

The sound of the bullet was small, contained; it had no reverberation. But time slowed down and I was caught with Paul in another atmosphere. His face twisted in surprise but he didn't go down.

"Cunt," he whispered, and with a great slow effort he heaved himself at me. He pushed against me and I went back, but I didn't fall, I kept my balance. His hands, those long and tapering fingers, groped clumsily toward my throat. And one more time I pulled the trigger.

I watched him go down suddenly, heavily, and I knew without looking that he was dead. He lay in front of me and I couldn't move. I was riveted by his stillness, his stone dead lack of breath. I heard a twig in the stove crackle, saw the fire shadows on the wall, heard night sounds out beyond the dirty windowpanes. I took a step back, and then another, as if the inert body at my feet could rise up and hurt me in some way. Of course he didn't move. I was alone, completely alone, in a sudden borderless emptiness that rippled out from that tiny room, raced across the Valley floor, and lost itself in the blackened night out beyond the unseen hills. My hand slowly came up and brushed my cheek; the reality of my own warm skin was an endless mystery to me.

I don't know how long I stood there, but a chill moved through me, a shudder that brought my senses awake. I felt the gun, now heavy in my hand, and, without thinking, I knew what to do: take it with me. There were rags in the car I could use to wipe off my fingerprints. I looked around; what else had I touched in this room, this dilapidated house? Nothing. Nothing at all. I couldn't see that I had left any footprints, but I scraped my feet along the bare floorboards to blur them just in case and, as I stepped to the door, I took up a fistful of my skirt to cover my hand as I unlatched it. I was halfway out before I looked back.

He was curled up like a baby, but one arm was flung out, its fingers spread fully, its palm turned up. Even then, I knew I would remember the undefendedness of that open hand. I took a deep breath and looked away. His eyes were closed and he could have been sleeping, waiting for morning, ready to reach out to me. But that possibility was gone forever, killed by a bullet, killed by lies. I closed my eyes and I felt nothing, no sense of triumph and no sense of loss, only the certainty that I had acted and there was no way now to take back that stone-still truth.

I drove out to the highway, all the time unseeing, as if the headlights of my car were drilling a tunnel and drawing me on. By the time someone found Paul's body, the gun would be gone, buried, with no way to trace it and the bullets back to me. "I'm safe," I thought, and then I heard the words and felt myself dissolve into all that irony. What place could be safe now, knowing what I knew? How would I judge—and who would judge me? Where would I find mercy?

I turned south, but I wasn't thinking about going home. Things were different now and I didn't know anymore just where home was. Maybe I would keep driving south, past L.A. and into Mexico—or maybe I'd turn north at some point . . . or east . . . or . . .

I switched the radio on. Dawn was a long way off and there was time enough to think about what I wanted to do. I didn't have to worry; NIGHT's money would take me anywhere I wanted to go. And wherever that was, I knew now I had the strength to get there. I was capable, could always do what needed to be done. It was simple, even if it wasn't easy. You just keep facing forward. And when the line comes up, you jump.

Printed in the United States
By Bookmasters